The Southern Magi

Book One of
The Divine Histories

Joseph D. Howard

To order additional copies of this book, contact:
Bookwhip
1-855-339-3589
https://www.bookwhip.com

*In memory of my Aunt Cynthia,
who gave me Benny and the Pancake Man*

PROLOGUE

T HE COTTAGE STOOD in a pit of darkness surrounded
by gray mist. The window absorbed light into its frame.
Two rooms were made for them. One room was given. They
stood where the three met, close to each other, steadily watching the
window as more light bit into it. A young girl stood between her
parents. Each of them smiled as she looked toward them. She had
hair like her father's, wavy and brown, but a face like her mother's,
simply mesmerizing. Ragged clothing covered their bodies; only
their faces were true. The man put his hand on her shoulder. His
beard was moderately well kept. Ears curved like small hooks, the
woman was tall and graceful. Her skin was much darker now; she
craved moonlight.

"You are to keep nothing from him," he said to the girl. "We
have lost too much time."

"But there's so much to tell him, Father," she said, staring up
at him.

"This is why it must be done in time. The shock will be too
much for him. The darkness will consume him," the man continued.
"You know what you will have to do."

"But we do not know this, Father. He may not—" she began.

"We are counting on it," her mother said. "It's your only way out, Alèynor. Meet her in the Terran system, and bring her back to our world."

"But what if she travels with the others? What if all four of them arrive together?" she asked, turning to her mother.

The desperation on her face sank like a stone. Despite her years of preparing, the dreaded day had never seemed so impossible. She prayed confidence would grow on her as they spoke.

"If they do," her mother said, "then it will be much easier for you to find her. If what we fear is to come to pass, he will need the two of you now more than ever."

Her father moved toward her. She was slightly shorter than he was. His relaxing brown eyes swirled in front of her. The curve of her mother's ears drew her attention up to her.

"Cassandra, you will have only one chance to escape this prison. You must be sure it is her. If she does not travel with him, then you will be trapped in the Terran system until he is strong enough to retrieve you himself. This *must not* happen. We will not be able to help you. We …"

"I know," the girl said, saddened. "But I can take you with me! I don't want to leave you here."

Her mother lowered herself and looked down into her daughter's hazel eyes. "We will never leave you." The woman smiled. "But this must be done, Alèynor."

Her mother spoke in her native tongue. Father and daughter were immediately caught by her dulcet voice. Within seconds, another sight caught their eyes. The gray light from the window shined in a little harder. Each of them looked to it, watching it. It pulsed three times—three long, steady pulses. Her father quickly reached into his pocket. He took out a scroll. There was a purple jewel the size of a dime in the center of it. He handed it to his daughter, and she quickly placed it behind her back.

"You will be our voice," he said. "Take him to the oasis and ensure maximum security. Reveal this to no other."

"What if he doesn't like me? What if he hates me?" the girl asked.

"You can do this," her father said. "You are much stronger than us."

"She should gather her strength," the woman said to her husband. "He should be coming soon. It may not be very long before she is needed."

Her parents led her to the room that was given to them. It was small with no window. The walls were painted with a vivid map revealing the outside world she dreamed about. There were hand-drawn icons over the Forest of the Moon, Aryvandaar, and the city of Numaia. She lay down as her father kissed her on her forehead. They left her in the room as they went back. The gray light had stopped pulsing. Cassandra stared at the map, letting her dreams bridge the gap between hope and fear.

1

A Hollow in Middlecreek

THE AIR TASTED like ashes. He gulped. His frail little chest nearly pumped out of his body; his clothes were too small, constricting him. There were alarms outside the house, an unfamiliar wailing. The windows on the second floor were being broken through as strange men in even stranger uniforms called out to see whether anyone was still inside. He tried to cry but failed. Something ran in behind him and picked him up as if he were a beach ball. He turned around, trying to put a face to his rescuer, but all he could see was a golden light. He latched on to his rescuer, tighter, knowing he would take him to fresh air. The little boy closed his eyes. When, surrounded by streams of burning flames, he opened them, he saw his rescuer, holding his hand in the back of another wailing machine. He shook his head to see strange men in strange uniforms next to him, touching him. The rescuer absorbed his tears.

"He is not leaving me!" his rescuer shouted.

"But, sir, we have to check his vitals. He's wearing a medallion, sir; it could have burned into his skin, sir. We must—"

"He is not leaving me! I am his grandfather. Do what you must, but he will stay in my arms. Is that clear, boy?" he shouted again.

There was a series of strange pokings, but the boy kept himself close to the man who called himself his grandfather.

"He'll be fine. The fire didn't cause any serious damage. The medallion ... it's unburned. But how is that—"

"Are you quite done?" the old man said.

The boy looked up at his rescuer. His hair was curly and brown like the boy's was. The older man's clothes were just as damaged as the child's were. He held on to him, weeping softly into the child's burned clothes. He lifted the boy from his shoulder and placed him on his knee. The old man gave him a warm, forced smile, still trying to calm him down. Every tear evaporated before it touched skin. For four seconds, the old man did nothing but smile and look into his matching brown eyes.

"Everything's going to be okay now, Nolan. You are safe here. You survived," he said.

Evvvverrrrything ... is ... goooiiing ... to ... beeeee ... ooooookayyyyy, the boy heard, in a strange array of distorted sounds. Sniffling, Nolan began looking around to see that everything was beginning to swirl around him, like a colorful cotton candy maker. He kept seeing oranges.

Gasping for breath, Nolan's body jerked up into the air. He lay back on the bed, looking up at the ceiling, placing his hands behind his head. Nolan couldn't help but get the feeling that he was forgetting something—anything to wash out that memory. Running his hands through his wavy brown hair, he looked around his room as if he was trying to find something, but everything was in its proper place—the larger dresser to the right of him with a large mirror attached, his flat-screen TV hanging above the wall. His Xbox was still on, but it had faded out.

Looking to the left of his TV, he saw it: the confirmation—the newspaper clipping announcing his parents' death. "Family Broken by Fire." The only picture shown was of his grandfather holding him in the back of an ambulance. He had changed so much since this picture. Fifteen years. The only thing that was the same was the medallion hanging from a silver chain. He put his hand on it, wishing he could remember when his parents had given it to him. They said it was an electrical fire. No one could have stopped it, but only Nolan and his grandfather had survived. He looked up at the newspaper clipping again. It was a closed-casket funeral. The fire had left no respectable memory of his parents. He didn't remember too much about the funeral. The only thing he could still remember was the smell of fire and the taste of ashes. His grandfather had given him a new start in a new town, one where he wouldn't have to walk by the first home he ever knew while the people's pity pulverized his young pride. *Wylies are proud, not pitiful. Never forget that, Nolan.* Nolan could almost hear him say it when they moved to Texas.

As the sounds of the room sat still in the early morning, Nolan stared at his medallion, which was now lying flat and hitting the tender flesh above his heart. It was the size of a chocolate chip cookie as wide as his thumbs meshed together. The old silver necklace had an image of a giant tiger on it; half of the tiger was painted white and the other half black. There was writing on the back in a thin circular line. No one he knew could read it. His grampa walked in to see him lying on his bed.

"Nolan, are you okay? I heard screaming," his grandfather said.

"It's nothing, just a nightmare," Nolan lied. He was too old for this.

"Are you sure?" he asked.

"Yeah," he said. "I have nightmares, Grampa. Nothing to worry about."

"Do you want to talk about it?" he asked.

The days of Nolan talking about his nightmares had passed, especially this one. He had already heard the story. His parents were new to town. A vacation turned into a job offer, which turned into a new home—and ended with a double funeral.

"What are you doing up?" Nolan asked.

He pulled a shirt on over his head. His medallion was underneath. Sitting on the edge of the bed, he listened.

"You woke me up," he replied. "I was in my study just across the hall—"

"Reading." Nolan laughed.

"You guessed it. There's a new article on the Big Web—"

"Internet," Nolan said and chuckled. "We talked about this, Grampa."

"Fine, on the *Inter-Net*."

Nolan let his grampa tell him more about some article he'd found online, but he couldn't shake the dream. Why had he been dreaming about his parents after so long, and why had it been that memory? It could have been any other memory about his parents—his parents hugging him, moving into a new place, giving him a toy—anything—but not fire. No matter how many times he dreamed it, it still felt vivid. Seeing his grandfather's smiling face as the conversation drifted into more articles on the "Big Web," Nolan was calmed by his friendly face, and perfect teeth lined up as if they were waiting on the scrimmage. His grampa was remarkably healthy for someone his age. His hair was thick with brown curls not flowing past his ears. Gray had just started touching his sideburns. Watching his grandfather return to his study across the hall, Nolan turned on the TV where he would spend the next few hours wasting his Saturday morning as he had done nearly every Saturday since he'd graduated high school three weeks earlier. It was the best way to drown out a nightmare. In between *Call of Duty*, he picked up the large green cup on his dresser. Drinking last night's apple juice, he was able to keep himself awake in between games and check the occasional e-mails. Just more bullshit about applying to colleges he had never heard of. Nolan took another sip of his apple juice. It still tasted funny no matter what his grampa said. He'd heard somewhere—on the Big Web, most likely—that this new brand of apple juice was healthier than what they had drunk before. It made the taste sweeter than what he was used to.

Once noon chimed on the clock in the living room, Nolan knew that was his indicator to get ready. His grampa had always allowed him to have the early mornings to himself, but they always had lunch together. Always. Nolan took a shower and got himself ready for the day. His friends were coming by later to hang out. They didn't really have plans; they were just going to drive around, maybe hit up the carnival. A firm knock was heard throughout the house. Nolan knew instantly who it was.

"The door's open!" Nolan heard his grandfather shout.

He would make his way downstairs to the kitchen in no particular rush. Dressed comfortably, he walked out of his room and past the guest room, bathroom, and study on the second floor. As he descended the stairs, his childhood flashed back again. The pictures were from age three to his high school graduation with lots of memories of all the activities he had done growing up, mostly sports. He had tried them all—from baseball to lacrosse—but none of them lasted more than a few months. "It just makes you well versed," Grampa had told him. Seeing all the pictures of his grampa and his friends, Nolan wished he had at least remembered what his parents looked like. His grampa's description could only go so far. He had no pictures—well, other than the kindergarten picture he had drawn when he was five. He didn't think his mother had orange hair.

As he ran down memory lane almost as fast as he could, the front door was the first thing he saw. It was partially open, which meant that Henri had been the last one to enter. He sighed as he closed it, right on schedule. Making a quick left, he saw his grampa making sandwiches in the open kitchen located directly in front of the living room, where the History channel was beaming. Nolan leaned against the island counter while Henri and Emmett joined him on either side.

"Seriously, you know, you really should lock your door. That's probably what happened to those Jensen people over in Percy," Henri said.

"Seriously," Emmett imitated. "You sound like a valley girl. What's up, man?" Emmett said, getting a slight head nod from Nolan.

"You want any help, Mr. Wylie?" Emmett said.

"You boys go sit down. I'll take care of lunch. Consider it a post graduation present," he said and smiled.

"It was a present to graduate," Henri said, nudging Nolan.

Henri and Emmett had been his friends since kindergarten. Henri had grown up the most since then. Tall, clean-shaven, and a smartass. His long black hair, which always looked sleek as he tucked it behind his ear, was almost touching his shoulder now. Emmett was almost the complete opposite. He had short, hazel brown hair and unbelievably blue eyes. What he lacked in height, however, he made up for in muscle. Now that they were out of school, he was enjoying growing out some facial hair. A brisk five o'clock shadow made them all a little envious. His hair always grew the fastest, but it wasn't public knowledge. Emmett liked to keep his hair short. He said it was less work he had to do in the morning. Still, it looked good on his baby face.

"What's for eats, Grampa?" Nolan asked.

"Aw, just some chicken breast I cooked up on honey wheat." He smiled, preparing the last of them. "Emmett, you still like honey mustard, right?"

"Yes, sir," he responded.

The three of them sat together as his grampa made the last of the chicken breasts. They looked out of the bay window, waiting for someone to do it.

"So I pulled a Wylie the other day and caught myself watching the History channel. Did you know that they found some new mummy hidden in one of the pyramids?" Emmett smiled.

Nolan watched his grampa's face light up with excitement about old news. His grampa was fascinated with history. He spent so much time reliving the past even his phone lived in another era.

"They actually discredited that; turns out it was a little boy who died in the pyramid. Remember, Nolan, I told when you got up. Historians were surprised it hit national news. People thought he was the pharaoh's son," Grampa said.

Nolan sat back and almost listened to his grandfather talk more about the differences between mummification and the actual remains. By then, he was an expert at this. Nolan looked over to his friends and smiled. He put his fist in the air and bumped it with Emmett's. Their hands softly exploded as they whispered, "Yuuupp." Henri threw his hands in front of himself with a what-about-me look on his face, to which, Emmett and Nolan, without words, said, "You shoulda pulled a Wylie."

"So what do you kids have planned for the rest of the day?" Nolan's grandfather asked, bringing them each a chicken sandwich served with potato chips. He turned to get their drinks, but Nolan had beaten him to it. "Thanks, son."

Nolan smiled. He knew that his grampa only called him "son" when he did something that in his words "your father would have done." He looked forward to those moments because for a second, he felt like he knew his own father. They each had a cup of apple juice in a tall glass.

"I don't know. Henri?" Emmett said, taking his first bite.

"What? You assume I have a plan?" Henri stated, food still moving in his mouth.

Emmett and Nolan shared a still look.

"Do you not?" Emmett said.

Henri grunted before putting his sandwich down and—they were thankful—swallowed before his mouth opened again. "Well, maybe …"

"Exactly." Emmett chuckled.

"You should've placed a bet," Nolan said.

"I woulda won too," Emmet said, leading to a laugh. "Just like last time."

"Maybe!" he exclaimed and smiled slightly. "Maybe, we can head over to the carnival. Uncle Joshua says—"

"Don't you mean Principal Drake?" Nolan laughed.

"He's not our principal anymore. I wonder if that means we call him Joshua or Mr. Drake," Emmett said. "It's all Lily now."

"You know my mom hates when you call her that," Henri said. "Her name is Lilith," he said, imitating his mother. "If I named her Lily that would be her name."

Turning his head, Emmett said, "Why is your mom so anal about nicknames? Besides, I don't see your *mother* here, do you, Nolan?"

"Boys," Nolan's grandfather said. "Be respectful of his mother's wishes even if she's not here."

They nodded.

"Why would we go to the carnival anyway?" Nolan asked. "We don't need hours anymore. What else you got?"

"It's supposed to be really good this year. They repainted the Ferris wheel. And besides, since we don't have to work it this year, it might be nice to actually ride something."

"There have been plenty of things ridden in the carnival," Emmett whispered as he tapped Nolan's shoulder.

Nolan knew this was going to happen. Some habits put up a fight. The Middlecreek End-of-School Carnival was held every year, the weekend after finals. Principal Joshua Drake, along with the other principals from the four neighboring schools, two elementary and two junior highs, got together to hold the annual Middlecreek carnival in the old football field. The profits would be equally split by each of the five schools. It was easy money for them and a good start on next year's volunteer hours.

"That's sounds great. Maybe you'll see some old friends." Nolan's grandfather smiled.

"I doubt it. Most people hate that thing," Emmett said.

"Not everyone." Henri laughed. "Besides, what else is there to do in this town?"

"You're not gonna eat, Grampa?" Nolan asked.

"Unfortunately no, I had half a sandwich from last night in my study. Besides I was just in the middle of this news spread on the Big Web."

"Internet," Nolan corrected.

"Stubbornness must be a family trait," Emmett whispered.

"Why do you like history so much, Mr. Wylie? I'll never understand that. It's old news," Henri responded.

"As they say, knowledge is power," he said, before making his way back upstairs. "You kids have fun; trust your instincts." He chuckled, shaking his finger at Nolan as he left.

Nolan continued eating his sandwich, not looking forward to going to the carnival. His ex-girlfriend, Lindsay, was probably volunteering. She did *not* take it well, but it was long overdue.

"What's up with that *never understand* shit?" Emmett said, once Mr. Wylie was upstairs. "You're the go-to guy." Two thumbs were thrust in the air as Nolan smiled.

"He's more like a random-fact generator," Nolan said. "Who cares how ice cream is made? Or where beer first came from?"

"Or how the invention of the steam engine *changed the world*. I swear, man, one of these days, you're gonna find something useful to talk about."

"Shelby seemed to like what I had to say," Henri said, ever so cocky.

"Please," Emmett said. "Shelby's had a crush on you since freshman year. That was an I'll-never-see-you-again fuck."

"How is Shelby?" Nolan asked. "She still working at the smoothie place this summer."

"I think so. I haven't talked to her in a few days," Henri said.

"Let me guess," Emmett said. "Since Wednesday night. You give us all a bad name, Henri."

"At least I put my name out there," Henri said, laughing. "No one likes a hater, Emmett."

"No one likes a motherfucker either," Emmett grunted.

"Don't fucking call me that," Henri said.

"I'm not the one sharing his dick with the family."

"Hey, I did not know that was her mom!"

Nolan listened to the two of them bicker on like an old married couple. He looked down to his medallion. For some reason, it felt heavier than normal, as if he had a small sack of pennies around his neck.

"So, Nolan, you ready to go?" Henri asked, taking him out of his confusion.

"Huh? Yeah. I just got to put some shoes on. And get my keys," Nolan said.

Nolan made his way up to his room and quickly put his shoes on. Sweat was still masking a scent on the back of his pillow. Spraying some Febreeze, he tried to cover up the nightmare. When he made it downstairs, Emmett was placing all of their dishes in the sink.

"Off to the carnival, we will go," Emmett announced as if it were some eighteenth-century joust.

"Shotgun!" Henri shouted quickly.

The Wylie garage was more organized than either Henri's or Emmett's. It was home to the two cars of the house, Nolan's grandfather's Lincoln Cadillac, which no one else was allowed to drive, and Nolan's silver Mustang, which he had named Carmen. As they made their way to the car, Nolan pushed the garage door opener.

"Damn it. I forgot my keys. Hold up," he said.

Halfway toward the stairs, Nolan felt another unfamiliar weight. Placing his hand on his left pocket, he felt the impression of his keys. Turning back, he met Henri and Emmett outside his car. Revving up his Mustang brought more joy than he could possibly imagine. He kept it neat, just as his grampa did with his car. It was his way of appreciating everything his grampa had done for him. Since everything they had had burned in the fire, his grampa did his best to replace those memories. Besides, it was calming having his grampa's trust to leave the house almost whenever he wanted. After pulling out of the garage, he made his way out of the neighborhood, as Emmett tried to change the radio station.

"Never touch the radio, man!" Nolan laughed.

"Aw, come on. Are you still on that? You play the same shit every day." Emmett laughed.

"You gotta respect the classics," he replied.

"All I'm saying is you need to try something new. Get some real music," Emmett said.

"Yeah, because you're so open-minded!" Henri chuckled, rolling down his window.

"About some things, I am," he snapped back.

"Please," Henri said. "Every time we go out, you eat the same damn thing *every damn time*. Quesadillas and—"

"A Dr. Pepper," Nolan said. "Oh, don't forget about the face."

Emmett looked at him as he scrunched his face as if he were holding a menu. "You know it's true. You be searching for those damn quesadillas."

"So what? I like what I like. If I wanted to try something new, I could," Emmett said.

"All that talk, no game," Henri said. "Just like *everything* else you do."

"I got game," Emmett said.

Nolan knew he was trying to sound confident. He admired that about Emmett. Steady. While Henri was known for making his way throughout the high school, Emmett was more of the reliable guy, a man of his word. Girls liked that, well, some girls. Driving back toward the high school made Nolan realize how *not* little their town was. Middlecreek was home to about fifty thousand people. It was a quiet suburb in Cyrus County in between two neighboring cities Percy and Tessa. Everything had a story behind it, like Albertsons, where the boys had their first and only attempt at shoplifting at eleven; Mr. Wandengo's Sportatorium, where all the latest sports equipment was kept in full stock; and of course, Auntie Mae's Ice Cream Shop. Every kid in Middlecreek made at least one trip there over the summer. Their (now) old high school, Middlecreek High, was located just past the Super Wal-Mart but right before the main highway going toward Percy. It was hidden behind some trees with the community center in front of Parker Lake, where Nolan got to second base with Michelle Rockford. Everything had a memory. Once you made it to the high school, you'd be surprised you ever missed it, it being the crown jewel of the Middlecreek. With their football earnings, the school looked almost new again. Two floors of classes, some portables behind it, an outside weight room, a small football field, a pool, and a track field, it was impossible to miss for anyone attending. Nolan couldn't believe he would no longer have to drive there every morning, listen to the same lessons, and see the same people. He was a high school *graduate*. He could go wherever he wanted now, but the decision had already been made less than a year ago. Nolan, Henri, and Emmett had agreed it would be smarter for them to stay behind from a big university and go to Wilson Community College for two years. They wanted to enjoy being the big fish in a small pond a little while longer before they rushed off into adulthood.

The parking lot was in back of the school, where normally a sticker on your windshield would be all that you needed to stay there, a sticker that was still stuck to Carmen's windshield. Finding a decent parking spot was virtually impossible, so Nolan had to settle for sweat seat. Nolan had nicknamed them sweat seats because afterschool, you could always smell the football team practicing. Luckily, for them, the carnival took over the football field so they wouldn't have to endure a true sweat seat.

"Come on. I promised my mom I'd ride the Ferris wheel with Lilith," Henri said, leaving the car.

"She's fifteen; you still gotta ride rides with her?" Emmett laughed. "Our parents got it right the first time, didn't they, Nolan?"

"They didn't need a redo," Nolan said, as they all made their way onto the hard concrete where they used to race to get to class on time.

"It's tradition, all right," Henri replied. "Lilith's probably waiting for me."

Tradition had always been a big deal to the Roland family. Every Sunday night, his parents would have dinner at their house, and on occasion, Nolan and Emmett would show up.

"So I'm gonna meet up with guys from the team. Meet up later?" Emmett said.

"Are you gonna have any money left?" Henri asked.

"Don't you worry about me. I always get mine," Emmett said.

"Seriously," Henri said.

"You say that word a lot, you know? Nolan, come on, man. Move your ass," Emmett said.

"Did you guys hear that?" Nolan asked.

Nolan turned his head; he could swear he had heard a loud cry for help. The sound, which was more like a shriek, was behind him. He thought it was nothing until he heard it a second time. It sounded like a woman or maybe a little girl.

"Hear what?" Henri responded.

"That shriek," he said.

"I didn't hear anything," Emmett replied.

"Come on. We gotta get to that carnival," Henri said, continuing to walk.

"I gotta check this out," Nolan said, turning around.

"Come on, Captain Save-a-Ho; it's probably just a pet bird or some shit. Let's go! Mrs. Pierce is in the dunking booth this year, and I've been practicing my throwing arm all week," Emmett said.

"Getting a few midnight strokes in," Henri said and laughed.

"Shut up," Emmett said.

"You seriously don't hear that?" Nolan said, as the shriek got louder.

"Uh, let's go check it out," Emmett said. "Before he hears it again."

"Two out of three." Henri chuckled, making his way toward the mythical sound. "But we better be back before the lines get too long!" he shouted, only to be ignored. "I don't wanna keep Lilith waiting."

With Nolan leading the way, they made their way through the cars, unaware that they were being watched from a far by a familiar face. It took them a few moments to get to the portables. Nolan had asked if anyone could hear the shrieks now, and he was comforted by small head nods from his friends. *At least I'm not crazy*, he thought. They thought they had narrowed it down to one possible place: the corner between the first portable and the emergency exit at the end of the gym. It was where some students went to smoke during off periods. The only way to get there was to use the emergency exit door, which had been broken for as long as they knew. No one knew about that place except students, and since the school doors were locked, they wondered how anyone would have gotten there in the first place.

"Let's get out of here," Henri said. "It smells like weed and vodka."

Nolan led them around the corner. They were surprised to see a man dressed in a black cloak in between the school and the portables. He looked old; there was gray hair almost flowing from the hood of his cloak, and he smelled rotten. As he looked at them, they saw a red symbol burning on his head. It pulsed in front of them.

"Did his tattoo just move!" Emmett shouted.

Nolan never thought that he would think this, but he was creepy for an old man. He stood up against the fenced gate with his hands covered by the length of the cloak. His arms were in front of him like that girl from *Bewitched*. When the old man looked at Nolan's shirt, he smiled, raising his head from the shadow. There was something burned on the man's forehead. A tattoo. They saw it more clearly now with the help of some sunlight. It looked like the three points of a trident, but the middle one was longer.

"Give me your medallion, young Moon Dea," he demanded. The hood of his cloak covered his face, but his voice was booming.

"What!" Nolan shouted. "How can you see that?" Nolan asked, taking it from underneath his shirt. The medallion still felt heavy.

"Let's just go," Henri said softly. "He's probably just a homeless guy. A crazy, creepy-ass homeless guy."

"Who are you?" Nolan said, ignoring him. "How did you get back here?"

"And where the hell did that screaming come from?" Emmett asked.

The man's face got very tense as if they had somehow upset him, but none of them seemed to care. They were simple questions. The cloaked man said something in a foreign language. None of them had ever heard anything like it before. It was lyrical and terrifying as if he were singing along next to a mortuary choir.

"What did you say?" Henri asked.

Immediately, the boys were surrounded by multiples of his reflection. Nolan looked around, as did Henri and Emmett, frightened and frozen. Each one of his multiples formed a circle around them. The hands all reached with an incredible length. It resembled an enormous clock, rotating and ticking each of them, demanding Nolan's medallion. Nolan instinctively put his hand on his medallion. *What the fuck is going on?* He felt himself being pulled backward, but his feet weren't moving.

"Foolish hollow! You shall never remove what is not yours to have!" Nolan shouted, in a deeper, older voice. Nolan could hear the voice, but it wasn't his own. He tried to speak but couldn't. His hands were pulled to the terrified shoulders of his friends. He could see what was happening, but he had no control of it. His body transformed into a golden orb. It quickly spun around his friends, taking them inside the orb as well. As their bodies moved, they could feel everything as if they were packed too closely into an elevator with a dozen people. Comfort was the last thing on their minds. They moved as fast as the speed of light—probably faster. It felt like hours before their feet hit solid ground again. They yelled at the top of their lungs, but it was nothing but an echo behind the school. When their bodies landed, Emmett and Henri threw up. Nolan vomited as well, but there were traces of blood in his. He kept vomiting for a few more seconds longer than his friends did. When the last drop left his mouth, Nolan looked over to his friends. He was sure they were wondering the same thing.

What just happened?

At the entrance to the carnival, the watchful eyes of Principal Joshua Drake were pointing up with his shaggy brown hair covered by a blue hat. He was wearing his favorite shirt with the yellow rose in the top left corner and blue jeans. He was definitely the coolest-looking principal in Middlecreek, and he took pride in that. The golden orb pierced through the clouds like a thread though a needle. All of the years of planning and the day had finally come. Keeping them under lock and key had been so cruel but shamefully necessary. Joshua knew they would be angry, especially Nolan but they had no choice. He moved the hair behind his ear, keeping his gaze on the heavens. He was the final protector, ensuring their departure was not followed or traced. He watched for moments longer than he needed to. These types of situations required extreme delicacy. So much would be changing for them, and they would have so many questions. Those questions could lead to swift anger toward some many valued lives. They couldn't do it here; the risk was too great. Neutral ground would keep them safe until they were ready to understand why so many things would be different now. *A few more moments, just to be sure*, he told himself. The sky was still clear and empty of all its fury. Never twice would a day like this occur. Picking up his phone, Joshua held his finger on one number and waited for the ring. Terrans made such crafty things.

"They came just like you planned," he said, before listening to the short reply and closing the phone to return to his responsibilities. "I'm sure they will arrive safely, Your Highness, but they won't be happy about it."

2

The Prince and the Magi

"WHAT THE HELL just happened!" screamed Henri. "Oh shit, not again!"

Nolan, along with his friends, each grabbed onto their stomachs as they vomited more onto the ground. Nolan vomited for the longest time again, being hurled over for more than a few minutes longer. There was still blood in his. No one spoke. Nolan had no idea what was happening. Whatever it was that had spoken from the medallion was gone. He was pulled back, but he was in so much shock, he couldn't say anything. The olive-skinned graduate looked up in the sky to see a giant sun hovering above them, but it was blue, a royal blue. *What's wrong with the sun?* he thought. Nolan looked around to see that they were in some kind of forest, but he didn't take the time to look closely at it because that would have made things real. In a dream, all you had to do was let things happen, just as he had done that morning; he would wake up soon enough. Opening and closing his eyes did nothing but make things feel more and more real. Nolan had seen an image of a sun like this before, but it was in his science class back at school. He was amazed at what he remembered since Mrs. Pierce's class seemed so distant to him. It had only been a few weeks since she had given him his last final, but he could still remember why he too wanted to see her dropped in a pool of water at the carnival.

Nolan could still remember her saying, in her grimy voice, "Zphysics surroundsz us. Let thisz always be with you. Live long and prosper." Seeing her pudgy fingers do the Vulcan salute made her students laugh every semester as they walked out of her class for the last time. If only she were here. She might know where the fuck they were. What Nolan was looking at was called a blue super giant. More than three times the size of their own yellow sun, it was said to be among the hottest and largest stars in the universe. Blue super giants were extremely rare and, as far as he knew, nowhere near Earth.

"Man, your shirt … it's … glowing, Nolan!" Henri shouted as he pointed.

Nolan looked down to see that it wasn't his shirt glowing; it was his medallion. Nolan pulled his medallion from under his shirt. It was glowing a golden color with black streaks around the light. He had never thought gold could be so terrifying. What kind of family heirloom did shit like this? *Wake up! Wake up!* he shouted in his mind. Nolan closed his eyes, and he tried to take the medallion off, but it was not coming off. Every time he tried to pull it off, the medallion froze at the base of his chin and forced itself back to his chest.

"I can't take it off, man! What the fuck is this thing?" he shouted.

"I don't know, man," Emmett replied, as he walked over to him, trying to help him remove it. Henri had walked over there as well, but neither of them could help.

"What the fuck?" Henri exclaimed.

They heard rustling coming from behind them. They frantically looked around, trying to see what it was. A man walked out of the shadows in a white and gold cloak. His hair was red and rustled by the wind, yet his clothes were neat. He was shorter than they were as he walked with a smile toward them. The man was elderly with vanilla skin and lime-green eyes. Wearing a thin gold chain around his neck with what looked like a little dragon surrounded by a circle, he walked proudly with nothing taking his attention away from them.

Nolan's body froze in front of them. His eyes were blank, and his feet couldn't move. Henri and Emmett tried to wake him. Nolan felt something overtake him again, and again, he was powerless to stop it. His medallion was still glowing, but his friends were still at his side. The medallion must have taken over again. He shouted, but no words came out. No one could hear him! When at last he could hear, it wasn't his voice, but the same voice that had saved them from that creepy old guy back in Middlecreek.

"It has been so long since I've been able to breathe fresh Devanian air," said the voice from Nolan's body.

The voice sounded like his grampa, a little deeper though. Nolan could hear the voice, but he couldn't stop it. It was loud and booming. He had never been more afraid in his life. Was he possessed? Possession was just something people watched on TV shows about ghosts or some shit. What was that word he said? *Devanian?* He kept yelling out his friends' names, but nothing came out. He could hear and see everything around him as if he were watching his own life through a TV screen, but he could not control himself, not anymore.

Your Highness was the only phrase the man with the neat red hair in front of them could utter as he bowed on one knee.

"My reign has long been over. Are you the one meant to usher us in?" the voice replied.

"Yes. He suspected you would be able to find them if he was threatened. He will be relieved that you arrived here safely. Inter-realm travel is very difficult on the body."

"Yes, I was able to breach worlds with little difficulty. It is the only way I could cross. The bond between them must be stronger than I thought."

"How long will the effects of the spell last? Surely a possessive spell cannot …"

"Excuse me!" Henri shouted. "Can someone explain to us what the *fuck* is going on here?"

Henri reflected Nolan's inner fury with their prolonging conversation. Henri would hate it if he said it aloud, but sometimes he was just like his mother. She was very, *very* attentive to plans and rules. Unexpected changes made her irritable and loud. Henri's patience for all of this confusion had just reached its limits. His friends' fear would overpower their established friendship. Henri and Emmett had now backed up next to each other. They were as far away from the two of those things as they could be. Nolan didn't blame them. If he could, he would be right there with them.

"Henri, Emmett, all will be explained shortly. You are safe, here," the spirit from Nolan's body replied as they looked, dumbfounded, at him.

"I was safe at the carnival!" Henri shouted.

While normally it was Emmett who was quick to snap back, Nolan could imagine what Henri was feeling. The Ferris wheel was tradition, damn near an obligation. He had never missed one since Lilith was in junior high even when he had to start working them. Having your mother's brother as your principal gave him more than a good relationship with the teachers.

"How the hell do you know my name?" Emmett whispered, his voice sounding more like a grunt than a quiet whisper.

Nolan knew the fury was rising in Emmett. His anger wasn't as swift as Henri's was. Emmett held on to it as if he were shaking a can of Dr. Pepper. It was only a matter of time before Emmett exploded. That was when Nolan and Henri could relax. Emmett was their quiet storm whenever he was ready to put all that muscle to good use. The red-haired man in the cloak was walking toward them with a frozen face.

"I'll fight an old man if I have to!" Emmett yelled, fists formed.

"Don't worry, children. You're on Wylie Isle, the summer palace. My name is Zachariah Kingsley, senior librarian of the Cystlian Towers. I can explain everything; I assure you."

"Somebody sure as hell better!" Henri shouted.

"Have you located him?" the spirit asked.

"Not in the vicinity, Your Highness, but I cannot be certain. Perhaps if you—" Zachariah Kingsley said.

"Not now. He would be able to pick up the connection instantly. We must get to safe ground. He must have discovered the same thing my son did. There was a hollow waiting for us in the Terran system. Please escort us to the summer palace, Master Kingsley," the spirit said.

Nolan thought the worst as his friends remained still. Maybe this guy was taking over Nolan's body and leaving *him* trapped in a medallion? *This could be the end of me*, he thought. Just when he thought, he was slipping to the other side, he felt something wash over him. He could not explain the warm sensation rising through his back. Since he could not speak to anyone, he finally got a chance to look around the island. Every ounce of peaceful and pleasant thought melted in a stream of bountiful colors laid before them. The trees were thin, like palm trees, and had fruit the size of coconuts hanging from its branches. It wasn't as large as he would have thought an island to be, but it did look bright. The trees soared overhead. He couldn't hear anything on the island, which surprised him, but he didn't have anyone to answer his questions so he didn't bother. Where was he? His mind looked over, and he could see an animal or something move within the shadows of the trees. Through the shadows, it looked magnificent. Its white fur and black stripes reminded him of the nights that he would stare out his window into space, looking at the same image on his medallion. It looked like a white tiger; he had never seen anything so grand in his life. He wondered if it had anything to do with his medallion. Those black beady eyes were looking directly at him.

He did not know what it was, but he thought it was talking to him—at least in his mind. *Welcome home, Nolan*, it echoed in a low, older tone. Could animals talk to him in his head? How did it know his name? Nolan knew what it was, but he could not say anything. He did not even know if he could think of anything. If he thought something, would that creature be able to hear or was it like a one-way street? It didn't matter; instantly, the white tiger disappeared.

"Master Kingsley, I believe it's time for an explanation," the voice from Nolan's body replied, looking to see that the boys were still terrified.

"Of course, Your Highness," uttered the mysterious Zachariah Kingsley. "Henri and Emmett, follow me. I will explain everything, as I promised."

"What's up with that sun? Where are we?" Henri asked, still keeping his distance.

"The blue sun?" Zachariah said. "I imagine it must seem foreign to you. The realm you are in is much older than your adoptive home, farther beyond the science of the Terrans. We exist in the Deva Loka on the planet known as Deva Prime. The blue sun is the center of our universe, and the red moon is our single satellite."

"Planet? As in more than one?" Emmett whispered.

"You did not think you were alone, did you?" Zachariah asked. "I am told most Terrans do not believe this anymore."

Zachariah and Nolan walked in front of them, and they kept their conversation quiet as they followed. Nolan could barely hear them, but he tried as best he could.

"This guy's crazy, right?" Emmett asked.

"I don't know, man," Henri said. "I mean look around. They have a blue sun, man! This shit is definitely not Earth!"

"Then why are we here?" Emmett asked more softly.

"I don't know how, but we have to get Nolan back before we leave. We can't seriously leave him behind in this place," Henri said.

"You're right," Emmett said. "Let's just get Nolan and get the hell out of here."

"Is that a palace?" Henri shouted.

The beauty of the summer palace froze them at the entrance. A long corridor in front of them was made of stone with small red pebbles embedded in the texture. The path to the castle was green and had pillars alongside it. The castle was the largest structure on the island, separating two large grass plains. Green pastures were generous with light-green trees and bushes with bright red and yellow flowers. Two stone figures were protective of the entrance door, one of a marble tiger roaring and another a marble dragon with its wings spread wide. Zachariah and Nolan walked in front of Henri and Emmett, who were shocked but still impressed. The entrance to the castle was made of black wood. The door had two knobs in the center of its wooden frame. A thick silver lining welcomed them as the doors opened before them. The castle looked traditional in size and shape; it was four stories tall and made of stone like a British castle. Its massive size could have contained anything and everything in their houses back home. The castle was covered in red and white paint with handcrafted flower petals on the tiles. There had to be at least twenty rooms, counting the outside windows. At the top of the castle, a peak about four feet tall with a circle surrounding eight symbols watched over them. A blue-green sun was setting behind them. It was about three times the size of their sun, but from their position, it looked distant still. They had never had such a close view of a sun before. It cast a shadow on the peak that stood in front of them, revealing a shadow of the strange symbols. This did not help though; they still couldn't read it.

Just as Emmett tapped Henri's shoulder, Nolan felt his head turn, but he didn't command it; someone else wanted him to see them. Either way, his attention was temporarily redirected before he saw what they were looking at. The moon behind them, rising slowly, was red and twice as big as Earth's moon. The red moon was staring at him. It moved slowly as the blue sun sat across the sky. Nolan was expecting the red moon to create a red moonlight, but it was white, just like it was at home.

"Welcome to the summer palace. I imagine you must be hungry. Come; I'll show you the dining room," Zachariah said.

Zachariah led them through the front door. The castle was even more beautiful on the inside. As he walked in, there was a large set of stairs on his left-hand side. The stairs wired up to the second floor and continued to the third. The stair railings were golden, and the stairs were white with a different pattern on the tiles. Pictures of what they guessed were his family and friends hung on the walls. The picture frames came in all sizes and colors. The pictures looked hollow, and the images were frozen. Blank faces were the common feature in all of them. They were dressed in heavy robes and crowns.

Two creatures walked down the stairs and welcomed Zachariah and his guests by bowing their heads. The creatures looked bigger than average monkeys. They had black fur and beady gray eyes. Their long tails moved like snakes. Without either of them touching it, the door behind the boys closed with an abrupt sound. They turned around in shock.

"Did those monkeys just close the door without touching it?" Emmett asked.

"I don't think they're average monkeys," Henri said.

"If these things aren't monkeys, what are they?" Emmett asked.

"Please prepare dinner. I have come with the Southern Magi," he said.

The monkeys' faces widened as they looked up. Each of them looked at the others and grunted. The one on the left pounded his chest and told the other one to follow him. Their thick tails danced with delight as they made their way into the kitchen. When they were safely inside, the doors closed as if they had their own will. Did the monkeys do that or the house? They were surprised as they left to go to the kitchen. Within moments, the table was being set for four people as if they knew they were coming. White and light-brown dinnerware was set in front of them, but no one was hungry. Emmett and Henri sat on the same side while Nolan sat opposite. *I don't blame them*, he thought. They did not speak at all at the table, still in a dreamlike state. Zachariah sat at the head of the table. The monkeys carried the food out from the kitchen. Nolan couldn't see into the kitchen from their current seating, but the door was still swinging, revealing more golden and white tiles. They placed a giant boar in the center, and the second monkey brought out sides that were foreign to the three of them but smelled sweet. The door opened two more times, as plates came out with dessert and bread. They did not even care about the food; they wanted answers, especially Nolan. Zachariah served them each a part of the meal. Henri and Emmett kept their distance from his hand as much as they could. Nolan had no choice but to sit down and stay calm. The three of them each got a serving of whatever it was in front of them, but no one was touching forks or spoons.

"I have already answered that question, Emmett. This is the summer home of the royal family where we are all welcomed guests," Zachariah said.

"Did you read my mind?" Emmett whimpered.

"I can read the minds of others, yes," Zachariah said. "Is this not common in the Terran system?"

"Common! Are you fucking kidding me? Talk about invasion of my fucking privacy. And rude as hell," Emmett said. "What are you, some kind of alien?"

"You are the alien here, Emmett," Zachariah said.

Nolan was almost proud Emmett's fury was reaching its peak. Even Henri had to look up. This wasn't like Emmett at all. He was normally very respectful of his elders, but apparently, that didn't include mind readers.

"I was born with it, Henri. My grandfather had the power as well," Zachariah said.

I think it is best if you hear the truth now, Nolan. Just listen, the voice said again.

Nolan was confused. How could he hear that guy in *his* head when he couldn't even move his own arms? He looked down to see that the light over his medallion had left. It had happened so quickly he wasn't even sure it was real. His friends didn't notice. He looked over to Zachariah, and he wondered what he meant by "power." Hoping that this would work now, Nolan opened his mouth.

"I see Nolan has returned to us," Zachariah said.

"How did you …" Nolan began, but Zachariah only smiled.

"Whoa! Nolan, is that you? How the hell did that happen? Where were you?" Emmett asked.

"I don't know. Whoever was in control just … let go," Nolan said.

"Cool. Let's get the fuck out of here," Emmett said as he stood.

"I'm afraid you cannot, Emmett," Zachariah said. "Only a Divine Dea has the power to travel between realms, and Nolan is too young. I do not think he will have the strength, let alone the knowledge of how."

"But he got us here? He can take us back," Emmett said.

Nolan didn't even know where to start with that. He had no idea how he had brought them there—wherever that was—and he had absolutely no idea what a Divine Dea was.

"Mr. Kingsley, what do you mean 'power'? Is that how we got here?" Nolan asked. "Did I do this to us?" He looked at the food in front of him, but he refused to eat anything.

"Please, call me Zachariah," he said.

"Well, Zachariah, what *did* you mean? How the hell did we get here?" Henri asked.

"I have much to tell you, so please bear with me," Zachariah said.

"That's never a good sign," Emmett stated.

Zachariah sat at the head of the table, taking a deep breath as if he was preparing to give them a horrible memory. He took a small bite, chewed, swallowed, and spoke again.

"You were right, Nolan. You did bring you and your friends to this world. As the Moon Dea, you have the power to travel between worlds."

Moon Dea, that was the same thing that thing had called him.

"The hollow," Zachariah corrected. "It was sent to the Terran system to find you. Thankfully, you were able to get here before you could be captured."

"But how ... did I do that?" Nolan asked.

"You had help," Zachariah said. He pointed to Nolan's medallion. "The man you heard when the three of you arrived here, his name was Lucian Samson *Wylie*. He was and still is Nolan's great-grandfather, the father of Amos Bartholomew Wylie."

Nolan's eyes bucked as he looked at this *Zachariah*. He had been possessed. Somehow, some way, he had been possessed by some kind of spirit from his own family.

"He possessed me!" he exclaimed.

"He endured a terrible punishment for over seventy years to ensure you arrived here on this day. Remember this, Nolan," Zachariah said.

That was a very strange way to avoid the question, but before Nolan could question him anymore, Zachariah had shifted his attention to Henri and Emmett.

Zachariah continued, "Henri and Emmett are also what we call Deas, just as I am. This simply means you have *powers* similar to a god. You were brought here to fulfill your destiny. As your birthdays passed in the Terran system, the cycle is complete and your powers have reached their maturity. Now you must hone them."

Nolan and Henri looked down to Emmett. He was right about that. Emmett was the youngest of the three of them. They had gone to a casino not even a week ago to celebrate.

"How do you know our birthdays?" Emmett asked.

"Well, that's simple. Nolan is the eldest followed by Henri then Emmett. You were each born only a couple years apart from each other."

"That's not true," Henri said. "We're born in the same year. Emmett's birthday is in June, mine is in April, and Nolan's is in February. We're months apart."

Nolan knew what Henri was doing because he always did it. With all of the trivial information he stored in his memory tank, he loved poking holes in people's stories. It made him feel smarter. It also made him a dick.

"Ah," Zachariah said. "You're right."

Henri smiled.

"By Terran standards. Our weeks and months are quite different from those with which you were raised. Nolan was born in the summer, the season we are currently in. They are two hundred and six days in the summer. Does that cover the gap between Terran months?"

They tried to do the math in their heads, but none of them was able to answer fast enough. Still Zachariah smiled as he looked at them. Zachariah now looked only at Nolan.

Try it. Call for something.

"Call?" Nolan asked.

"If the legend is true, then one of your powers is the ability to move things with your mind alone. Telekinesis. Perhaps a display of your power will confirm what I have just told you. Go on; try it," Zachariah said.

Nolan was not sure what he was supposed to do, but it wouldn't hurt to try. He wanted to do something simple to prove to this guy that he was completely off his rocker. He threw his left hand into the air, aiming for the fork below him. He tried it many times, growing more and more content with the result.

"See? I can't be your Moon thingy. I don't move things with my mind, and I'm not magic. Now please just take us home. You got the wrong guy." Nolan looked over to see his friends' raised eyebrows. He knew that they had been expecting the same result that he was giving them. He was normal; he knew it. His friends were proud of him as they were sitting back in their chairs, laughing in their heads. They were happy to see that Zachariah was wrong about Nolan. Now he would have no choice but to send them all home where they would forget this whole thing ever happened. Nolan looked back over to Zachariah, whose frustrated look received no sympathy from any of the boys.

"Concentrate." Zachariah was still confident.

"See? I told you I'm not one of you! Just send me home!" Nolan said.

"It is you and only you!" he said.

"I told you, you're wrong!" Nolan said.

"Just try, Nolan!" Zachariah said again calmly. "Concentrate! Your powers have been dormant for years. It will take more than one try to awaken them again."

Nolan tried several more times, waving his arms around like one of those guys directing planes. Zachariah continued to encourage him. No matter what he did though, nothing happened, no bright lights, no sudden movements, no anything. *Still*, Zachariah told him to try.

"I did! I'm not magic!" he shouted, pounding his fist on the table. Quickly all the silverware on the table went flying into the air and streamed straight to the ceiling, leaving deep impressions. Four sets of knives, spoons, and forks were frozen above them still as they were only moments ago. Nolan was speechless. How the hell could this happen? What had Zachariah done to him? Put him under a spell? He backed up out of his chair. Nolan was staring at the ceiling.

"You are Moon Dea, Nolan. Your powers are connected with your emotions, eternally linked to your soul. Just as all of us are," Zachariah said.

"Nolan! What are you?" Emmett yelled.

Henri and he just stared at Nolan as if he were a zoo animal, some creepy, freaky-looking zoo animal. Nolan couldn't even look at them, let alone hear them. *What am I?*

Do you still think me mad? Zachariah's voice was in his head again.

"Move out of the way, you little *monkeys*!" Emmett yelled again, when he tried to leave.

Nolan's first thought was envy as Emmett tried to get up. Maybe if Emmett left fast enough, he could escape the effects of whatever spell Zachariah had cast on them. However, the big, pleasant monkeys weren't letting him. They kept urging him to sit down, shaking their heads as they guided his bottom back to his chair.

"How do we know you didn't use your own magic to make him do that? Why should we trust you?" Henri questioned.

"I can *only* read minds, Henri. Even if I knew a spell to make this happen, it would have no effect. My powers are limited. His are nearly limitless."

Nolan didn't understand. How was it possible that he could only read minds? Every bit of magic he had ever seen on TV allowed everyone an equal opportunity to do magic, not just one kind. Something wasn't right about this. But then again, with a blue sun and a red moon, this wasn't his world anymore.

"Have I given you reason not to trust me? I told you I cannot—"

"We don't know that that's true!" Emmett said. "We don't know anything about this place! Whatever you did to Nolan, undo it and make us normal again and send us home!"

Nolan was still in shock. He didn't even hear what Henri or Emmett had said after that. What had Zachariah done to him! He wanted to go back home where he was normal. Rocking back and forth, he wished, prayed this was all still just a dream.

"Normal? Oh, but you *are* magic, both of you. I told you; you are *all* Deas in the same family, as you are now, just like me. Nolan is not the only one. I thought you would know this when Nolan used his own powers. Nolan was just the beginning." Zachariah began. "The eldest sons of the raven-haired Rolands, Henri, have had the power to master the element of wind for nearly two hundred years. Their powers were dormant for much longer than that however. It wasn't until Emperor Magnus Wylie discovered them that their powers rose again to their true strength."

"Emperor," Nolan said, cutting Zachariah's words in half. "Are you saying I'm some kind of prince, too?"

"The Sun and Moon Deas are the two ruling families, yes. They reign over the Northlands and Southlands respectively. Magnus Wylie was the first. He blessed the Roland family along with seven others, reviving their powers over the eight elements."

"Raven-haired Rolands," Henri said, as his own black hair shook recklessly. "That's crazy! We're not magic; no one in my family is. They would have told me. They would have told all of us!"

"The Planet of White Moons is very dangerous to our kind. Exposing the lot of you, especially Nolan, to its energy could have destroyed the realm in which you resided. Deas pull energy from the sun, the moon, and the earth. On this planet, there is a natural balance to prevent us from draining the source. On the Planet of White Moons, however, there is no balance for us. Death always follows the white."

"There is only one moon on Earth," Henri said.

Nolan was suddenly revived as well. Dangerous? How could a white moon be dangerous? He looked up to Zachariah, hoping for explanation. Zachariah ignored Henri's facts. He said it was for this reason they were not allowed to practice magic in the Terran system. Only a Dea whose powers were outside the elements would not disturb the natural balance of the Terran system.

"And who would have been able to do that?" Emmett asked.

"Why a Wylie, of course, Amos Bartholomew Wylie to be specific," the senior librarian of Cystlian Towers said.

"Grampa?" Nolan asked. "He used magic to keep us there?"

"To give you a normal life, to learn the ways of the Terrans," he said.

"I'm not lying, Emmett." Zachariah smiled.

"Stop reading my mind! You're sitting over there like you know everything, but you don't know anything, not about me, Henri, or Nolan. You're wrong about us," Emmett roared. "We're not weird!"

"You think magic is strange, do you? As a son of Merciful Markus, I expected you to be more open-minded! Your father is very well—"

"Listen, here you, old man. You do not know shit about my dad. You have no idea who he was or what he did. So you just shut up!" Emmett shouted.

It was like watching a volcano erupt. Nolan and Henri remained quiet while Emmett rose from his chair. They knew more than anyone that talking negatively about his late father was the best way to get him upset. Markus Bradley had been on a research trip to India last year. He was a geographical consultant for research facilities. The plane had run into an electrical storm over the Pacific and crashed into the ocean. They spent months trying to find him or any of the crew, but there were no survivors. They were told to prepare for the worst. At the funeral, Emmett had barely cried, but his mother wasn't as strong. His father had no family, and his mother's could care less about their half-breed grandson's father.

"I did not know," Zachariah said.

Every muscle in his face was overcome with weakness. Nolan knew he probably had an unwelcome guest sharing in his memories of Markus. He was the father everyone wished he or she had—fun, adventurous, and always smiling. Markus was the parent they called when they stole some small toys from Albertson's. They didn't even want them; it was just a rush. Markus didn't give them a lecture like Henri's mother would have. He told them life was too short to waste time doing meaningless shit. Then he took them to Principal Drake, who was just Uncle Joshua to them at eleven. They spent hours working on his backyard and his front yard while Markus and Josh drank beers on the patio. Theirs was a friendship that Nolan and his friends aspired to have.

"Markus … dead," Zachariah said. "We thought there might be a different way for the transference if you were born among Terrans.

I … I met your father at Cystlian Towers, Emmett. It was I who helped him identify the artifacts he retrieved from his adventures around the world. The day he brought back the hippopotamus seal, I thought—"

"The what?" Henri asked.

"The hippopotamus seal contains a sacred object used to contain the strength of one of the first daemons. This seal gave Markus the same powers contained on the seal, the ability to control the element of earth. He was one of the first to travel to the Terran system. He is … *was* a great man and a good friend. Tell me, is Joshua Drake still in his company?"

"Uncle Joshua?" Henri said. "They were best friends."

"In more than one world, young Henri. They both worked for the Towers, along with me," Zachariah said.

Nolan saw Emmett's fury cooling itself. He tried to get up again, but this time, the tail of one of those monkey things stopped him.

"Despite this awful news, there is still much more I have to tell you. It is no coincidence your powers lie in the eight elements. It is because of your powers, the three of you are the next generation of magi. Henri, since your element is wind, you are called the Southern Wind Mage; Emmett, you are the earth mage; and, Nolan, your element is water, making you the Southern Water Mage," Zachariah said.

"Now you tell me that I have to be something else too? What's wrong with you?" Nolan shouted. It was bad enough what happened with the forks and then being a prince and now *this*?

"Water is the element of the moon. This much the Terrans have gathered for themselves," Zachariah said. "Who would be a stronger water mage than you?"

Nolan didn't hear any of that. This was way too much information for him to process. He could *maybe* understand this whole power thing, but being a prince? That was ridiculous. Having power over water was even more unlikely. The three of them looked around at each other without any words. None of them knew what was going on, but there was nowhere to go. They had to sit down and bear it. They just wanted to go home.

"I don't know what language you're talking in, but it makes no sense," said Henri, ready to leave now more than ever.

"Our world is in peril, young ones. The two cycles of magi have been reborn, and it seems they will have to answer the same question as their predecessors. The world needs you, all of you," Zachariah said.

"All of us?" Nolan repeated. The two big, pleasant monkeys looked up at Nolan before looking back to Zachariah.

"The magi are the guardians of the eight Devanian elements, protectors of the physical and spiritual. The physical elements, you should be familiar with—water, fire, earth, and wind. The spirit elements are the mind, the heart, light, and hope. The power over these elements lies within each of you. Each of you is the given the title mage, distinguishing you from other Deas, but together you are known as the magi."

"What's the difference between the two groups?" Nolan asked hesitantly.

"Physical and spiritual, two worlds rotating around each other endlessly. They are more similar than different. These elements are linked, stronger than you know. They are wedded in a way: water with mind, fire with light, earth with hope, and wind with the heart. Spiritual energy is used to shape the core within us all. While it is used much more internally than externally, it has proven itself strong enough to stand on its own.

"So does this mean we can fly and do spells?" Nolan asked jokingly.

"Like witches," Emmett said, looking at Nolan.

"Wee-chez?" Zachariah asked. "As in the spell casters of the Terran system?"

"Yeah …" Henri said. "I don't think we're witches."

"I guess we'd be wizards, huh?" Emmett whispered.

"You are Deas, not wee-chez or wee-zards," Zachariah said.

"What is a Dea?" Nolan asked.

"A Dea is a being that has the soul of a god and with that comes … certain power. Some can read minds; others can change the winds. The possibilities are growing more ever still. For eight

Deas, however, their powers are rooted in the strongest of any magic known to our kind: the power over the world, a mage. Along with their power, each mage is blessed with a staff given to them from the stars. The staffs are used to center your powers in order to prevent them from running rampant. They help you hone your skills. You'll use them until you have complete control of your powers. But unlike the others, you, Nolan, can perform a spell of any kind because you are also a spell caster," Zachariah responded. "Is that a gift the wee-chez can perform as well?"

"Let me guess, they have to rhyme too, don't they?" Emmett said, still chuckling.

"To awaken true power, spells must be matched with their male and female counterparts. Spell-casting Deas have long been foretold to use this power to invoke the gods to do their bidding. The more powerful the pairing, the stronger the link. For a Dea to—"

"But I thought we were the magi? You said we couldn't use spells," Henri said, hoping to catch this guy in a lie somehow.

"You can only use spells that reside in *your elements*, but even they require the same kinds of pairings as any other spell. The magi is only a title. Without it, it would be impossible to distinguish you from any other race. Do not be mistaken; you are both Dea *and* mage."

"Other races?" Nolan asked curiously. This was too weird to be real.

"Beside Deas, there are four other races in our world: Elves, Dwarves, Ankkns, and Kingskin. Elves are immortal. Dwarves and Ankkns have been blessed with long life." Zachariah could tell they were wondering about lives of Kingskin so he told them Kingskin live between eighty and a hundred years.

"Yes, Henri," Zachariah said, chuckling. "I guess they aren't so blessed. According to legend, Mother Maia took years away from Kingskin after King Omar believed himself wiser than she."

"Goddess? Gods? Magic? So what? Am I supposed to believe that mermaids, fairies, and centaurs are real too?" Emmett laughed.

"Why, of course, Emmett. They are among many dangerous creatures in this world. Do not treat them blindly," Zachariah said.

Nolan watched Emmet's face drop with a confused look of utter shock. Nolan knew he was just kidding about the mermaids and stuff. Zachariah wasn't.

"What about daemons? You said something about the first daemons. What are those?" Nolan asked quickly.

"Wait ... You mean demon demons!" Henri shouted. "What kind game are you playing here?"

"I believe the demons you are referring to are a different matter completely, Henri. I've done my best to study literature about your realm, but it is very limited here. De-mons are evil where you come from, yes? In this world, they are known as day-mons. Perhaps if I spell out the word, it will help you understand: D-*A*-E-M-O-N. Daemon."

"That's Latin," Nolan said. "It means an intermediary between humans and god. Well, I guess that makes sense in a world of gods and magic."

"I see your grandfather has kept up with the Wylie tradition of learning Latin. It is a language we share with the Terrans. And yes, it does make sense, doesn't it? There are two kinds of daemons in this realm: domesticated daemons, which we now call beasts, serve as farmhands and food and wild daemons who can summon immense power, similar to a Dea. Beasts include red chickens, horses, manure pigs, harvest hogs, et cetera. Over the centuries, they have become powerless in their servitude to assist the living."

"So," Nolan began. "Since Deas have the souls of gods and daemons are the intermediaries, does that mean ..."

"Why, yes, Nolan, I see the Wylie blood even in its youth is quite cunning. The magi each receive one daemon who will guide them in this world. Here, I shall show them to you."

The monkey-like daemons led more daemons out of one the shadows from the kitchen. They looked and walked proudly. One resembled a tiny bear cub with midnight-brown fur and strong, beady eyes. Its tail was short and fuzzy, hanging but inches from its body. The second was an owl-like bird about twice the size of the owls they were familiar with; it had brown and yellow wings and a sharp beak. Its claws were sharp, and its wings were well trimmed.

The last was a large seal with two sharp fangs outside of its face. The white leathery skin was unlike anything that Nolan had seen before. Its blue eyes were fierce as it walked on its two fins followed by a thick tail. These were definitely not demons from their world. They looked just like regular animals. Each of these daemons had a mystical symbol on its body. The seal had one on its fin.

"Those are the symbols from on top of the palace, aren't they?" Emmett asked.

"Each daemon is born with their elemental symbol hidden on their bodies. I am glad you noticed it, Emmett," Zachariah said.

"You've got to be kidding me," Emmett replied.

Zachariah introduced them. "Oris is a honey-back owl, the daemon of wind, so his mage is Henri. Gebb is a storm bear from the Stormy Forest of the Outlands, the earth daemon, so his mage is Emmett. Pani is a silver seal, the water daemon, so his mage is Nolan," Zachariah explained.

"So these are our guardians," Nolan asked. "They're so small."

Zachariah laughed. "Only these daemons have the power to change their forms, allowing them to be more—what's the Terran word for it—port-able. They have each been preparing for this moment all their lives."

"That doesn't make any sense? How did you know that I was coming ... today? Did *you* send that evil thing to bring us here? Or what is this Lucian guy?"

As they were getting out of their seats to see these daemons, Nolan was finally seeing the craziness in Zachariah's words. He had heard what he had to say, but he wasn't a believer. Despite Zachariah's confidence, there was still a hope that he was wrong. If he was right, everything had been a lie. Nolan wondered if Emmett and Henri were thinking that too.

"I cannot answer that," Zachariah said, calmly. "I have no way of knowing who sent the hollow after you. As I said, only a Divine Dea can travel between worlds, but there may be darker methods of inter-realm communication that I am ignorant of. The important thing is that you are here ... at last. Nolan was the first to begin the physical cycle, and Emmett was the last. With all of you here, you are at the peak of your destiny, but I may not be the only one who knows."

"Are you saying someone else may have sent that? Or are you just covering for my grampa!" Nolan shouted.

"Nolan, you don't actually believe your grampa did this, do you?" Emmett wondered.

"How else can you explain what's happening?" Nolan snapped back. "He said my grampa was the only person who could use magic outside this place! What if he did do it?"

"But he's your grampa," Henri said. "You can't think he actually—"

"Look around," Nolan said. "Zachariah, those monkey things, this place, what I did with the forks! This can't all be a dream. Someone sent us here. This place is real. What else are we supposed to think?"

Nolan didn't want to think it, but it was the only thing that fit. His grampa had kept this from him his entire life, looked at him every morning and made him feel normal. But he was just a freak! An alien!

"Your grandfather would never use white magic to get you here. He did not want this to happen this way, but they left him no choice. He had to prepare," Zachariah said.

"How do you know?"

"We had a plan," he replied. "How did you think I knew to be here? Your grandfather was to arrive with you later in the day. He wanted to wait until after some event. I don't remember the name of it. Some … some great wheel, I believe."

"The Ferris wheel," Henri whispered. "That's why he encouraged us to go and have fun."

Was it true? Did his grampa really plan all of this out?

"But how?" Nolan asked. "How would have he have talked to you?"

"Lucian. While only Divine Deas can travel between realms *physically*, spirits do not require such limitations. A hollow, young magi, is a spirit lost to white magic. I was in the Towers but a few days ago before I arrived here. Your grandfather has been planning this your entire life. I am sure he is heartbroken he cannot join us."

Nolan didn't want to believe this. Grampa? Lying to him all this time? He wished things had gone the way his grampa wanted. Then he would be explaining things, not Zachariah.

"Now you want me to believe that we all have these *powers* and that my father was this *inter-realm* magic person. That's impossible," Emmett said, picking up where Nolan had left off. "How is it that I can control the earth? I mean if that were possible, I could tear this place apart, right? You said my dad had the power; that doesn't mean I have it."

"The eldest child inherits the hippo seal. This I am sure," Zachariah said.

Nolan could tell he was still shocked by Emmett's lack of belief. Nolan looked at Emmett.

"I hear what he's saying about your dad but—"

"Don't … Nolan. My dad was not … he wasn't, okay, so just—don't," Emmett said.

"We're all learning something new. Just sit down," Henri said.

"Everyone's making me sit down! What if I don't want to?" Turning around, Emmett waved his hand over a wall, and he turned around almost as quickly. The wall he waved at immediately blew up into a thousand pieces. The rocks were everywhere. The sound from the explosion could have awoken a man from the grave. Emmett covered his face, trembling in fear. Nolan couldn't see the forks anymore.

"Oh my god! What did I do? What did you *do* to me?" Emmett shouted.

"Don't point that thing at me," Henri said, forcing Emmett's hand down. "Now do you believe?" he shouted.

"Oh, what a wonderful display of magic!" Zachariah said, clapping his hands.

"But the wall?" Nolan said. "Aren't you worried?"

"Watch carefully," Zachariah said.

The three of them turned suddenly to see the exposed forest around them. The rubble on the ground was smashed to pieces.

What were they supposed to be looking at? Everything was destroyed. Emmett destroyed the palace just like he said he would. The rubble then began to quake, moving slowly at first and then incredibly fast. As if they were pulled by strings, the stones reappeared on the wall. When they did, a thin blue line matched all the broken pieces together. Within seconds, they couldn't even tell that the wall was once a pile of broken stones. It put itself back together.

"A living relic spell, equipped with auto repair," Zachariah said. "Didn't I tell you? This is a safe place. Your powers come from your emotions. The important thing is that you believe. Your powers are already advancing as you stay here. This is a great sign." Zachariah smiled, almost completely ignoring the once-gaping hole.

"Yeah, I guess …" Nolan said, as he looked at Emmett, remembering his own magical display. Emmett was breathing heavily, and he could not stop looking at the destruction that *his hand* had done. Henri and he were soon next to him, smiling.

"You're just like me, now." Nolan chucked.

"Seriously, man, I didn't know you had it in you," Henri said.

"I kinda did." Nolan laughed.

"I'm a freak," Emmett whispered.

"We've always been freaks apparently." Henri laughed. "Now there's just a name for it. What do we have to do now?"

"Just rest," Zachariah said. "We will continue tomorrow. We are nearly in third passing."

They had no idea what he was talking about, but they followed him anyway. Zachariah showed each of them where they would be staying as he walked them up the stairs. Each of their little protectors followed them. All of their rooms were on the second floor. There were about six rooms on that floor, but only three were to be used. As they walked up to their rooms, they passed three rock statues sitting in the hallway. The first statue was of some sort of beast they didn't recognize; it must have been one of those new creatures Zachariah was talking about. It had two arms and a large tail with spikes at its tip. The second statue was of a tree; it was small and stood about four feet on top of a pillar. The third statue was the most unusual. It was the largest with two incredibly large creatures on one pillar. They were fighting, frozen in time. The creatures were a giant tiger and a flying dragon, just like the ones they had seen outside. *What's with the tiger and dragon?* Nolan wondered, as he looked to his medallion.

Once Zachariah showed their rooms, which were all next to each other, the daemons followed their magi inside. He told them to get some rest. They had a busy day. Nolan was standing in the room as Pani was lying on the floor. The room was twice as big as his bedroom at home. There was a large bed in the center with a glass on top of a dresser equipped with clothes for him. The closet was next to his dresser. At the edge of his bed was a smaller bed for the silver seal. He had a window to his right. He could see the beauty of the island as nightfall came. It was actually smaller than he thought an island would be; he could see the water from his window. Nolan sat on the edge of the bed, looking out of it, a part of him hoping that he wasn't dreaming. The small trees were smashing into each other as the wind blew. Nolan looked out to the red moon. It was the same color he pictured Mars would be. The craters were so large, full of possibility. He didn't know how long he looked out to the moon, but for a few moments, it was just Nolan and the red moon. Then he remembered he wasn't alone. Nolan looked to the silver seal in front of him. His skin was smooth, but the tusks were a little frightening. It looked at him with large crystal-blue eyes.

"So, can you talk? Or do you read minds like Zachariah?" Nolan asked.

The silver seal turned to him, with confusion on his face.

"Why, of course I can talk to you," the silver seal said in a deep masculine voice. "What kind of guardian would I be if I could not communicate with my mage?"

Nolan's jaw nearly hit the floor. He almost fell over himself.

"You talked!" Nolan said.

"Is that not what you asked?" There was another few seconds of awkward silence before the silver seal spoke to him again. "I am sorry your grandfather could not be here with you," he said, moving closer to him. He looked up at him with wide blue eyes.

"Me too." Nolan sighed. He didn't know what more to say to him. He was talking to an animal or a demon or a daemon or whatever.

There was a knock on the door. *Emmett,* he thought, *at least that's the same here.* Emmett walked in with his daemon followed by Henri with his daemon. They had looks on their face just as he did.

"They talk?" Henri said. "Did you know they could *talk?*"

"I've never missed Middlecreek more in my life," Emmett said, with Gebb behind him. "This is too freaky."

"Yeah, I didn't have anything to do in my room so I found Emmett and then we came in here," Henri laughed with Oris behind him. The daemons quickly made their way to the floor where they would do nothing but sit down and listen.

"I know it seems weird, you guys, but I think we have to accept it. I mean, look at the facts. Emmett did blow up that wall and me with the fork thing. Now I guess we just wait for you, Henri," Nolan said.

"You might be waiting for a while." Henri chuckled. "Wind? What a lame-ass element."

"But doesn't this just seem a little strange? Why is this happening to us? Why now? What *cycle?*" Emmett asked.

Gebb the storm bear rose up from behind Emmett. "It's because our world needs you." His deep voice also did not fit his small body. The daemons spoke as if they were parents.

"What do you mean?" Henri asked.

"The Mafia …" Oris the honey-back owl said, then he stopped for a moment. "They intend to use their magi against you."

"The Mafia?" Emmett said, laughing. "Does *Mafia* mean the same thing here as it does at home? Do you even know what that means?"

"Do you?" Gebb, the storm bear, said. "The Makaian Mafia has been hidden for hundreds of years. They use magic for all the wrong reasons. For centuries, they were unquestioned, but as the Divine Deas came to power, their wounds unto the world were healed."

Mafia, Nolan thought, *run by magic?* He tried to picture *The Godfather* combined with giants and mermaids. Nolan couldn't help but chuckle.

"We can talk about this more in the morning, please; we must let them sleep," Pani said.

Nolan knew Emmett and Henri wouldn't feel comfortable sleeping in their rooms so they all crashed in Nolan's room. Nolan was able to pull some blankets out from his closet. It was just like when they had sleepovers in kindergarten. The daemons were asleep first. Nolan got down from his bed, and the three of them lay on the floor like they used to when they were kids. But that was back when they were still called Terrans.

"Ya'll up?" Nolan whispered.

"Yeah, we couldn't go to sleep either. Will we ever be able to go home again? What about my parents and Lilith?" Henri asked.

"At least your parents have some clue. My mom has no idea. How am I supposed to tell her, especially when I don't even know what's going on? When will I see her again? What's wrong with me?" Emmett asked.

"The same thing that's wrong with all of us. We're freaks. Whether we like it or not, we *are* here and we don't know how to leave," Nolan replied.

"Everything we ever knew was a lie," Emmett said.

"Not everything," Henri said, yawning. "Remember Zachariah said Mr. Wylie wanted us to learn. What do you think he meant by that?"

"I don't know, but I doubt it's physics or any of that crap," Emmett said.

"Who knows? I don't even know who he is anymore. Emperor, prince, I can't be a prince," Nolan said.

"I'd rather be a prince in a foreign land than a stranger," Emmett said. "At least that way, you can get the best of it. Who knows? Maybe you got servants or a shitload of money."

"Maybe but I think you're speaking for one now." Nolan laughed as he pointed to Henri.

Henri had fallen asleep fast. His snoring was just beginning to ease its way into their conversation. He always was the first to sleep and the last to get up. Old habits died hard.

"Emmett, I know this is a lot to handle, but we're gonna stick together through it all. You know that, right?" Nolan said. "At least until I figure out how to get us back home."

"This shit's unreal, man."

Emmett nodded before he fell asleep on the floor as Nolan layback down on the ground. Their first night in Deva Prime was definitely unforgettable—silverware and walls. They slept quietly, with the exception of Henri. At last, Nolan slept. He felt himself slip into a part of his subconscious that he had never felt before. It was almost as if he was dreaming. He looked down at his body to see that it was in full color. He looked down to see the room, but he couldn't see his friends or the daemons. There were just white outlines of their bodies. He walked over to the bed as a swirl of golden light appeared beside him. The light continued to swirl until it became a person. He was an older man, wearing royal cloaks with a mystical symbol engraved on them. It looked like a tiger. Everything around Nolan was just as real as when he was awake, but there was no color, only white outlines of things he had once seen. He didn't see his friends anywhere, nor did he see this daemon that was supposed to protect him. Out of fear, he looked down, searching for anything to grab. Soon it was just him and the white outline of an old man in front of him. His hair was wavy, touching his shoulders. The man was taller than Nolan was, with a very respectable sense of stillness. He watched Nolan carefully as he spoke.

"Hello, Nolan."

Nolan recognized that voice. It was the same voice that had brought him and his friends to Deva Prime, the same one who was talking to Zachariah when he first met him, which only made him worry even more. *This is definitely not a dream.*

"Dico me, Lucian. Tantus sum atavi," Lucian said in a deep, mystical voice.

"Is that Latin?" Nolan replied. *How do you know that?*

"Latin is a language we share with the Terrans. I trust Zachariah told you."

"Why did no one tell me?" Nolan asked.

Nolan knew his anger was misplaced, but he didn't care. Lucian looked so much like his grampa, he couldn't control himself. And he was the one who had brought them there—and the one who had possessed him.

"Do not blame your grandfather. He had a difficult choice," Lucian said.

"How the hell would you know what kinda choice he had? Aren't you dead?" Nolan asked.

Nolan couldn't even look at Lucian because he reminded him too much of his grampa. He didn't even know where he was anymore. Was he awake or still asleep? Lucian remained calm as he looked at Nolan.

"This place is called Suspension; it lies between the physical and the spiritual worlds. Everything you see is real but only to those who can see it. In this reality, your body will be sleeping normally, but your spirit will still be active, stuck between two realms. Here, you can see me just as I am. It is not much, but it is the best I can do. With the connection to my physical body broken, my powers are very limited."

Nolan felt bad, but honestly, he could have cared less about some dead guy and some kind of limbo place. With all of this new life being confirmed by his little magic trick downstairs, he couldn't believe his grampa had lied to him all his life. Better yet, he couldn't even be there to explain it to him now. Instead, some faceless ancestor or a friend of the family had to tell him something he should have known years ago.

"How is it you can talk to me through this?" Nolan asked, holding up what would have been his medallion.

"I cannot talk to you *through* it. I can speak to you *because* of it," Lucian said.

"What's the difference? You were the one talking to Zachariah before we got here. My grampa sent you there to get us. Why?"

"Yes, he did. Spirits can travel between worlds, but it is not as simple as it sounds. I had to find you, Nolan."

"He knew that you were looking, right? For my medallion?" Nolan asked. "Why didn't he tell me when I was home?"

"Amos didn't find out until recently. I reached out to him once your powers began to manifest," Lucian said.

"And how long ago was that?"

Lucian took a deep breath before replying, giving Nolan a second to wonder how he would reply. Would Lucian even know?

"Not too long after Emmett's birthday. I trust Amos would have had to allow your powers to grow again. This would have taken a few days."

"So everything I ever knew was a lie? How was I able to live a normal life?"

"Magic, specifically your grandfather's. He supplied you with everything you would need to live a normal Terran life on the Planet of White Moons. He did the same with Henri's family and Emmett's. We did what we had to do to ensure your safety."

"How can *you* do *anything* when *you're* dead!" Nolan snapped.

Nolan looked down to his knees. Why was he so angry now? He was just talking to Emmett about accepting this life. Somehow, seeing Lucian pulled something out of him.

"There are many things I did before I died. Teaching my only son was one of them."

Lashing out at Lucian almost made Nolan feel better. If his grampa were there, he definitely would be. They needed to understand what they did to him!

"Why couldn't I have learned about magic at home then, huh? If he was able to give me a home, clothes, and everything else, why couldn't *he* have told me?"

"Your powers are too strong in this realm or ours. Your grandfather was the only one who stood a chance against you, but even he wouldn't have been strong enough to teach you. One bad dream and you could have destroyed everything you loved. The Planet of White Moons is dangerous to our kind; it disrupts the balance within us!"

"It's white *moon*, just one, no more!" Nolan shouted.

"Planet of the White Moon, my apologies!"

"But what about Emmett and Henri? They have powers too. They could have helped! I think I deserve to know why I was lied to for so long!"

Nolan was getting angrier by the second. It felt good.

"Markus Bradley wasn't the first mortal we sent to the Terran realm. We know how dangerous it is!"

Nolan was surprised Lucian had the same tone he had now.

"We tried, decades before, to send some nonliving beings to the Terran system. Too much energy was pulled from their white moon to sustain their magic. Hundreds of thousands of Terrans died in a terrible hurricane. Believe me when I tell you, there is a reason why your magic was restricted in the Terran system!"

Nolan looked at Lucian's face, seeing the anger and sadness wash over him. He didn't think it was possible for a ghost to be able to show that kind of emotion, not unless he was Casper. He tried to process this as Lucian quieted down. His parents? Were they the victims of this inter-realm journey? He couldn't escape it. Their death must have had something to do with it. Lucian knew something.

"So, you're saying I've always been this way? My family? My parents?" Nolan asked.

"Your father, my grandson, was born a Dea like you."

"And my mother?"

"An Elf," Lucian said.

"An Elf? Seriously? With the ears and everything?"

For some reason, Nolan didn't think he meant Christmas elves. How could he be half Elf? A half Elf, it sounded like a bad comic book. The more Nolan thought about his parents, the more he started to piece together what Lucian had just told him. *They died for me.* Nolan wondered if his parents knew the risk when they took him to Earth. He wanted to know why they chose a planet that was so dangerous for him. While he knew they would be happy he was safe, what was the cost? From a hurricane to a house fire, Zachariah was right: death followed the white moon. Upset at his grandfather for lying to him all his life and worried about what made him so fucking powerful that he couldn't even be told about his own heritage, Nolan couldn't help but wonder if everything he had ever been taught was nothing more than a lie. If he couldn't trust his family, whom could he trust?

"How do you speak Latin, a Terran language?" Nolan asked.

"There are many similarities between us and the Terrans. This was why we wanted to study them, learn their history, perhaps understand this unseen connection."

That may fit. If the Planet of the White Moon was so dangerous to them, there had to be some other reason Nolan was sent there. But why? He needed to know more.

"What about you? How are you alive in Suspension?" Nolan asked.

"My spirit lingers on until I know you are safe."

"I'm not safe now?" Nolan asked.

Lucian smiled as his head turned. Nolan's face was just as intense as before.

"When I feel you have safety been secured, my time will be over."

"How?"

"As always through you."

"I don't understand."

"You will."

"But if we're all Deas, why aren't my friends here with me?" Nolan asked.

"Only you can see me. As Zachariah said, your powers will grow here. All will be explained in time, Nolan. Be patient," Lucian said.

Patience was not Nolan's strong suit. His grampa used to say he was just like his father. Nolan now wondered how true that was. He pulverized Lucian with questions about his powers. What were they? Why couldn't he use them before today?

"My only assumption is that your grandfather stopped giving you a binding potion, a rather powerful one to be honest. Depending on the strength of the potion and with someone of your power, you would have needed a monthly potion to keep your powers from manifesting under intense emotions."

"I think I would know if Grampa gave me a potion every day," Nolan said.

"Not necessarily. It could have been mixed in with your favorite drink, perhaps even with your daily meals. He would have started giving it to you when you were a toddler so by now it would taste normal to you. Has there been any change in your diet recently?"

Nolan would have known if he had been given a potion. Wouldn't he? There was no big change in his diet lately. His grampa almost always cooked his meals though. But … *the apple juice.* He remembered earlier that afternoon when he was playing video games and the apple juice tasted different. His grandfather must have stopped giving him the potion just about a month ago, when he coincidentally found the article on the Big Web, which meant that he knew this was going to happen. That hit him hard.

"I have a life back home. A great life," he pleaded. "I have to give all that up?"

"This is your *true* home. With time, you will understand. Rest for now. The sun shall soon be with us. Do not be afraid; now that you have returned to us, everything will be okay. I will keep you safe, Nolan; I promise you," Lucian whispered.

Nolan felt his eyes get heavier and heavier but not by his own command. His body became weak, and he felt himself fade away into a different region of his mind. The last image he saw was a smiling Lucian sitting on his bed.

3

Dea Meets Daemon

THE NEXT MORNING, Nolan cracked his eyes open, stunned at the sight of his slumbering squad. He still half expected them all to wake up at his grampa's house, after getting totally shit-faced after the carnival. But here they were on a planet called Deva Prime. Was this their destiny? Some grand decision had brought them together. He wanted to believe that was true because it was much easier to accept that than the worst alternative—that he had done this to his friends, trapped them in a life on an alien planet filled with powerful strangers, a giant blue sun, and a mob of magic. He didn't know how he did it, but he brought this on them, taking them away from everything they loved. And they stayed, like a puppy following the pack. *They didn't leave*, he thought. They should have. Henri and Emmet needed a real pack leader, not some half-ass prince from another world. He put his head back down, staring at the ceiling. It still looked like he was sleeping as Nolan heard the door open.

"Good morning, Magi," Zachariah said. "Meet me downstairs as soon as you're ready. There is much to learn. Here are some clothes for the day."

Zachariah placed some clothes on top of the large dresser next to him. The clothes were color-coded. Nolan assumed they were for each element they were apparently guardians of: Nolan had blue, Emmett green, and Henri gray. Emmett looked through them to see that the symbols were just like the ones he had seen at the top of the summer palace.

"Hey, look! It's those symbols again," Emmett said, showing off his new clothes.

"Isn't it the symbols of the elements? Zachariah said the daemons have them too, right?" Henri asked.

Nolan looked over at the silver seal, who was his guardian. He saw the symbol for water on his tail. He looked at it and then slowly looked at the back of his medallion. They were similar. The Internet had been little help to him when he had tried to translate it. His grampa was never able to give him a straight answer either. Now he could add that to the list of things he didn't know about himself. As he got ready, the first thing Nolan remembered was the conversation he had had with Lucian the night before. He didn't tell his friends about it. There were enough weird things going on. Nolan wanted to know more about the first time these people came to Earth. Lucian mentioned a hurricane. How bad was it and when?

"Look at me; I'm a little Zachariah," Henri said as he walked out of the bathroom fully clothed. Nolan and Emmett already had their clothes on.

"We look like cheap Power Rangers," Emmett added.

The three of them were messing around for a little bit, reliving their childhood a little longer, knowing that they would never wear clothes like this back home. They looked like the clothes that they had seen in history books but not as poor, like middle-class, royalty. Their daemons were silent as they prepared themselves, blending into the shadows of their playfulness. Nolan wondered for a second why they were so quiet, but he liked it. They looked like animals back on Earth, but there was some kind of mystery behind their eyes. Zachariah said they had powers as they did. He was curious to see how much like Pokémon they really were.

"Well, it's official: I'm uncomfortable." Emmett laughed.

"I don't know; it's not that bad," Nolan said. "At least there's matching pants."

"We better head downstairs now," Pani said.

Nolan was starting to see that Pani was like the lead daemon. He wondered if that meant he had to be a leader too. Henri was their lead guy. He always had a plan. Emmett was the muscle. Nolan was just the third opinion. Once they made it downstairs, the house looked as if no one had blown up a corner of the wall or sent several pieces of silverware into the ceiling either. Instead, they were standing in the same dining room they had entered the previous day. Zachariah, along with the two monkey daemons, led them down a hallway until they reached a door with a white knob. Zachariah walked them in. The room was very clean, cleaner than a room should be. Looking up, he saw books floating above them as if held up by some invisible bookcase—hundreds of books with titles Nolan couldn't see.

After the last of the daemons made it inside, the door closed itself, just like the front door did yesterday. A ray of blue light emitted from each of the books, creating an image before them. It was a boy. He couldn't be older than seven, but there he was with dirty hair and old clothes. Nolan swore he could smell manure.

"Is that a hologram?" Henri asked.

"Hall-a-gram? I am unfamiliar with this Terran term," Zachariah said.

"An image that can talk," Nolan said, translating for Henri.

"Why don't you ask him?" Zachariah said. Nolan didn't wait as he asked the little boy in front of him.

"Yes, I can speak. I am a *stimulated image manifesting organized narrations*."

"He is also referred to as SIMON. You see all of the books on the ceiling? They are each a piece of SIMON. All the knowledge within these books rests in him. He provides a visual and verbal articulation of books. Here in the SIMON room, your questions can be answered more clearly. Tell us of the magi, SIMON," Zachariah instructed.

"Magi," SIMON responded. "*Magi* are the plural usage for the word *mage*. A mage is a physical manifestation of the eight elements. They are its protectors, vessels, children, and guardians. Beginning with water, each mage is born after the first: water, mind, wind, heart, fire, light, earth, and hope. In the sixteenth month after the birth of water, the magi cycle is complete."

"What is the magi cycle?" Emmett asked.

"Magi cycle," SIMON said. "The magi cycle is the balance of magic in this world. For thousands of years, the magi cycle has kept balance of the physical and spiritual. The magi cycle is the center of all magic. However, during the White Ages, there was a rupture of the cycle, causing a division between the magi, male and female, good and evil. Eight of the magi have remained true to the ancient ways and eight became lost."

"The lost magi," SIMON continued, "have thus begun a new cycle, which is counter to the true cycle. With division among the cycle, magic has become weakened. The original magi have attempted to uphold its traditional values and restore balance to the world, but they have not done so without difficulty. As long as the division is kept, neither cycle will regain its former strength and our world will suffer the consequences."

Nolan stood there, looking at the silver seal to his left. This was why he needed a guardian, those lost magi. They wouldn't be as strong as long as another competing cycle existed. Looking around at his friends, he could see he wasn't the only one thinking this.

"The lost magi, SIMON, what are they called now?" Zachariah asked.

Nolan had almost forgotten Zachariah could read minds.

"The lost magi," SIMON said. "The lost magi are also known as the Makaian Mafia. They have introduced an alternative manipulation of the sacred elements. Using this imbalance to their strengths, they deal with many criminal activities. Their most notable crime was illicit drugs, gambling, theft, and organized murder."

"So I guess they do know what a mafia is," Emmett whispered.

"But what's a Makaian?" Nolan asked.

"I'll answer this, SIMON. Makaians, Onerians, magi, and gypsies are the four types of Deas in this world. The majority of Makaians are inside the Mafia. They believe themselves superior to all others. The Makaians have been responsible for every major crime known to our world and at the center of every major war. Nothing is beneath them," Zachariah said.

"They're still around?" Henri wondered.

"They were unbeatable. Hundreds have tried, but none were successful. Their numbers were just too great. But when the Divine Deas first came to power, only they could strike fear into the hearts of the Makaians, providing counter curses and remedies to the drugs they created. The most famous of which was the addiction absolver, which was formulated by Emperor Magnus Wylie," Zachariah answered.

"What's the addition absolver?" Henri asked.

"*Addiction* absolver," SIMON said. "Addiction absolver is a refined potion, which relieves a person of drug addiction. The potion was first created through the combined efforts of Emperor Magnus Wylie and the Southern Heart Mage Leah Channing. During the Second Age, Emperor Lucian Wylie and Mage William Channing were able to perfect the potion by expanding it to all known drugs."

SIMON must have only spoken when there was a question.

"Drugs are legal?" Nolan asked. "Because of Lucian?"

"Yes," Zachariah said. "This was one of the more serious blows to the Mafia."

Nolan looked at his friends with a timid smile on his face. Inter-realm drugs? He was sure he wasn't the only one who wondered what kind of drugs existed there. All drugs legal!

Nolan tried to picture a world where addiction was absolved with a potion. How would that work? Take a sip and you'll never smoke crack again? *Damn, rehabs would go out of business. And Lucian had helped. The same guy who possessed him.* Zachariah had said Lucian paid a terrible price to get them there. The only thing Nolan could think of was how he yelled at him last night. But why was he so angry with him? He didn't even know the guy.

"Explain the relationship between daemon and mage, SIMON," Zachariah said.

SIMON nodded. "The relationship between daemon and mage is a sacred bond. The two reincarnations provide strength to each other that cannot be equaled. This was evaluated more exclusively during the White Ages. It was revealed that magi were stronger, both spiritually and physically, when they were paired with their daemonic equivalent. The two provide balance for each other, feeding off the energy of the other. While true magi are linked to wild daemons, those who have become lost are also connected to lost daemons."

"What are lost daemons, SIMON?" Nolan asked.

"Lost daemons," SIMON said. "Lost daemons are also known as horned daemons, the daemon of the Makaians. They will have horns made of bone and blood erupting from their foreheads. This is often speculated to be a sign of superiority. The blood horns are the result of unnatural white magic spread throughout the daemonic lifestyle."

"So they have daemons just like we do, these lost magi?" Henri said.

"Yes and no. It is true that they are paired with lost magi, but they are unavailable to the Mafia's magi," Zachariah said.

"But why … SIMON," Henri said. "Why aren't the Makaians allowed to have horned daemons?"

"All horned daemons are contained within a secluded section of the Underworld. It is accessible only through the stone portal within Snow Mountains. The portal can only be opened through eight elemental eyes. Horned daemons were forced to reside there at the end of the Second Daemon's War."

"The Second Daemon's War?" Emmett said. "There were two Daemon Wars?"

"Yes," Zachariah answered. "The first was territorial between creatures and daemons. The second was much more organized. It was during this time horned daemons came into being. For centuries, the Makaians attempted to bond with wild daemons as you do, but the relationship was not nearly as strong. This led to the creation of blood horns, which were added to wild daemons. The first daemons of these nature are called the Omegas. They are the horned daemons to the Mafia's magi. The relationship between mage and daemon is just as sacred as SIMON said," Zachariah continued. "It is a spiritual and physical connection between daemon and Dea. Thank you, SIMON. That will be all for now."

SIMON nodded and then disappeared like a gust of wind. Nolan looked down to his silver seal. They were both reincarnations, paired with each other. Still it felt like an unfair advantage. Then again, it was the Mafia.

"So these daemons?" Emmett said. "They bring us spiritual enlightenment?"

Zachariah smiled. "You must protect each other. They are just as important to the cycle as you are. This was, I assume, the reason why the Northern Magi attempted to recreate this bond."

"Northern Magi? Does that make us the Southern Magi?" Henri asked.

"Yes, it does. In previous years, the distinction has only been in the location of the water mage's birth, but it has changed substantially. The first mage to become lost was a Northern water mage. As you heard, the cycle begins with water. Every mage born after him will follow his cycle. Each mage in this cycle would later become lost as well. The southern water mage remained true, therefore protecting all the magi below him. All magi known as the Northern Magi will be a descendant of the first lost magi."

So it doesn't really mean anything. Nolan thought it was very strange that one mage could determine the fate of the others. The first mage was more than just a guardian of water, but why him?

"One person can change the world, Nolan," Zachariah said. "But you are right. The names of the cycles are just names. It is a simple distinction. Despite you being born before the northern water mage, you are the southern water mage."

"Because there are two cycles instead of one?" Nolan asked.

"Yes, Nolan."

"So which one was born first? The North or the South?" Henri asked.

"With every birth of the truest eight, the falsest ones shall follow in wait," Zachariah said.

Nolan wondered if that was from a spell or something, but Zachariah didn't elaborate.

"The Northern Magi intend to undo the restriction of actions on them. When their horned daemons were imprisoned, they attempted to free them—thus the origin of the Civil War. The two sets of magi fought over the stone portal. This was the most destructive war our world has ever seen. Nearly all of the magi died in the process, but the portal remained closed."

"I'm still not sure what you want us to do. This isn't our war," Emmett said.

Zachariah was quiet as he led them back to the front door, which led to the palace garden. As they walked onto the patio, they saw the living beauty of the tiger roses and orange poppies growing just along the wall. Under the blue sun, the garden was full of life. Statues and hedges were shaped into animals Nolan had never seen before, and they were staring down at him. There was one fountain flowing to the left of them. Nolan saw a large patch of green as tall as the palace. He wasn't sure how deep it was, but it was a maze or something, a perfect picture of a peaceful palace. It wasn't until they got outside where the large blue sun heated the morning sky that Zachariah responded to Emmett.

"Whether you like it or not, Emmett, this is *your* war. If Amos had not organized your arrival here, there would have been other means of retrieval. I know you worry because your Terran mother knows not of this realm, but do not be afraid; if you wish to leave, I can arrange to have you sent back to the Terran system. But if safety is what you seek, you will not find it among the Terrans. Death will *always* follow the white."

"No ... I ..." Nolan heard Emmett whisper.

Nolan knew what he was thinking about. He was thinking it too. His grampa did have a plan, but something changed. Something neither of them really understood. They couldn't be safe in ignorance anymore, especially after that hollow thing found them at school.

"I can't begin to understand how difficult this must be for you, for all of you. I know it is much easier to accept this when your family knows where you are, but you are here together. You will never truly be alone. Friends can often be closer than family."

Nolan noticed Emmett's daemon, Gebb, smiling up at him.

"The longer you are here, the more advanced your powers will become. Just enjoy each other's company here and get to know each other while I prepare for the remaining magi."

"What are we supposed to do now?" Henri asked.

"Spend some time with your daemons. Enjoy the garden," Zachariah said.

Except you, Nolan, Zachariah said. *I will need you to stay behind.* Emmett, Gebb, Henri, and Oris started to walk off into the garden. They tried to sell happiness with their faces but not even Nolan was buying it. Pani was beside him as he waited with Zachariah.

"Aren't you coming, Nolan?" Henri asked.

"Nolan and I have a little more talking to do. He will be with you shortly," Zachariah said. Emmett looked at Nolan a little longer than Henri did. Quietly, Emmett went outside. Nolan and Pani stayed on the patio.

"Nolan, as you well know, you are unlike any other mage in the either cycle. Never has there been one with such dualities. There will be times when you do not feel like yourself, but I must advise you to always be very aware of your emotions. These dualities can be disastrous when mixed."

"What do you mean?" he asked.

"I mean no matter what occurs, you must try to remain calm in any situation. Can you do that for me?"

"Okay, I can do that," he said, sheepishly.

He wondered why Zachariah had told him that, making him wish he were the telepath. *Be calm. How difficult could it be?* Zachariah had said they were safe there. If his grampa trusted him, maybe he should too. Nolan met up with his friends outside. He explained to them the advice Zachariah had given to him. They were just as confused.

"Stay calm?" Emmett asked and smiled. "He said we were safe here. Why would you need to control your emotions in the safe place? What's the worst that can happen?"

Nolan tried to picture the worst, but without even knowing what his powers were, he wasn't sure what he should be expecting. Could he make water or just control the water around him? And what about the medallion around his neck? Zachariah said he was a spell caster. Was it because of that? That didn't sound too bad, he guessed.

Morning led into the afternoon as the three Terran magi attempted to bond with their daemons. Emmett was still too shocked to know they could understand him, but this didn't stop him from speaking very slowly and loudly to Gebb. The storm bear didn't seem to mind too much being spoken to like a foreigner in his own world. Henri tried to remain a little calmer talking to the honey-back owl like a small child. Nolan was the only one who tried to actually have a conversation with his daemon. He used to stay up late and talk to the newspaper clipping on his mirror, wondering if his parents could hear him up there. At least this time someone was talking back. After they got bored and hot, Zachariah fed them lunch in the kitchen, if you could call it lunch. He tried to make food they were accustomed to, but it ended up being a strange concoction of vegetarian lasagna, coconuts, and artichokes. After seeing Zachariah barely keep his fork in the air, they knew there was no point in eating whatever it was he made. They went exploring again after filling themselves with bread and fruit from the table. Zachariah remained in the house as they extended their search of the palace as well. In the back, they saw a large balcony overlooking a small maze. Around it, they assumed were hedges cut into the shapes of daemons. Henri suggested they give it a try. When they got lost, it was his fault.

"Why did you make us come in here in the first place?" Emmett said, after they saw the same peacock hedge for the seventh time. "Who knows how long we've been in here?"

Nolan looked up at the blue sun. It moved like their sun, and judging by the position, it was nearly sundown. Had they wasted an entire day?

"So we've been walking around? That's the point, isn't it? Besides, you said it yourself; we're safe here, so why not?" Henri said.

"Why not? Because I'm hungry as fuck! And I tried that *stuff* Zachariah tried to feed us. My stomach has been going crazy. Do they even have bathrooms in this place?" Emmett asked.

"I'm sure they do, right? They have places you go to … uh … relieve yourself?" Henri asked his daemon.

"The lavatories are located on the first and third floors," the honey-back owl said quietly. "Would you like me to fly ahead and find a way out?"

"Yes, please!" Emmett shouted, but Oris remained still.

"Are you kidding me?" Henri said. "This is awesome! It's no fun if he just tells us."

Nolan wasn't *that* surprised that the owl stayed. Henri was apparently *his* mage, not Emmett. He knew eventually Henri and Emmett would make him be the tiebreaker. It was his responsibility to their friendship, the downside of being in a trio. A part of him did want to get out of the maze, but another part looked forward to finding a way out. But it was getting late …

Turn left.

Nolan immediately recognized the voice as his ancestor, Lucian's. Rather than argue or even explain the new voice in his head, Nolan took a left. *Turn left*, he heard again, when they came to another fork. With Lucian's advice, they were led out of the maze before sundown. Henri and Emmett were thankful to Nolan's sudden luck. He didn't want to tell them Lucian had helped him through—the upside of being possessed.

Zachariah and the two monkey daemons were standing at the back entrance of the palace. The red moon was starting to make its nightly journey across the sky. Nolan felt strangely comforted by the presence of the red moon. It was much larger than the moon he had seen his entire life. Back home, he would have to get a telescope to see the craters of the moon, but here, all he needed to do was look up. Again, Zachariah ruined the mood with food as he tried to feed them. This time, it was what they guessed were taco shells stuffed with pasta and strawberry jam. They had never been happier to see bread and water. Halfway through their discussion of the maze adventure, Emmett excused himself "to find the can," which Nolan translated. The storm bear led him to the bathroom on the first floor, leaving Henri and Nolan to more awkward conversation with Zachariah.

"We will have to remain here another night or two," Zachariah said. "While the ingredients for the deconstruction potion mature. Then we will make our way to the next mage in the cycle. I believe he is in the Green Valley."

"So, we just find them?" Nolan asked. "And this true magic just activates?"

"Something like that, Nolan. When the time comes, the truest eight shall wake, and we must accept our fate," Zachariah said.

This was the second time Nolan thought Zachariah sounded like a rhyming tape recorder. He wondered if he had practiced what he was going to say while they were in the maze. As curious as he was to hear what Zachariah meant, Henri spoke.

"How are we supposed to find them?" Henri asked.

"With the three of you arriving as you did, they will undoubtedly know something has changed. They'll feel the cycle nearing completion. At least those in tune with their spiritual training will."

"So we just wait here until the potion brews?" Henri asked.

"Deconstruction," Zachariah corrected. "It's a means of magical travel. I've been gathering the ingredients since the day you arrived. The black covers haven't reached their full maturity yet. In a couple days, all I will need is the activation spell. Then we can make our journey."

"Why do you need an activation spell?" Emmett asked as Gebb led him back to the table. "You're magic. Just make it work."

Zachariah smiled. "Refined potions can only be completed by spell-casting Deas. I am a Dea, yes, but not one with the power to cast spells outside my element. They are very rare in this world."

Judging by the way Zachariah looked at Nolan, he felt like he knew what he was going to say. "I'm a spell caster, right?"

"Yes. Every member of the royal families is. Spell casting is one of the most powerful gifts known to us. It allows a person to do nearly anything." He paused as he looked at the confused faces. "You are wondering how I was able to practice magic without spells. This must be a requirement of the Terrans. Magic, at least in this realm, is very practical and very limited. Deas, especially ones such as myself, learn the specific methods of our magic rather than *all* spells entirely. I can only cast spells that are connected to the element I control, connected to my own soul. Since my ancestor was a mind mage, I can only create spells that are strengthened through me. To put it simply, mind spells belonging to a mind mage would have no effect if another mage spoke them. They cannot summon power they do not have. Spell casters did not have this limitation for reasons that are too complex for you to understand."

This seemed rather limited. Nolan wondered how many spells a person could make about a person's mind. Couldn't be that many.

More than you could ever imagine, said the still familiar voice in his mind.

"That's why we're still here, isn't it?" Emmett said. "You need Nolan to activate this potion so we can leave. You're as trapped here as we are."

It was obvious Zachariah didn't approve of the way Emmett said "trapped here," but it did make sense. They had gotten there because of Nolan's power, whatever that was, and now they needed him again to leave. The responsibility staring at him made him wish he knew how to use his powers. *What if I can't say the spell right? What if I fail? We'll be stuck here.* The longer he sat there, staring at the questionable meal in front of him, the more he wished there was some other way.

"Then how did you get here?" Nolan asked. "Why can't we just leave with you?"

"Sadly, young magi, I arrived here through a boat leaf. It cannot carry us all."

Nolan saw none of them knew what that meant and they weren't asking. There was all this huff about bringing them to this realm and uniting some cycle and now they were stuck here on an island. This had poor planning written all over it. *What were you thinking, Grampa?*

"We just stay here? Until this potion is ready?" Henri asked. "What are we supposed to do?"

"I am quite glad you asked! You see, when a mage is born, they receive their daemon within their fifth year of life. This allows them to bond more intimately. Due to unfortunate circumstances, all of the magi were not able to receive this blessing. This brings the three of you to an untimely delay. You lack the spiritual connection required to forever bond you with your daemons."

"Spiritual connection?" Emmett asked. "Are you saying you want us to bond with them?"

"It is more of a requirement than a desire. The closer you get, the stronger you become."

Zachariah then suggested that each of them spend the next few hours speaking with their daemons privately. He asked them to stay in their rooms in order to do this. Nervously, each of them looked at their daemons, unsure what they would talk about. Without saying another word, they walked back to their rooms and closed their doors. For about ten minutes, Nolan just looked at the silver seal in front of him. His skin was leathery smooth, like he had just gotten out of the water. The seal, Pani, stared at him with nearly lost puppy-dog eyes. Each time Nolan moved, those crystal-blue eyes followed.

"Why aren't you in the water? Like all the time?" Nolan asked.

"Magic. I am the only one able to do this," Pani said.

No doubt this was because of Nolan. He must have needed to be able to protect him whenever Nolan needed it. That still made him wonder though.

"The Mafia," he said, expecting his daemon to react, "what have they done since all drugs were made legal?"

"They now deal more deadly magic: dangerous artifacts, undetectable poisons, even fake talismans guaranteed to grant one unlimited power, like the one around your neck."

"Talisman?" Nolan asked. "This is a talisman?"

"Yes, an object deemed sacred by a god," Pani said.

Nolan quickly looked down to the center of his chest. He had almost forgotten about his medallion. Ever since he couldn't take it off when they got there, he hadn't really given it any thought. At least there was one thing in common between this world and Earth.

"Hundreds of people had them, believed them to be protective," Pani said.

"How would you know? You live in the ocean, don't you?" Nolan asked.

"You'd be surprised by what you find at the bottom of the ocean, Nolan," he said.

The Makaians didn't sound nearly as bad as Pani had made them out to be. So what they did a little black-market stuff? From the sounds of it, no one was really hurting. The rest of the evening faded into dreams. Pani fell asleep on the side of the bed, on his own private cushion. Nolan was expecting to hear Emmett's knock on the door, but he didn't. Instead, when he opened his eyes, he was back in the white outline he had visited the night before. Like last night, everything looked real and colorless except him. He was just as real as when he went to bed.

"Hello, Nolan," he heard from behind him. Lucian was standing there, his wavy hair mysteriously touching his shoulder. He looked so much like Nolan's grandfather.

"Why am I the only thing in color here? Everything else is just an outline. Why not me?"

Lucian gave Nolan a stern look as if to say, "Rude much?"

Nolan didn't care. With people lying to him his whole life, he felt he was entitled to be a little rude.

Seeing Nolan wasn't going to amend his question, Lucian responded, "Only beings in the physical world will appear vivid in Suspension. Everything else—the windows, this room, this palace—is nothing more than a shadow of its physical self. A mild comfort for those of us remaining here."

Nolan was somewhat surprised to learn there were more lost spirits in Suspension. For some reason, he only thought of the man who possessed him, the man who trapped him there.

"I heard you speaking with Pani about the Makaians?" Lucian said.

"How can you hear me? No offense, but you're dead. You're not even in this world, the physical one, I mean," Nolan said.

"This is difficult, I can imagine, so I will do my best to simplify it. Until my soul is at peace, the powers I had in the physical world are still transferable in Suspension. Therefore, I can speak to you through our mental connection."

"You're a telepath, like Zachariah?" Nolan said.

"Yes, that is one of my gifts," Lucian said.

"But you can't come into the physical world?" he asked.

"I can possess you if you like, but I'd rather not do such—"

"That's not what I mean. What happens if you cross over into the physical world, without possessing me?" Nolan asked.

"The only other way for me to enter the physical world is to be summoned. Even then, it is very powerful and dangerous magic and it would not last forever," Lucian said.

Nolan tried to wrap his head around it, but that didn't help. He wanted to know how Lucian could have possessed him from Earth. In this realm, possession made a little more sense, but according to Lucian, someone would have had to summon him to Earth. But if someone could send a spirit to Earth, why couldn't they bring a person?

"I came to warn you, Nolan," Lucian said, bringing Nolan back from his distraction. "It is true what Zachariah has told you about a mage feeling when another is near. He failed to tell you this also applies to the Northern Magi. They will undoubtedly be looking for you and your friends. The Mafia may be minor in the Terran system, but here, there are none of equal threat. You must, no matter what you see or hear, do your best to remain calm. There is no safer place for you to be than in this palace."

Nolan slept quietly that night. He dreamed about his parents' death again. This time, instead of crying, he was yelling. "How dare you do this to me! If I am to suffer for another's mistake, so shall they for mine." More ramblings came out of his toddler mouth as the fire raged on. None of it made any more sense than the last dream. *I did nothing wrong … I would never let them fall … Your lack of trust is infuriating … I was destined to do this!*

4

The Second Fire

E MMETT'S HARD KNOCKS woke Nolan the next morning. He couldn't remember what his toddler mouth had said. He got ready as quickly as he could to meet them downstairs for breakfast. Pani watched again with crystal-blue eyes until Nolan opened the front door. Zachariah's breakfast was by far the worst of his attempts at making food they were accustomed to—eels in some kind of gray sauce, fish eggs (which, for some reason, smelled like vomit), and some kind of brown concoction with peanuts. The only thing that looked remotely interesting was the fruit. It wasn't the same apples and oranges they had expected from Earth, but they at least didn't smell. The two monkey daemons quickly removed their untouched plates.

"Is it normal for daemons to do housework like this?" Henri asked. "With all that magical power they have, shouldn't they be a little more respected than that?"

Nolan wondered if that was what the honey-back owl and he had talked about last night or if Henri had come to that conclusion on his own.

"Daemons are not house pets by any means. The daemons you see before you, white-palmed gibbons, were sent here, along with your guardians. They helped me secure the palace from intruders, from both Dea and daemon penetration. This way, no one can pierce your minds or your daemons' minds to find our location. They clear the tables of their own accord. They view your daemons, the Alphas, in the same way Deas refer to the magi."

"And what way is that?" Emmett asked.

"A respectable one. Your guardians are just as important to the cycle as you are," Zachariah said. "You will see."

After breakfast, Zachariah again asked them to spend time with their daemons, but this time, he didn't ask them to stay in their rooms. Since it was Henri's idea for them to walk that maze and get lost, it was only fair that Emmett was allowed to pick their next little adventure. He chose to explore the interior of the palace. Nolan was exceptionally content with this. If this really was the summer palace of his ancestors, he was more than curious to see what it contained. The next few hours were spent with them roaming the palace, opening doors and climbing stairs; they found nothing too exciting, which bored Henri to pieces.

Nolan, however, was mesmerized by the grand style of the palace. If this was the summer palace, he could only imagine how beautiful the regular palace would be. On the first floor, down a wide hallway, there were portraits hanging on the walls. They were beautifully drawn with gray pillars between them. The frames were as tall as Nolan was, with the same symbol crafted along the golden sides. The symbol was a white tiger with a crescent red moon behind it. Three stars hung in the sky. Underneath each frame was a silver plaque, with a name written on it. The first frame they saw was of a man with the same olive skin and wavy hair as Nolan. He had a very stern face and wore more clothes than he needed. A long black robe hung behind him and a golden crown rested on top of his head.

*Magnus Valerian Drokke Amado Wylie, Divine Emperor of the
Southlands.*

"Look, Nolan," Henri said. "He's wearing the same medallion
you are."

Nolan looked closer and saw the exact same medallion as was
hanging around his neck. The black-and-white tiger on the cookie-
shaped medallion hung in nearly the same place despite Magnus
being taller. Zachariah *was* right. He was a prince, at least according
to this painting. Hearing his name called out again, this time from
Emmett, Nolan walked down in front of another painting. This
time, it was of a family. Magnus was in the center, seeming much
more content than he was in his solo portrait. To his left was a
darker-skinned woman with long brown hair. She looked Native
American or maybe Hispanic. Each of them had a crown on his or
her head and a matching smile. Playfully laughing beneath them
were too little boys, twins. They were just as regally dressed as their
parents, but the artist had somehow captured them nudging each
other.

*Emperor Magnus, Empress Taini, High Princes Lucian Samson
and Daedalus Simeon.*
Captured 21.6.37.

"I guess captured must be some kind of date," Henri said.
"Which one do you think is the year?"

Nolan didn't hear him. He was too memorized by the portrait.
Pani stared at him as well. He didn't even know Lucian had a brother.
It wasn't the lack of information that had him staring. They were
happy. Maybe if his parents hadn't chosen Earth as his foster home,
he could have grown up there and been raised as a prince.

"Hey!" Emmett said again as the storm bear followed. "It's Mr.
Wylie! Check this out!"

Shaken from his hope, Nolan followed Henri to the portrait
where indeed his grandfather's face was staring at him. Wearing
the same regal clothes as Magnus, equipped with the crown, Amos

Wylie was considerably younger than Nolan remembered him. His hair was still wavy, but there wasn't a trace a gray, not that there were many at home either. The only difference between Amos's and Magnus's portrait was Amos was not wearing the medallion around Nolan's neck and his name wasn't as long.

Amos Bartholomew Wylie, High Emperor of the Southlands.
Captured 125.13.41

"I wonder why he's the high emperor and not the divine emperor," Henri said.

"I don't know. Is it just me, or does his name seem shorter?" Emmett said.

Nolan turned around as his friends tried to imitate his grandfather's regal figure. Freezing instantly, he barely noticed Pani was standing next to him. His parents.

Theodore, Illariel, and Nolan Wylie.
Captured 147.14.31.

His father was just as tall as he was with more waves in his hair than any other Wylie. Illariel, his mother, was nearly as tall as her husband. Light-brown hair flowed in deep curls from her head. Her eyes were blue pools swirling in front of him. It was then that Nolan noticed his mother's ears. They had a curve near the top, making them just a little bit longer than his father's. Lucian was right; she was an Elf. Neither of them were wearing any kind of formal wear— no crown on either of their heads. Only one thing mattered to him: *Those are my parents*. Nolan looked deeper into the portrait of his parents, searching for himself as a baby. He didn't see it. Smiling, he saw his father with his hand clearly on his mother's stomach. He couldn't help but feel responsible now. His parents traveled with him to the Terran system when he was a kid. They tried to give him a happy life, but instead something went terribly wrong. They wound up in that fire. Inter-realm travel was dangerous, just like Lucian had told him, just like the hurricane. Had he been the reason why they died? Did he bring them to the fire by accident?

A hand touched his shoulder. He looked to his left and his right. Henri and Emmett too were now staring at the portrait. They didn't say anything but looked at his parents. It felt hours before anyone said anything. Each of them was wondering what Nolan's parents would have been like. What kind of music would they have liked back home? Would they have let Nolan have a later curfew than his grandfather? No matter how many questions they launched on the portrait, they knew it wouldn't answer. Rather than drag them away from the picture, Nolan was the first to continue to walk down the hallway of portraits. He stopped every time he came to one of his parents. At some point, he stopped seeing portraits though. Only silver plaques were placed below empty frames, four to be specific, on the formal side of the hallway.

Tomas Hortensio Wylie, Grand Prince of the Southlands.

Pellya Lucretia Wylie, Grand Princess of the Southlands.

Nolan Othorion Helayko Wylie, Divine Prince of the Southlands.

Cassandra Aleynor Wylie, High Princess of the Southlands.

The other three Wylies had to be the cousins he never met. The oddest thing about these empty frames was Nolan's name. His grandfather never told him he had a middle name, let alone two! He kept trying to read them over, hoping it would somehow fit with his first name, but it didn't. Hearing his name called out for the second time by Emmett, he quickly caught up to them. It was time for lunch.

Zachariah's face lit up with the same fire that bloomed in his hair when he heard that they had explored the palace, only partially referring to their need to bond with their daemons as well. Nolan was tempted to ask him about the other Wylies or even his own name, but he couldn't get the image of his parents out of his mind.

Before he knew it, Zachariah had asked them to spend more private daemon time. Nolan sat in his room as Pani sat down in front of him. Being forced to bond with his daemon had done everything but make him want to. Throughout their little exploration of the palace, the three of them barely gave any time to the daemons only inches away from them. With every blink, he saw the image of his parents and his unborn self. All the stories his grampa had told him suddenly made him question how much he knew about them. His father definitely was not a soldier, and his mother wasn't a teacher. They were a prince and an Elf. An Elf? Nolan kept touching his ears, wondering if his would ever grow like hers did. His grampa had filled his head with nothing but lies about them. He didn't say it in front of his friends, because the daemons were so close, but that was the first baby picture he had ever seen of himself. Everything was destroyed in the fire. Deciding not to misplace his anger with Pani, like he had with Lucian, he changed the conversation entirely.

"Is it true? What Zachariah said about daemons having respect for you and Oris and Gebb?" Nolan asked.

Pani's thin mouth smiled. "Yes. For Deas, the magi represent the strength of the gods and unity of the elements. The same applies to daemons. We were the first seeds of magic."

"The seeds of magic? Were daemons here before Deas?" Nolan asked.

"First came the Elves, then the Dwarves, Ankkns, Kingskin, and lastly Deas, in terms of people. For daemons, the only beings that came before us were creatures. Each creature is the direct connection to a god. The mermaids, for example, are the daughters of the moon, you."

Nolan couldn't help but give a questioning look to the daemon at his feet. Him a god? It sounded nice, but he had a hard time comprehending all that it meant. If there were really gods who used to live in this place, where had they gone? And why was he chosen to do this? Thankfully, before Nolan got a chance to think about it, he heard Emmett's knock. Not waiting for Nolan to respond, Emmett quietly opened the door as the storm bear called Gebb stood to his left.

"Where's Henri?" Nolan asked.

"He's downstairs trying to show Zachariah how to make a real meal. I think he's just as tired of that shit as I am. Who the hell eats eels? Are you all right, man?" Emmett asked.

Nolan knew what he was talking about, but he didn't want to talk about his dead parents in front of the daemons. He tried to show Emmett, but Emmett read faces as quickly as he understood quantum mechanics.

"Are you all right? You got a weird look on your face. You saw your parents downstairs. I was just checking on you. Believe me, I know how you feel."

Nolan's shoulders dropped. He wanted to shout, "How could you? You had both your parents! Your dad hasn't even been dead a year. That doesn't compare to a lifetime of loneliness!" But he just shook his head and got up from the side of the bed. He wondered why he felt so angry at Emmett. There was no more talk about dead parents for the rest of the day. Henri had found them a couple of hours later after failing to make an edible Terran meal. It was obvious his mom cooked all their meals. The suggestion then was for Zachariah to make something non-foreign to him. Anything had to be better than jam tacos or eels in gravy. After another exploration of the palace, they found a few more rooms but nothing like the Hall of Memories. Some of the rooms were locked though. Walking around the palace was more of a milestone than any of them had predicted. Whenever they found a room or a statue that looked interesting, they tried to remember to come back to it, but they never could. Once a few hours passed, and the three of them were utterly lost, they spoke to their daemons, hoping one of them knew the way back to their rooms. When they did make it back, Zachariah was walking up a narrow hallway as the white-palmed gibbons stopped behind him.

"Oh, good, I was hoping to run into you three. It's time we activated the potion," Zachariah said calmly.

They had all forgotten about the potion that would take them to the other magi. Zachariah led them into a room with cabinets full of potions in little wooden vials and jars of ingredients. Some of them were moving. A black cauldron was resting above a fireplace. They could hear light bubbling. With a thick cloth, Zachariah picked up the small cauldron and placed it in the middle of the wooden table in front of them on top a small metal plate. The plate sprouted arms, and within seconds, it stood before them holding the cauldron up. Each of them looked down into the cauldron. Zachariah was the only one who backed away with a smile. Nearly at the bottom of the cauldron was a gray liquid still bubbling. There couldn't have been half a cup bubbling around in there.

"How is that supposed to be enough to get all of us off this island?" Emmett asked.

"Little in quantity but surpasses in quality. This is more than enough for our travels. We only need to get off the island and into the Southlands. Now we only need the activation spell, then a few more hours of brewing, and we'll be ready to leave in the morning," Zachariah said.

Everyone turned to Nolan, making him wish he could give his medallion to someone else.

Zachariah walked over to him confidently and spoke. "You can do this. Refined potion making is remarkably simple for spell-casting Deas. The activation spell for this potion is *intorqueo*. You must say it proudly and very pronounced—in-tore-kwi-oh."

Zachariah told Nolan to place his hands on the sides of the cooled cauldron. The one-word spell turned in his head. *Clear your mind*, Lucian had told him. Nolan was hoping Lucian would come to his rescue as he had in the maze, but that was all he heard from his ancestor.

"In … tore … kwi-o," he said as slowly as he could. Opening one eye, he looked down into the cauldron. It was the same.

"Your powers come from your emotions, Nolan. Just like you did with the silverware, if you are timid, so are they," Zachariah said.

Nolan tried to think about how he felt when he first arrived. Shocked. Angry. Confused. Angry again. How could his grampa lie to him about all of this wonder!

Now! Lucian told him again.

"Intorqueo!"

The gray liquid began to glow a bright-golden color. The potion turned several times on its own before slowly stopping itself. Once it was smooth again, the potion changed from its gray liquid color to a soft pale-blue when the bubbling continued.

"Excellent work, Nolan! With a little push, you've done splendid! I knew you could do it all along! It's in your blood!" Zachariah said joyfully.

Patting Nolan on the back, Henri and Emmett peaked over the cauldron to see the color change. They were almost as happy as Zachariah was. Picking up the cauldron again, Zachariah placed it back over the fire. The sound of bubbling roared as they went into the dining room. As they walked into the dining room, the mouthwatering smells caught them off guard. Each of them sat down in the same place they had sat a couple of days ago. This time, instead of the white-palmed gibbons serving dinner, Zachariah did. On two separate trips, Zachariah brought a large pot of stew and a basket of tortilla-like bread. He poured each of them a plentiful amount of stew, leaving the basket in the center of the table. He brought out three plates of food they had never seen before. They smelled just as good as the stew. As Zachariah walked over to them, he placed the plates at their feet. Daemon food. Nolan couldn't believe he had never noticed the gibbons brought their daemons food too. That would explain why they were so quiet whenever they ate. Zachariah said it was salmon stew and the bread was called honey fold. He showed them why as he folded the bread in half before dipping it into his stew. When Nolan did the same, he barely tasted the salmon at all. The stew made the bread ten times sweeter than he would have thought. He could see he wasn't the only person thankful Zachariah had given up his experimenting with Terran food.

Throughout the small talk at dinner, Nolan kept replaying the image of himself making the deconstruction potion. He really *was* magic. Looking at the medallion around his neck, he had never been prouder to be a Wylie. *If only Grampa had been here to see me.* Going upstairs for more quality daemon time had never been easier for him. As much as he wanted to continue to talk about his amazing display of magic, his curiosity was spiking. He wondered what kind of magic he could do next. From the second he closed the door, he looked down to his daemon.

"What other spells are there for me to try?" Nolan asked.

"Why? Were you thinking about reading one?" he asked.

"Well, I was thinking about making one. I've seen it all the time on TV. All I have to do is make it rhyme, right?" Nolan said.

"T-V? I doubt they would have …"

Nolan didn't hear the rest. For a second, he forgot that he wasn't at home. He didn't know how to explain it to Pani, but maybe he could show him. What was the worst that could happen? It just had to rhyme. All spells had to rhyme—at least that was what he remembered from old TV shows. That was the worst part, but hey, it was in his blood. The trick was figuring out what he wanted to do. He didn't want to try anything too dangerous. Zachariah was the first person in his mind. Maybe he needed a taste of his own medicine.

"I want to read minds …"

What rhymes with mind?

"I'm not sure that you should," Pani began only to realize that he was being ignored as he continued.

"For a short period of time … Allow me to hear their thoughts— uh, proving I'm not here for naught?" *Naught,* he thought, *not the best word, but what else rhymes with thought?* Nolan was thoroughly excited; he wanted to see if his spell worked. He walked outside his room to test it. As he walked out, his head became an awakened tornado. He fell to the ground. Voices filled his brain faster than an empty cup under a waterfall, not just the voices in the house but even the ones outside. Every living thing outside was in his head and some of them were even in a different dialect. He couldn't shield himself. It was too overwhelming. He couldn't figure out which voices were his friends and which weren't. Pulling on his hair did nothing but make his spiritual pain physical as well.

"Nolan! Nolan!" Pani shouted.

"My head!" Nolan didn't know what the big deal was. It looked so easy. The pain was increasing now. He wasn't even able to hear himself anymore. The harder and harder he thought, the more

Lucian came to his mind. As Nolan screamed, Henri, Oris, Emmett, and Gebb ran into the hallway, but they only made it worse by shouting.

What have you done? Lucian said.

Why isn't it working?

Spell casting is not an easy action. I can neutralize the spell, but I don't have the strength to do it here. I'll need to take you to a place where our powers are stronger.

Whatever, just make it stop!

Place your hand on Pani and shout out "Magnus's Oasis." I can handle the rest.

Not even thinking, he stretched out his hand to a scared Pani and shouted, "Magnus's Oasis." His body was the first to become a golden orb. Then in less than a second, it spun around Pani, absorbing him into the mass. Nolan felt just like he did the first time he was jammed into a crowded elevator. Nolan and Pani quickly left their friends with dinner-plate eyes as they frantically ran out of the room.

Nolan looked around the unfamiliar territory and sat down quietly. He didn't know where he was, but Lucian told him that he had to go there. He honestly didn't care where he was. This was paradise compared to the hell he had created for himself; maybe magic wasn't as easy as he thought it would be. He waited for a few seconds before silence—pure, perfect silence—returned to him. Never had he been more grateful to have a dead guy possessing him. Gasping for air, he looked up to Pani. He couldn't hear voices in his head.

"I can't hear you!" Nolan shouted.

"I didn't say anything," Pani said.

"I know," Nolan shouted as he hugged him.

The hug was uncomfortable, but he didn't care. Wherever they were, it had strengthened Lucian and probably him too.

"Are you okay, Nolan?" Pani said.

"Yeah, I don't know what Lucian did, but yeah, I'm fine. I'll never try that again. Do you know where we are?" he asked.

"Magnus's Oasis, I assume," the silver seal responded.

"What's that, another spell?"

"I don't know, but you shouted that just before you teleported. Only Wylies can move from place to place without a spell or a potion. It's your inheritance. The distinguishing feature of your family; it's how you arrived here in the first place. I'm sure your great-grandfather will be able to explain. Can you try summoning him?"

"I don't know. I feel really weak all of the sudden; besides I don't even know how. I've only talked to him when I was dreaming."

"Dreams are the link between worlds. You have not spoken with him any other way?"

"He talks to me sometimes, but I've never started it," Nolan said.

Nolan knew Pani was expecting more of an answer from him. There was nothing he could do. Lucian had brought them to this place, but he had no idea where they were or how they could get back to the palace. He wasn't exactly in a big rush to go back to the castle though. Wherever they were, it was blissfully beautiful. A sense of unusual happiness stormed over him with every breath he took. A large shimmering lake was only a few feet away from him. The bright-green grass spread for as far as he could see. Despite having no apparent source of light, this land was unusually bright. Several of the flowers looked like they had been polished.

"I wonder if Zachariah knows about Magnus's Oasis. Maybe it's a Dea thing?"

"It's possible, but this land does not look like anything in our world. That lake shouldn't be that gray," Pani said.

Following the silver seal's pointed flipper, he looked closer into the water. It was gray, storm cloud gray. For a second, he thought it might have been a large amount of deconstruction waiting to be activated. As tempting as it was, he was in no rush to use magic without knowing the right way first. After a few more moments of awkward silence, Nolan looked up to see that the skies were darkening. *What is going on?* The place that they had called peaceful was soon everything but. The land around them began to quake, and the trees began to shrivel. The bright-blue clouds ran to hide and reveal an angry face. The face looked almost identical to Lucian's, except his hair was mangled and loose with large streaks of gray hair along the sides, which could only mean one thing. *His twin brother,* Nolan thought, *the guy from the portrait!* His name had come up blank to Nolan, but he knew he was a Wylie. Pani looked up as Nolan stared at the forming clouds. The silver seal quickly jumped in front of Nolan, harshly staring at the gray cloud as if thunder and lightning were only moments away.

"How sweet. I've been looking for you, my little lost prince. How lovely it is to finally meet you in person," the dark voice shouted from the clouds.

Before Nolan could even get a word out, his medallion was glowing again. He knew what it meant as he felt Lucian take over. When he did, Nolan felt a surge of power that he had never felt before. He was confused; he thought Lucian was weak, but if this place gave him the strength to fix his little spell, who knew what it had done since he had been talking to Pani? Daedalus was the name he uttered before the face stopped smirking. Daedalus seemed unaffected by Lucian's presence after a moment however.

"Drifting into white magic, are you, brother?" Daedalus chuckled. "Do you honestly believe possessing this boy will make you any stronger? I have already killed you once." He laughed. "It would be ridiculously simple now!"

Daedalus killed his brother! That couldn't be. They looked so happy in the portrait. What went wrong? Nolan's faith in Lucian had somewhat weakened. He had no idea what could have made Daedalus kill Lucian, but he knew he had succeeded.

"Daedalus, you mustn't do this! You are a Wylie; you have a solemn vow to uphold!"

"Vows can broken, can't they, *brother*," Daedalus replied. "I knew Amos would protect his sacred cycle. It was only a matter of time. Thank you, Nolan, for falling into the innocent temptation of magic. It'll be the death of you and your friends. You will always regret your first spell now."

With those final words of departure, no one had to say anything. A fountain of questions sprang out of him, but none left his mouth. Again, he had brought his friends into harm's way. He desperately hoped Zachariah's and the daemon's magic would leave them protected. Before long, he had control of his body again. Still unsure how he could summon Lucian, he hoped he could hear him in Suspension.

"Where are we?" Nolan asked.

You don't need to speak so loudly. I can hear you just fine. Nolan looked down to Pani, but it was clear he couldn't hear what Lucian was saying to him. *This place is called Magnus's Oasis, the center of all Wylie power. In this place, our powers are at their strongest.*

"So that guy—the guy who *killed you*—is just as strong here as you are?"

Daedalus cannot enter the oasis thanks to a blood binding lock. This was why only his head appeared. He must have used astral projection.

"So, he did kill you! And now's coming for us. Do you think he'll be able to find my friends at the—"

Don't! He may be still be listening. Yes, my brother is the reason I am dead, but our tale is not for this day.

"This is all my fault! If I hadn't made that spell … you wouldn't have …"

Before he could even finish his sentence, Pani spoke. "This is *not* your fault! We knew, all of us, that the summer palace could not protect you for long. Why do you think Zachariah had you prepare the potion today? We knew this day was coming. Your grandfather prepared for this too," Pani said.

Grampa had a plan? Still? His daemon's foresight made him feel a little better. Nolan still had a ton of questions for Lucian. But he had more important things to worry about.

We must return now. I will bring you back safely. Whatever happens, remain calm. I am here with you.

This was the third time, he had told him to be calm. *Why were his emotions so damn important?* As long as Lucian was there, he was protected; he knew that now. Lucian took over the body and placed his hand on Pani's shoulder as they teleported him back to the summer palace. Lucian had brought them just outside the front door. When Nolan opened his eyes, he wished he had kept them closed.

The summer palace was on fire.

Nolan ran out from an orb, nearly landing on Emmett, Henri, Zachariah, Oris, and Gebb. The fire was golden with a white center, consuming everything from the garden to the maze in the back. Everything was roaring. Black smoke rose into the air, making it even more difficult to breathe. The fire didn't consume the palace like he thought, but then he remembered what Zachariah had said: *A living relic equipped with auto repair.* As fast as the fire was consuming, the palace was trying to rebuild itself. Two forces were locked in a sanctum of chaos and magic.

"Nolan!" Henri and Emmett shouted.

"What happened?" Nolan asked.

Emmett was the first to speak.

"After you left, Zachariah said you might have gone to some special Wylies-only thing. He took us down to get the deconstruction potion, but it wasn't ready. We tried to wait for you, but then someone busted through the front door. Those monkeys tried to stop them, but someone stabbed them. We barely saw it. Zachariah used some kind of magic to stop them from seeing us. We picked up the potion and ran for it."

Henri continued for him, "We tried to lose him in the maze, but he wasn't following us. It wasn't long before we saw some big-ass bird over the maze. Oris tried to blind it, but it didn't work. But when the fire spread to the maze, we just ran around the corner. The cauldron fell as we were running, but we think we lost that guy."

"You thought wrong," a seductively sly voice said.

Nolan was expecting to see Lucian's twin, but he wasn't there. Each of them turned around to see a young, handsome blond-haired man, holding two thick daggers in his hands fifty feet away from them. Daemon blood was still dripping off them. Zachariah stretched his arms in front of them just as Pani had done. But the blond-haired man didn't back down.

"I'm not here for you, Kingsley," he said. He threw the knife quicker than anyone could react. Nolan's eyes widened.

"No!" he shouted.

Zachariah was the only person he knew in this realm! He couldn't let this happen! He didn't care that everyone told him to be calm. What was the point of being magic if he couldn't use it when he really needed it? No one said anything. The knife was frozen midair, a foot away from Zachariah's chest. Zachariah's eyes bucked at Nolan, glee raining from his eyes.

"Nolan Wylie," the blond-haired man said.

Nolan had never heard his name sound so eerie. The knife dropped in front of Zachariah, but the man didn't care. "The little would-be orphan prince."

"How did you get past the gargoyles?" Zachariah asked.

The blond-haired man sucked his teeth and shook his finger, smiling. "Amos isn't the only one with clever tricks, Kingsley. If he's not sharing his, why would I share mine?"

A golden orb identical to the one Henri and Emmett had seen before landed to the left of them. The man smiled again. When it materialized, Nolan felt like he was back in Suspension. Daedalus and Lucian looked identical in every way but their hair. Where Lucian's wavy hair was neat and trimmed, Daedalus had wild hair and much more gray. He walked alongside the blond-haired man, staring at him and not the magi.

"We cannot kill them, Calais; you know this," Daedalus said.

The man called Calais ignored him as he stepped forward. "They say you were raised an orphan, little prince. What wonderful lies. To tell a boy his parents are dead when they could not be more alive."

"My parents are dead! They died protecting me!" Nolan shouted.

"Protecting you?" Calais gave a hearty, high-pitched laugh.

Daedalus chuckled softly.

"Is that what they told you ... or is that what you've been telling yourself all these years? Think about it; has anyone ever told you the story about your parents' disappearance? Ask him now. Ask Zachariah Kingsley about your beloved parents."

Nolan knew he had to be lying. They had to be dead. All the years he spent crying himself to sleep, the fire—he remembered how they died. That dream had been plaguing him his entire life. Was that magic too? Did any of it really happen? *Everything we ever knew was a lie*, Emmett had said their first night. Furiously, Nolan turned to Zachariah, the only person who hadn't lied to him. There was fear in Zachariah's eyes as Nolan shouted, "Tell me he's lying! Tell me they're dead!"

No words came out of Zachariah's mouth, but his eyes said, "I can't."

Turning back to the two people in front of him, Nolan was shouting again, demanding they tell him what happened to his parents. Daedalus placed his hand on Calais's shoulder, trying to lead him away. Calais kept walking with a smile.

"They're alive, of course, trapped, but alive." He gave another high-pitched laugh. "But not from lack of trying …"

"Calais," Daedalus whispered.

"Get your hands off me! He asked me a question, not you!" Calais said.

Nolan didn't care that Calais was walking closer to him. He had to know what happened to his parents. And they couldn't kill him; they said so. Without even thinking about it, he began to walk closer to the handsome blond-haired man. No one could stop him. Much closer than they were before, Calais lowered his voice.

"You were taken from this world, little prince, not out of love but fear. Your parents abandoned you on that pathetic planet of Terrans. If your grandfather had not tried to find you, you'd be dead. We spent decades trying to recover you and bring you *home*, playing with your parents for information. It was a true delight I still enjoy. We knew you'd come back for them, if you survived, and then you bring yourself to the *old oasis*. What a foolish little would-be orphan you are. Want to watch while I make your dreams come true?"

Nolan couldn't move. "My parents … are alive."

"Nolan," Zachariah whispered. "You must—"

"Shut up! You're as bad as Grampa. Every word that comes out of your mouth is a lie!"

"They're all liars, Nolan."

"Calais," Daedalus said.

"Every one last one of them made you foolish and weak. They will always lie to you. It's all they know how to do."

With his head turned, Calais made his move. Pulling the knife out, he pressed it inches away from Nolan's throat. He was leading Nolan back to where Daedalus stood.

"But don't worry; you're safe with me now, little prince," he whispered into his ear.

As the forever fire spell consumed the palace ahead of them, Nolan could think of nothing but his parents. Was Calais telling the truth? Was anyone? The blade got closer, almost drawing blood. Everything he had ever known was a lie, a blood-boiling lie. Every part of him wished his grandfather was with them so he could ask him. But how could he trust him? He had never told him anything about this place, about being a prince. Lucian attempted to speak with Nolan, but he didn't even respond. It was too late. Nolan's anger at everyone on the island was growing at a rapid speed. He was angry at Lucian for bringing them there, Zachariah for lying to him, Calais for torturing his parents, Daedalus for killing his brother and indirectly bringing them all there, and his grampa, for everything in between. Everyone in front of the burning palace stood back with fear as they looked up to see that the clouds were moving. The cloudy night sky was suddenly becoming clear. All they could see was that large red moon staring down at Nolan. *He* was doing this somehow. Zachariah pushed Henri and Emmett back as if the burning palace was safer than being in Nolan's path.

"Nolan? You have to stop this," Emmett said sternly.

Nolan's head fell over. In the blink of an eye, Nolan had firmly grasped Calais's knife arm. As his head popped up, he had a vicious smile on his face and his eyes—they were as black as the sky. The suddenly dark stares complemented his olive-skin as he maintained perfect control. They all looked up as the moon began to recede back to the clouds as its inherit power manifested before them in mortal form. Everything around them could feel this new presence standing before them. When he started laughing, heads turned with fearful curiosity.

"I don't need protection, you worthless little changeling ... but you do." His voice was no longer his own; it was more youthful and dominant, completely sure of itself. Nolan grabbed Calais's arm. As if he were a washcloth, Nolan thrust his arm in front of him, smashing him into the ground, eyes still black as night. Calais dropped his knife. With the blink of an eye, Nolan appeared in front of him, kneeling beside his blond hair.

"Memories rushing back, changeling. Your pathetic species was nothing more than soulless copies of true children," Nolan said in his new voice. "Must I help you remember your failure?"

Nolan's hand was inches from touching Calais's face before a golden orb circled around him. The two beings left in a single orb. Nolan laughed aloud. He looked over to Emmett and Henri. He couldn't see them, but Nolan could hear them.

"We're not leaving here without him, Zachariah!" Emmett shouted.

Nolan could hear his voice was louder as he walked closer to the burning palace.

"Nolan?" Emmett asked.

Nolan looked around, but he couldn't determine where the voice was coming from.

"You have to stop. Whatever this is, it's not real," he said as his heart raced.

"Emmett Bradley, are you the one who thinks you understand what it's like to be an orphaned child? Because you don't, but I can fix that," Nolan said, his voice searching for him. "Where are you, son of Markus? You think this is some illusion, some Terran magic trick? The only illusion here is burning behind you. I know who you are, you worthless half-Terran. Your weak father abandoned our world to breed with those lesser beings. Why anyone would allow you to become a mage is beyond me."

"We have to get that thing off his neck!" Emmett shouted. "He wouldn't be saying any of it if he wasn't wearing it."

"You think I am possessed? The one you call Nolan. We are two halves of the same coin. We are a god! And you are nothing but feeble shadows," Nolan roared.

He was still Nolan physically, but mentally, something else was there. It felt just like when Nolan was taken over by Lucian, but this being was much stronger. Nolan tried calling out his friends' names, but nothing happened, just like before. Whatever this being was, it was more powerful than Lucian was. His ancestor was no longer answering his cries. This was what everyone was talking about. This was why they told him to be calm. Nolan could feel his mind getting weaker by the second.

"Zachariah, take down whatever this is! Where the fuck is that ancestor of his! Can't you do something?" Henri shouted.

"Is that what that is?" Nolan said and smiled as he moved his hands, searching for magic. "Zachariah trying to block me with a confusion spell. Magi magic is so *breakable*!"

"We don't have time. Henri, you have to—"

Zachariah screamed as he fell to his knees. Nolan moved closer to the screams. He thought only mind spells could affect the mind mage. Zachariah's powers were limited. His were nearly limitless. That was what Zachariah meant. Could he cast whatever spell he wanted?

"There you are," Nolan said with a smile.

"Maybe, if I use that spell that got us in trouble in first place. What was it—Sali dre dad ... something," Emmett whispered.

"The half-Terran dares to use my own tongue against me!" Nolan yelled at Emmett, laughing as he walked toward them.

"How did he hear me?" Emmett asked.

"You have much to learn about this world, half-Terran. It is like the Dea said, you *especially* are the foreigner here," Nolan whispered.

"The daemons," Zachariah whispered. "You must make them stronger."

"What?" they said in unison.

"Henri, your element is wind. If we can make Oris ascend, we can fly out of here."

"But I've never ..."

"Oh, I do hate whispering," Nolan said. "Almost as much I hate crying."

"We must! *Ah!*" Zachariah shouted. Before Nolan launched another spiritual attack, he heard Zachariah tell Henri to trust in his magic and trust in himself. Zachariah was still using magic on the Raven-haired one. They couldn't leave now. This was *long* overdue.

Zachariah continued to scream. Any second now, he knew the Dea's defense would break and Nolan could truly capture their vision and grace. *Pani, tell me where they are! Your mage demands it!* Nolan spoke to him through a telepathic connection. Pani's body froze as Nolan looked into the distance, searching for their bond. Nolan's magic was taking over him. Trying to fight it was useless; Nolan was still the southern water mage. Pani's body began to shake, and when he turned around, his eyes were blinking black. Nolan smiled and told his daemon to reveal himself.

"I'm … sorry," Pani whispered. "I … must … obey …"

Pani looked at the Southern Magi with sorrow. A glow surfaced around him, and he only pointed his arms to the sky. From there, he was speechless as a gigantic wave came from all around them, making them fear that they were on an island. It would wipe out everything that was in its path. Pani ran into the distance alongside his mage as the water came rushing in. Slowly, they could see the water hadn't touched the ground around them. Zachariah's defense must have protected them from the physical elements as well. No matter. The waves moved around them like cars moved around buses picking up passengers. Nolan's grin was devilishly proud as he rubbed the silver seal vigorously on its head. Their voices were so much louder now.

"No!" Zachariah said. "He knows. Do it now, Henri! While my defenses are still up! Quick! We don't have much time!"

"Do it, man! Whatever he wants, just do it!" Emmett shouted.

"Mage Henri, you *can* do this. It's in your blood," Oris said.

"Daemon of wind, mage of the kind, powers in sync, powers in twine, raise a daemon of expected fame. Show yourself as I proclaim!"

Breaking Zachariah's spell, Nolan was overpowered as a bright-gray bubble of light surrounding Oris blinded him, and he became a new daemon, a daemon with magnificent beauty and overwhelming strength. The creature stood on its two feet with wings that spread to all of the world. The wings of this creature were like those of an older, more mature owl. He now had two claws, orange with white nails. This was the owl that protected the wind mage.

"Everyone get on my back now! I'll take you somewhere safe; we don't have much time!" Oris bellowed. Now his voice fit his body. His voice was so authoritative that the magi felt they had to obey. Emmett, Henri, Gebb, and Zachariah piled on top, leaving Pani trapped in the gaze of his own mage. They flew toward the skies as the defense broke and Nolan's vision returned. With the defensive spell broken, Pani walked slowly toward his mage. The black-eyed shell of a prince was standing on the edge of the forest that shaded the burning palace. He stared at it and smiled. Amusement kept him frozen and dry as the water moved around him. When the sullen silver seal spoke, it sounded very forced. He informed his mage of their escape.

"Do you think me blind, daemon? No doubt Zachariah taught them the ascending spell. Let them enjoy the small victory they achieved. Ah, it feels so good to be back home. Oh, look at your handsome face. You're like a god, *but you're not.*"

Nolan wiped his hands over Pani's eyes, and the crystal-blue color returned. Pani thanked him and asked him how he should address him.

"Didn't you hear, daemon? Nolan and I are the same. Every time you talked to him, you were really talking to me. Now, tell me, daemon, what do you know of this island?"

"Only the summer palace, my mage." Nolan looked over to the palace as it was still burning and trying to rebuild itself simultaneously.

"Daedalus deserves his recognition. Combating auto repair with forever fire, genius. But to cast a forever fire spell, there must be an origin source."

Nolan stretched his hand toward the burning palace. A living stream of the golden fire followed him. In a straight line, it revealed a link. Nolan and Pani walked the path side by side, not saying a word to each other. The fire led them to a large patch of grass. It stopped just outside of something, but there was nothing there but trees and bushes. Pani stared into it, searching for the source.

"There is nothing here, my mage." His voice was still as forced as before.

"Daemonic magic, how foolish was my sister, giving so much to something so insignificant."

The daemon wasn't pleased with his remarks, but who cared? Nolan walked closer to the place where the fire stopped. He said something in a language that sounded like that of the robed man who had helped bring them to the Terran system. Backing away, Pani stared. A gray mist was broken in front of them. A large house appeared in its place. It was full of shaded windows. The house had not been well cared for, but still, it was there.

"Daedalus's secret haven," Nolan said.

Now they followed the fire inside the house. It hadn't stopped when they had. The door opened for them. Pani continued to follow his mage. As they walked inside, they saw that nearly everything was covered with a white sheet. The house was just as grand as the summer palace, but the shades were all drawn, blocking all light. It had once been a lovely home. Nolan followed the fire until it led him into a dark room. The room was large with nothing more than a large white caldron atop a fire. Shelves of books had been destroyed, their contents lying on the floor with dust covering them. Daedalus must not have used this place often. He looked around at pages that had been ripped from books. As he picked up one of the pieces, his face pruned up. He looked at one of the symbols, a carving of a trident with a high middle horn. He held the paper in his hand, and a black energy swallowed it, leaving ash on the floor.

The fire stream led to a jar atop a shelf. The same golden fire was burning within it. Nolan took the jar, showing it to the daemon, very impressed with himself. Firmly holding the jar, he slammed it against the ground. Once the fire felt air, the stream died. Nolan rose up, placed his hand on Pani, and teleported them back to the palace. It was much easier than before. When they got back to the palace, the forever fire had been extinguished. The palace was rebuilding itself much more effectively. The two of them were taken just outside the palace gates. As Nolan led the way, he was stopped. Each of the statues, the tiger and the dragon, sprang to life, growling. They stared at the black-eyed Nolan.

"Gargoyles," he said slowly. "What is the riddle?"

"There is none …" One of them spoke.

"Not for the likes of you …" the second continued.

Nolan's shoulders dropped. "I am the Moon Dea! Open these gates."

"Body you may have …"

"But spirit you do not … Leave this place, or accept the price."

Pani felt the firm grasp of his mage press into him as they teleported back to Daedalus's haven. Walking past the morbid house, Nolan found Daedalus's glass greenhouse hiding in the back. The flowers had a more dangerous appeal than anything else did. Black leaves and purple thorns were the most appealing as he slid past the decaying smell of life that lingered through the walls. The greenhouse was colder than the outside, as expected, and several flowers were moving on their own, some even attempting to hit him only to be burned and recoil. While many of the flowers were the same, he kept his focus.

Nolan looked in front of him and saw a dormant plant resting in a silver pot, but in front of it, there was a pedestal with words on it. *The protection plants. To call on them one must utter the words: uocat te, dominus.* Nolan read it carefully as he spoke the words. From the silver pot, a large root stretched up to the ceiling. The plant had a giant mouth with green teeth and stood just as tall as Nolan. Black and green were its main colors, but crimson-red petals were at its base. Their vines covered the entire greenhouse, like a blanket. The plant had roots that were sticking out of the ground, and once its mouth opened, his head turned to the left.

"You have penetrated our lord's defenses. How may we serve?" the plant asked.

"How far do your roots reach?" Nolan began.

"Our roots are embedded deep under the foundation of the home," the plant said.

"I need to discover a path into the summer palace," Nolan demanded.

"We cannot. The gargoyles defend more than the outside, my lord. Our limits are bound within this manor, none else. If there is ever a need for us to tell you that a danger approaches in *this house*, we shall alert you," the plant leader said as he seeped roots under the house into the ground.

"Why do you need to gain access into the summer palace, my mage?" Pani said, grunting as he asked.

"I need to find the others. Zachariah will have already blocked my vision of the Terran magi, but he cannot shield me from those under my own moonlight."

"The cycle will protect them, my mage. You may find them no easier than the others," Pani said.

"But there is one foster mage still among the Terrans. I will consume *her* with joy."

Only one man came to mind, the man who could help him find her. The boy's grandfather was in another realm, requiring much more than power. *Tell me where your grandfather is.* Nolan's eyes were opened by force as his darker half pushed them apart. He felt something invade his mind, forcing him to remember things he didn't want to—the day his grampa gave him Carmen, his first car; the newspaper article on his fake parents. The chicken sandwich his grampa had made for him. Nolan's eyes fell again. *Thank you.* He concentrated hard, placing his hand on the daemon. He closed his eyes and thought even harder, and when he opened his eyes, he was in the study of the house the boy grew up in. The study was different than he had imagined with a single window. An elderly man was closing the door of the office, and he looked up. He sneered as the sacred language of the gods had been written on the ceiling. It was fresh, written in red paint, preventing him from teleporting away.

The Wylie trapping spell was large enough to cover the ceiling in a circular formation. The spell was written around the Wylie crest with the language of the gods surrounding it. Once they were ensnared, there was no escaping. However, as Nolan had just done, it was possible to teleport into the trap but not out. Nolan looked over to see that the window had been painted over with black paint, the only light being four tall candleholders, giving off a terrible flame. The wooden desk was bare, and the old man was staring at him, shaking his head.

"Jaahn," Amos said.

Jaahn could see Amos was holding something. A book. The book was thick. He could see some kind of crest on the cover; it was an image of a tiger's head with three stars on the side of its face as the moon was positioned behind it: the Wylie crest. The same crest covered their little summer palace.

"Are you the one he calls Gram-pah," Jaahn said and smiled. "This is your home, is it not? How small it must seem. You wouldn't like me to burn this one as well, would you?" Jaahn said.

"Your words bring no fear to me, Jaahn. Return my grandson to his proper form," Amos said strongly.

"Would you like to speak with him?" Jaahn asked. Jaahn was concentrating on his dark powers.

Nolan was back again, for a moment, shouting out to his grampa. The moment lasted but a few seconds, as the sorrowful eyes of Amos Wylie made Jaahn chuckle with delight. His eyes closed again, and Jaahn was back, staring at the old man with a smile on his face.

"You think that book is going to help you defeat me? It did not help your grandfather, did it? It's secondary magic that will always cower before its elder," Jaahn said.

"This book is not for you. It is for him," Amos said. Amos then spoke in a language that sounded like something was stuck in his throat. The silver seal looked directly into his eyes, taking in every sound.

"You think the daemon can help you? How foolish you Deas have become in my absence! My sister's lesser beings are just more shadows," Jaahn said. "This is your fault, Amos Wylie! You kept me a prisoner in my own body! If you had not tried to stop me, your ridiculous problems would be gone!"

"There is another way," Amos said. "You will never be trusted again!"

"No simple Dea can send me back. All your attempts will fail, surely you must—"

"It is already done. Say hello for me."

Jaahn smiled as he heard the portal-creation spell.

"Four by four, I make the door, to a land across the shore. I am here but wish to be there, so I summon a portal and end this prayer," Amos said.

A door appeared in front of Jaahn. It was simple, like a door to a cottage. He kept his head straight; there was nothing he could do. Amos warned Jaahn to shield his eyes. Not a second later, the door burst open with yellow lights burning out of them. The light absorbed Jaahn as the door shut and disappeared.

The honey-back owl was flying through the wind with the Emmett, Zachariah, and a storm bear cub Gebb. They had been flying for what felt like an hour. Henri was still looking at the largest owl he had ever seen. When everyone else used magic, bad things happened, but Henri had saved them. Whatever spell Zachariah had told him to say saved them from … Nolan? It looked like Nolan, but it wasn't him. Could it have been another spirit that possessed him like Lucian did? Whatever it was, it was the on the rampage, masked under his friend's face. Zachariah said they would be safe in the castle, but he was wrong about *so* many things. Up there, in the sky, away from everything they thought was big and terrifying, they were truly free. But what happened?

"Did Lucian go AWOL or something?" Henri asked.

"Do you remember me telling you a Dea has the soul of a god?" Henri and Emmet nodded.

"To inherit a soul sometimes can come with a price. I'll explain more clearly once we've reached land. It is not safe to discuss it here."

"So it's true then," Emmett said. "Nolan's parents are alive? Why wasn't that the first thing you told him?"

Zachariah sighed. "Would he have believed me? Would you? We were going to tell him, but the emperor wanted it to be in a more comfortable setting. Amos was to be the one to tell him, not I."

"But you said only Nolan could travel between the realms. How would Mr. Wylie have gotten here?" Henri asked.

"The original plan, you remember, was for Amos to come with you. Fortunately, there are more ways to communicate than face-to-face, Henri."

"But they're his parents!" Emmett said. "He thought they died trying to save him! Do you have any idea what that's like?"

"Actually I do, Emmett," Zachariah said sternly. "Hearing the truth from a loved one makes all the difference in the world! Even Daedalus was trying to stop Calais from telling him like this. We feared this might happen, so we did everything we could to keep him calm. His parents were kidnapped when Nolan was but an infant. The world thought they had lost him, and if it hadn't been for his grandfather, they may have been right. Emperor Amos is the key. As long as he's alive, they are all protected. Amos was not going to reveal the truth until he knew Nolan was safe here, that each of you are. *The cycle* will protect you. The eight of you are bonded to each other. They will not dare kill you now. They still need you."

Henri was surprised how much faith Zachariah put behind the southern cycle. It was just a birthing circle. How could it do them any good? It hadn't helped them yet.

"Zachariah, we will be coming to the barrier shortly. Are you sure there will be enough?" Oris said.

Zachariah reached into his pocket and removed three pieces of lime-green paper. Before he got a chance to explain, there was a gust of wind from behind them. A fifty-foot-tall eagle towered over the honey-back owl, wings spread wide. Its golden beak froze under the red moon. Its amber eyes stared them down.

"What the hell is that?" Henri yelled.

"It is Roc the Ferocious Eagle," Zachariah said. "He patrols the barrier separating the three continents."

"Passes?" the eagle asked.

Zachariah held up the three passes. The eagle quickly grabbed them before examining them. "I do not see daemonic passes. It's been ages since I've tasted an owl this large. Hopefully you know how to swim."

"These are the Southern Magi, great Roc. Read between the lines. 'In accordance with the stars' intrusion of the way of this world, a mage shall be permitted to travel throughout any landmass with the accompaniment of his or her daemon. Such is the law as signed by High Emperor Amos Bartholomew of the Southlands.'"

Roc grunted but quickly shredded the passes with his talons. He then flew ahead of them to guide them. Henri didn't understand what barrier Zachariah was talking about it. The ocean looked just as clear on the other side. Roc scratched with great claws at nothing. As he did, they saw a spectral of colors emitted from the sky. A brown ring opened wide enough for them all to fly through. Henri turned around once they were safely through the portal. Roc was gone.

"What's the barrier for?" Emmett asked.

"After the Civil War, there was a barrier created separating the three continents—the Northlands, the Southlands, and the Outlands. Two patrol creatures prevent any communication between the three continents without authorization. Roc watches over the skies, and Roa watches over the waters. Only the emperors can travel without one. No magic can get through it, no exceptions, no survivors," Zachariah replied.

"Survivors? You mean that thing was gonna kill us?" Henri said.

"Roc and Roa are quite different. Roc prefers to eat his victims, but Roa is a cleverer creature," Zachariah said.

"Why are they kept apart? Was the war that bad?" Emmett asked.

"It's a long story, and I'm exhausted. We need to find camp for the night," Zachariah said.

5

The Cycle and the Curse

IN THE MIDDLE of a grass field, legs crossed, a tall young woman with flowing brown hair sat. Rolling her dark-green eyes, she continued to stare into the morning blue sun. Her arms dropped to her side. A long wooden staff nearly as tall as she was floating on its own above her. A red jewel was wrapped in small branches as it pulsed beside her. *"Bond with your daemon," he said. "Build a spiritual kinship," he said. "A mage needs to respect the cycle," he said.* Her daemon and she had been bonded since she was five, she said. Their spirits were entwined, she said. This was an enormous waste of her *time*, she had said. For last few weeks, every single afternoon, she had been sitting, waiting for some divine answer as if she didn't already know which magi were missing from the cycle. Of the eight elements, five were untrained and three of them were somewhat ready. It was their responsibility to protect the world, yet fewer than half of them had even seen it. Her time would be better spent trying to find them and get them up to speed. But *no*, here she was, planted on the grassy knoll atop a hill, waiting for some starry message that said it was okay to leave the nest now. From the moment her archmage had told her the cycle was nearly mature, she had been preparing to meet them. She had only waited for this moment since she got her daemon. Nothing was more important than the cycle and the true magi. The world had waited long enough. As a blue and white firebird the size of an owl flew beside her, fluttering her grand wings under the crisp light of the blue sun, she knew he was close. With black beady eyes, she landed beside her.

He's coming, Kandace.

"Great," she said. "Maybe he'll say I can stop now."

Kandace did her best to resume the meditative position, straightening out her back and lifting her head up toward the sun. A man in a gray cloak walked in front of her with his hands behind his back. His skin was colored like red sand burning under the scorching sun and he had a handsome face. His midnight hair contained no streaks of gray, yet she knew he had to be at least a hundred years old. With his hair tied behind his head in a very neat, tight scarf, he was extremely tall, especially to her. As his bare feet hit the ground, he shook his head.

"No point in trying now, Kandace," the man said.

Opening one eye, she said, "How do you always know?" Kandace stood up, picking up the wooden staff to her left. There was a red jewel at its head. With a tight squeeze, she held on to it, ready to move on from consistent sitting.

"Now that we've got the spiritual thing figured out. Let's do some physical training … please, Archmage Medhas?" Kandace asked.

"And what would be the point of spiritual training if you did not learn anything? Do you feel any change in the cycle?" Medhas asked.

"No more than I did yesterday. I felt … happier, just like you said. There must have been more than one," Kandace said.

"Can you tell me where any of them are?" he asked.

"No," she said and smiled. "How would I be able to do that?"

"How many remain?" he asked.

Her head dropped to her shoulder. "There are only three here, Archmage Medhas. You told me that. Me, one is Blackheart, and one is with the Meians."

"You are supposed to be focusing harder on your spiritual training, Kandace. Body and spirit—"

"… are one with us all, to make one weak the other will fall," she continued.

"Since you have obviously learned the lesson, you should have no problem delivering it. Sit and do not move again until you can tell me which of the magi have returned and which are still absent. There will be nothing else for you until this is clear. Do you understand?"

Frustrated and bored, Kandace sat down. The sun was barely up, and she was spending her day meditating when she would much rather be doing *anything* else. For the first hour, she created a fireball in her hand and bounced it from that hand to her staff hand. The second hour, she spent thinking of ways she could control her fire wakening spell. But the third hour, her body went cold, as if she had been dropped in Glacier Waters. Next there was a gust of wind, knocking her onto the ground, pushing dirt under her fingernails. When her eyes opened again, she picked up her staff and ran toward the cottage where Archmage Medhas and she lived. As she burst through the door, she saw him. He was standing in front of the fireplace, occasionally sending blue fire from his hands onto it. As the blue fire joined the roaring fire, Medhas turned around, placing his hands behind his back as he did so.

"I assume you have something to tell me," he said.

"I think I … felt something." As she quickly explained her short experience, Medhas nodded.

"You were cold, then knocked over, and *then* you saw the dirt under your nails?" he summarized.

"Yes."

"Interpret," he said.

"Okay, well, being cold is weird; it's the beginning of summer, but I wasn't just cold; it was like I had been dunked into … *water* … and then came that blow … *wind*. Two of them are here," she said very proudly.

"Close," he said. "The stars speak to us in many ways. What may seem simple to you requires great work on their part. Try again."

"So then, magi of water, wind, and … the dirt on my hand? Earth? That leaves the only missing elements to be light and hope," Kandace said hesitantly.

"Who are also known as?" Medhas asked.

"The Gemini Sisters," Kandace said. "They must not be here yet. So *now* can we do the physical training?"

"Did you thank the stars for their infinite wisdom?" he asked.

Her shoulders dropped again. "*Thank you, stars.*"

I don't know why he has to talk about stars like that. It's just a myth, pure spiritual energy … What a load of dung! Kandace said telepathically to her daemon.

His people have reverence for the stars. You ought to learn something from that. The chances of you meeting one are far greater than his own, the firebird said to her.

Opening the door that led to the outside, Kandace disregarded her daemon and her archmage. Her mother had tried to teach her about the stars and how much they needed to be respected. All of it was meaningless. The stars only intervened when the world was killing itself. And *that* would only happen if someone wasn't fighting to keep it alive. Kandace's duty was to the world, not all-powerful judges, whom no one could overrule. This world belonged to everyone who lived and breathed here—no one else.

Nolan opened his eyes slowly. He felt like he had just risen out of a coma; every muscle in his body ached. He was in the middle of some grassy field. Pani was next to him. There was what looked like a town somewhere nearby. Walking over to him, he wondered where they were. Nolan felt every vein in his head throb as he tried to sit up. Flashes of his grampa were deposited into his memory bank. When did he go home? More memories starting flaring—spells, fire, water, someone else in his head. *I just had the most unbelievable nightmare.*

It was no nightmare, Nolan.

Jaahn.

Nolan's body felt like it was being electrocuted as he lost control of it again. Everything went black. He could feel his mouth open again. Whatever this thing was, it was speaking, but he couldn't hear the words. Pale-blue light rose from his hands before they quickly disappeared into the sky. Jaahn's voice was strong and lyrical, like an opera singer's. Pani stood up next to him, sadder than he thought a seal could look. Nolan tried to call out to the daemon. Nothing happened. Why hadn't he been able to protect him? That was the point of having one! The Mob must have done something to him, or maybe it was Daedalus or that Calais guy. There was nothing he could do. More memories screened in front of him, but he wasn't sure how he was supposed to respond. He saw his grampa, a blond-haired man, a brother called Daedalus … his parents … Were they alive, or was that just another lie? How would he be able to tell? Whom could he trust? Henri and Emmett were nowhere to be seen, and neither was Zachariah. He thought maybe this thing inside him had hurt them. He had to find them. Nolan desperately had to make sure they were okay. It was bad enough he brought it to them, even though it was unintentional. He had to find them, but he couldn't. Something wouldn't let him.

Jaahn watched from a distance, seeing a young Dea on her knees with her hands covering her face. She was alone in the deserted village. Half the homes were destroyed; the other half had severe damage. If they had been closer to water, perhaps a hurricane would have left them in better condition. The only living thing in the area was the young Dea crying. Crying was such an ugly thing to do. Her blond hair touched her shoulders as she continued to weep. A wooden staff with a magenta stone stood on its own to her immediate left.

"She's a mage," Pani whispered.

Jaahn ignored him as if he already knew.

"But where is her daemon? Her guardian?"

"Let's go see if she knows where," Jaahn said.

Jaahn was leading them closer to the girl as the daemon remained quiet. The closer they got, the more destruction they saw. The village wasn't very large, but it was very populated. Dozens of homes were spaced equally apart from each other. Market stands were turned over, but there were no bodies from what they could see, except for the little mage in the center of it, spewing out those pathetic tears like a child.

"Is everything okay?" Jaahn said, seeing the young mage. It was eerie how much he sounded like Nolan.

Hazel eyes stared up at him as she grabbed hold of her staff.

"Who are you?" she asked.

"My name is Nolan, and this is my daemon, Pani. I'm one of the magi from the Terran system. My friends and I got separated. Are you another mage?" Jaahn asked.

"What's your element?" she asked, still sniffling.

"Water."

"The chill," she said, wiping a tear. "My name is Amelia, and this was my village of Blackheart. I'm the Southern Mage of … Heart." Amelia began.

Amelia, he thought tastefully. Oh no, she was crying again. "What happened here?" Jaahn replied. He could tell that she didn't want to tell him. She looked down to Pani. Tears started to fall. Jaahn knew how desperately she wanted to talk to someone. He was all ears, especially if it stopped the ridiculous sounds she was making.

"You can't tell anyone … *anyone*."

Jaahn nodded, rolling his eyes internally.

"*I* happened here. I'm cursed. A terrible force takes over my body, making me do unbelievable things to the people I care about. Do you have any idea what that's like?" She wept.

Jaahn sighed and shook his head, laughing in his mind as he thought of Nolan.

"Every fourth generation, the eldest girl in my family is cursed. My great-great-grandmother was tricked into taking a stone that contained the curse. By the time she realized what it was, the stone was gone. We've been cursed ever since. Our eyes burn white, and we destroy everything in our path."

"White eyes," he said, intrigued. *An essuda curse.* "No one has found the stone that contained the curse after all these years?"

"We've tried, but my great-great-grandmother didn't leave us much to go on. All she said was that it was blue," Amelia said.

"And the ancestry of the heart magi also runs through your veins." Jaahn could no longer hide his excitement.

"For the past hundred and sixty years," she said.

"And the gift, it is a generational blessing, yes?" he asked.

"I wouldn't exactly call it a *blessing*," Amelia uttered.

"But what happened to your hometown? Maybe I can help somehow," Jaahn responded.

Jaahn couldn't have cared less about the mage's plight, but he needed some time to think. An essuda curse required delicacy, but it was a tool of pure creation, not destruction. This blessing wasn't meant to be given to worthless Dea like Amelia. This was the seal of a god. Jaahn needed her power, but without that stone, there was only one way for him to get it. And she had to give it to him willingly. He needed her to feel comfortable to will her power from her soul.

Amelia said her sister was playing with her friends when she pointed out that her brother was being picked on. Amelia went to help. There were two kids, but they weren't from there. The boy was pushing her brother onto the ground. Amelia asked him what he was doing. He threw some kind of powder into her face, and she fell to the ground. When she awoke, it was morning and her village was deserted, including her daemon. She turned her head, thinking that she heard her name being called, but instead she saw a man in front of her. He told her he was the one who did this. She knew it had to be the curse, but she didn't know how he knew. Only the people of her village knew. He disappeared after that. Then Jaahn walked up to her.

"Truly fascinating," he said. *I have to get that stone.* He kept trying to sense where the stone was but nothing came to him. *I know it has been here somewhere. It'll be so much faster that way.*

Jaahn watched her search through all of the debris, looking for some kind of clue about where everyone was, and then she found a note from her mother, telling her the village was safe, staying in the next village over, Farmer's Hill. *Yippee for her,* he thought. He couldn't sense that damn stone.

"I couldn't believe that I had destroyed all their homes," Amelia said, nearly crying again.

Jaahn kept trying to focus on the stone, but he occasionally had to look at her. She was obviously oblivious to her true power, and he wasn't going to be the one to explain it to her. *It would only make things more difficult for me.* Turning his head quickly while she wasn't looking, Jaahn saw that there was someone watching them a few miles behind her, and he was not in the mood to share an essuda curse.

"Amelia, we should split up and try to find your daemon," Jaahn insisted. "She'll be able to help us."

"Okay. We need to find the other magi too. The cycle is nearly complete now. We're just missing the Gemini Sisters. Maybe that's why you're here?" she cried, looking up at him.

"Uh-huh," Jaahn said, already walking past her.

As she ran in search of her daemon, Jaahn went to find the spies. Once Amelia was out of sight, Pani and he teleported in a golden orb to reappear in front of a strange family. The woman was grotesque beside her overly handsome but short husband. A son stood between them, favoring his father—thank the stars. He looked at the boy as the lights went on. Both of them were there. Amos was cleverer than he had given him credit for. They would be his temptation, delaying his devouring of the magi while Amos and his little people gathered themselves. Even in their state, they were extra calories on an overstuffed plate. The boy looked at him with uncertainty, but at least he wasn't crying. Jaahn didn't bother looking at him. Whoever they were, they were expendable. Not wanting to waste any time, Jaahn grabbed the man's throat and lifted him up in the air.

"Who are you, and what are you doing here?" Jaahn shouted, crushing the man's throat with his bare hands.

"Your Highness, please, my name is Kali Hobbes, and that is my husband, Liam, and our son, Raymond. Please release him," Kali cried, tears in her eyes as she hugged her son.

Jaahn looked down to the medallion around his neck. He had almost forgotten it was there. It was a dead giveaway to any native in this world of his ancestry. Kali had dirty copper hair. She stood out in front of her son and husband. She wasn't nearly as odd looking and out of placed as she stood next to her husband. Her seductive golden-brown eyes were the only enticing attribute she had. Liam looked at her lovingly as Jaahn dropped him onto the ground. Her husband, who was ruggedly handsome with straight sandy-blond hair and bright-blue eyes, was much shorter than his wife—nearly four inches. Liam was dressed in country clothes. Kali stood next to their son, Raymond, who was in the happy middle. He had his father's handsome face and his height. He had his mother's weight, but he carried it better than she did. His hair was straight but messy and sandy blond. Jaahn stared at the boy, and his face lit up like a house on fire.

"Who brought you here?" he shouted.

"A man calling himself Daedalus. He refused to let us leave. He took my family and me from our home and forced us here. Please, we just want to go home," Liam said.

"And I gave all the credit to Amos. Even on opposite sides, the Wylies are still family," Jaahn said.

"The emperor, Your Highness?" Kali said.

Kali found herself grabbed at her own throat as Jaahn looked at her. He said he wasn't talking to her. If he was, she would know it because she would hear her name *fat cow*. The choking continued as he put his hand to his chin. On one side, there was the essuda and then *Raymond*. Amos and Daedalus had learned too much from Magnus.

"All right, I'll play along. How clever can they be?" Jaahn said. "Raymond, you're coming with me now." He released Kali. Her gasps made him laugh as if he had just witnessed her first marathon.

"*No!*" Kali shouted. "You're not taking our boy! Please we just want to go home! Do not take my son from me!"

"Say that word to me again, and I will rip the vocal cords out of your throat," Jaahn said.

Kali and Liam were speechless as they held Raymond between them.

"Why do you want me?" Raymond asked.

"Want? You'll just be good company! Now either you walk here willingly, or I make you watch them die! The choice is yours," Jaahn said.

Kali and Liam looked at each other as if any of them were strong enough to defeat him. A foul odor arose between them. Magic was masking as something else. They were hiding something from him, but he wasn't sure what it was. Jaahn wouldn't let himself be distracted for a *third* problem. The weepy, whiny girl would be back soon, and he couldn't afford to trigger another of her *episodes*.

"Don't hurt my parents, Your Highness. I'll come willingly," Raymond said.

"Please take care of my boy," she cried. "Please, Your Highness."

Jaahn couldn't stand crying. It was such a useless procedure that never changed his mind. Her fat tears made her even more unattractive as Liam held her in his arms. Liam could barely look at the god in mortal form who was taking his only child. This was for the best, Jaahn said; one day, Raymond would understand.

"Say good-bye to your parents. You may not see them for some time." Jaahn laughed, as he looked at the mother's tears.

Raymond walked into his parents' arms as his mother cried. Raymond looked at her for a moment before turning to leave. Jaahn grunted as he teleported Pani and Raymond near the girl again. She had found her daemon. *Great.*

"Which Alpha is that?" he asked.

Pani looked disgusted. "A rose tiger, daemon to the heart mage."

"And what are her weaknesses?" Jaahn asked more aggressively.

"I cannot know, *my mage*. Perhaps you should ask her," Pani said. "Useless."

"You do what I say when I say, Raymond Hobbes," Jaahn snared.

"Your Highness's words are law," Raymond responded.

"Just call me Nolan. Do you have any idea who I am?" Jaahn asked.

"You're … Nolan?" Raymond said slowly. "Would you like me to call you something else?"

"No," Jaahn said laughing. "That will make this much easier."

6

Walking through Questions

S LEEPING LAST NIGHT was the hardest thing either of them had done. Henri and Emmett woke up at nearly the same time. Zachariah was already awake. It felt like they had just been camping, except there was no breakfast waiting for them and a friend was trying to kill them. Other than that little blip, Zachariah told them they had to keep moving. Oris descended back into his normal form, flying slightly above them. Gebb was walking alongside Emmett. Ascending spells, as Zachariah told them, had a limited window. Still it was more than enough to bring them there safely. They were in the middle of a large forest, filled with thick trees and flowers. It was what they imagined a rainforest would look like. They could tell there were more than a few daemons with them. From the sound of it, there were more monkeys. They talked more than the monkeys back home. Here, Henri and Emmett sensed they were *actually* communicating.

"Before we go anywhere, you gotta tell us what's going on. Why are we running around everywhere?" Emmett asked.

"Yeah, it took us hours last night to find a *proper campsite*," Henri said.

"All right, Magi, but I'll be quick," Zachariah said. "We are in a land called the Outlands, home to all wild daemons. While they will not hurt you out of respect for your guardians, my life is not as valuable. As I told you last night, we have to keep moving so he does not find us. I was told to bring you here if for any reason the cycle was in jeopardy."

"I still don't get it," Henri said. "We just walk the forest until … something else happens?"

"You now know why we are moving, yes?"

They nodded.

"Then let's go."

It felt like they were back in the SIMON room. Gebb and Oris stayed close to their magi, but they were just as silent as Zachariah was. Emmett and Henri were getting restless with Zachariah's lack of answers, but what could they do? Neither of them was a mind reader.

Amelia should have been more aware. A few days ago, she sensed three magi had returned to Deva Prime. With the southern cycle nearly completed, she should have known the Makaians would try *something* but not this. The fact that they knew about her curse made her a danger to everyone around her. The cycle was already getting stronger. With just one mage, something stopped her curse for the first time. Maybe the magi together would keep her safe while she figured out how to control it. Nolan's sudden appearance was greatly appreciated, even though she knew he wouldn't understand. How could he? Maybe that was why it was so easy to talk to him. He was proof the cycle was working just like she knew it would. In the distance, the young rose tiger cub ran up from the surrounding forest. It didn't take long for Amelia to find her daemon, thanks to daemonic telepathy. The tears dried up when she saw her. Amelia watched, smiling. The rose tiger had an autumn-bronzed coat. Her velvet underbelly was a light shade of magenta. Her brown eyes were warm when her mage opened her arms. When the rose tiger was standing beside her again, they spoke.

"Amelia, I'm so sorry. I had to get the people to Farmer's Hill and then—"

"Bast, Bast, stop. I understand. I know," Amelia began. "Is everyone okay? I didn't hurt anyone, did I?"

"No, the village was able to escape long before any damage was unleashed. The only question I have is how? You weren't angry, and you haven't had an outbreak in years."

"Thanks to you," Amelia said. "It was Daedalus. I'm not sure how, but I know it was him. I've never felt like this before," she cried. "I just … I …"

"How did you break his magic?" Bast asked.

"It was the cycle. I don't know how, but right after the village escaped, I met another mage, one of the fosters. Remember, I told you three of them were already here. Well, he was my shoulder to cry on. I'm supposed to meet him back in Blackheart," Amelia stated.

"What's his name?" Bast asked as they walked back toward the village.

"His name? I think it's Nolan? He's the Divine Prince, the first mage. Who is that walking next to him?" Amelia responded.

Amelia saw her renewed faith reentering Blackheart with a handsome short boy. A little more than fifty feet separated them as they walked through the damaged city. Rubble was large enough for them walk over; even if it wasn't as clear as the roads had been before. Eeriness continued to drip over the village's borders as if there was still some danger. Every few feet, Amelia looked down at the destruction she had unknowingly unleashed into her hometown. She had been born there, with almost never a need to leave. There was no other home to her, yet she was the cause of its destruction. The cycle saved her. *Nolan* saved her. From a distance, she wondered if he could hear her silent thanks. When she saw the short boy walking beside him, she asked Nolan who it was.

"I found this young man wandering around; his name is Raymond. He was separated from his parents," he said.

"I'm sorry, Raymond. Are you okay?"

Raymond nodded.

"You must be the son of one of the new builders. We need to get him back to his family, but they must be hours ahead of us by now. If we leave now, we should be able to catch up. They're on their way to Farmer's Hill. There's another mage there. Maybe that's where your friends were headed," Amelia wondered.

"Sure," Jaahn said carefully. "We should start moving."

Henri and Emmett were smoldering under the heat of the blue sun. The forest's high trees offered less shade than they would have expected. Monkeys continued to chatter all around them as if they were talking to each other. The worst part about the walking was a combination of sweat and avoiding monkey shit on the ground. The walking, however slow, had long set its ways against the magi. Zachariah was the only one who seemed ignorant of their discomfort. He had been leading the four of them through Meditation Trees for hours. The leadership of the senior librarian was easily recognizable as fear. Neither Henri nor Emmett knew what was ailing Nolan. The hours continued to fly by, with less and less communication. Zachariah had insisted on ignoring them completely, especially their cries of exhaustion.

The ideal place to stop was in the center of the monkeys' chatter. The Alpha daemons couldn't understand what was being said, but they knew when someone was getting ready to warn them of an attack. Red papayas were hanging above them. Many of the monkeys were feasting on them. Zachariah said it was the fruit of knowledge, not for its window to enlightenment but for its tempting sweetness. The fruit was the favorite treat of all monkey daemons. In the middle of the forest, Henri and Emmett sat down, but Zachariah remained standing. He asked the daemons to bring them down some of the fruit from the trees above them.

"How much longer do we have to keep walking?" Henri asked, not eating the fruit in his hand.

"I do not know. If all else fails, the other magi should be meeting us here as well," Zachariah said.

"What do you mean 'if all else fails,'" Emmett said.

"If the Gemini Sisters do not reunite quickly, there may not be a way to bring Nolan back," Zachariah said.

"Bring him back? Are you saying he's gonna die without these sisters?" Henri asked.

"Not die," Zachariah said. "Just sleep. What's happening to Nolan is similar to his first arrival except instead of being possessed by another's spirit, he has fallen to his own soul."

"So this fall," Emmett said, "it's kinda your fault—well, you and Mr. Wylie." Emmett ate the fruit. It tasted like a ripe pear with the sweetness of a strawberry. He saw Zachariah's speechless face and kept eating.

"Yeah, it kinda is," Henri added. "You both lied to Nolan constantly, knowing he had this dark soul or whatever. What did you think would happen when he found out his parents weren't actually dead? Think he'd just *be calm?*"

"We thought …" Zachariah began. "All of us agreed it was better for Nolan this way. Growing up without the burden of knowing his origin, giving him a carefree life with the Terrans is what his parents wanted. It was what was best for him."

"And what about Nolan's parents? Were they okay with being dead?" Emmett asked.

"It was their idea," Zachariah said.

"What kind of parent wouldn't want to be a part of their kid's life?" Henri asked.

"Parents have to make tough choices," Zachariah said. "We do not want to leave our children, but we *must* do what is best for them. Theodore and Illariel had two options: have their child raised in imprisonment, or have him grow up free without them."

"So …" Henri started.

"A child should not be raised in captivity, young mage. They made—"

"The wrong decision. They made the wrong choice," Emmett whispered. "I understand where Nolan is coming from. My dad died a year ago, but there isn't a day that goes by that I don't think about him, wondering if he's thinking about me, wondering if there was something I could have done. I at least had a happy memory of the last time I saw my dad; all Nolan had was that fire. That's the only memory of them he's ever had. Anything would have been better than that. You should have told him."

"So then the fire," Henri said, "that wasn't real, was it? Was that Mr. Wylie too?"

The monkeys started screaming, interrupting Henri's question. Zachariah quickly stood up as if Jaahn was right behind them. Pale-blue lights came soaring through the air from behind them. Zachariah shouted, "Run!" and the magi and their daemons followed him deeper into the forest. He was shouting, "It's impossible! We are protected!" Still, the three of them ran from the two balls of blue light. They tried to outrun the light, but everywhere they went, the light followed. Zachariah tried to block the energy from them as he had blocked Jaahn earlier. It had no effect. Zachariah yelled at them when he realized they weren't tracking the magi. The pale-blue lights were targeting the daemons! No sooner had he said this than Oris and Gebb quickly proved his theory. A pale-blue light hit each daemon square in the chest. Emmett and Henri watched. Zachariah stopped.

"What did he do to them? Does this mean he can find us?" Henri shouted, nearly out of breath.

The daemons stood in front of Zachariah. He placed a hand on their heads and concentrated. Emmett and Henri saw a brown light wash over his hands. After a few seconds, Zachariah's hands dropped.

"Those were spiritual attacks," he said. "Physically, they're perfectly healthy, but Jaahn has done something to their spirits."

"Animals have spirits?" Emmett said.

"Daemons," Zachariah corrected. "Daemons have spirits and souls, just as we do. I cannot determine what Jaahn has done to them, but it cannot be good. Do you feel any different?" Oris and Gebb shook their heads.

"But isn't the mind a spiritual element?" Henri asked.

"Yes, it is, Henri, but unfortunately, I am not trained in daemonic spirituality. Not many people are. Ankkns are the only people left who spend daily time with wild daemons."

"So we just have to wait?" Henri asked. "Until something happens. Again."

"I'm afraid so. Jaahn has access to magic far behind my capabilities," Zachariah said.

"But why? Why the daemons?" Emmett asked.

"They are connected to you, the magi, the cycle, more than you can possibly understand. This is why I wanted you to bond with them in the summer palace. Jaahn must have seen the connection and used it against you."

Henri and Emmett continued to follow Zachariah deep into the forest. The four of them walked more nervously than ever. With their daemons in front of them, they decided to take advantage of being in the back.

"What do you think Nolan is doing right now?" Henri whispered.

"I don't know," Emmett said.

"You think he'll be all right? And what about his daemon? He left with him too? Why isn't he protecting Nolan? Aren't they supposed to protect us?"

"How does he protect Nolan from *Nolan*? Remember what Zachariah said about the daemons being connected to us? Well, whatever happened to Nolan affected his animal as well."

"So what happens to one happens to the other?" Henri stopped for a moment. "And Nolan just did something to *our* daemons. But he wouldn't know about daemon-Mage relationships, would he? I mean we don't even really know. How could he?"

"Whatever's in Nolan, it's *definitely* been here before," Emmett said.

Oris and Gebb stayed close to their magi, gazing at them. They were closer to their daemons than they had been back at the palace, staying within inches rather than feet.

7

The Elven Magi

A S HIS LONG blond hair hung from his head, he closed his eyes and sat against a wall with his legs crossed. He remained as still as he could with a large wooden staff standing directly in front of him all on its own. The staff was much older than he was and had a brown jewel at its head. With milky skin and gray eyes, he focused on his thoughts. First passing had left his room full of the early sunlight. The light touched the open window, bouncing off the large mirror behind him. His curved ears and narrow eyes looked into his grandfather's gift for just a moment. The Elven glass had rings of gold circling it. It was much taller than he was, nearly touching the ceiling. He closed his eyes again. Insight always came much sooner whenever he looked into the mirror. Its powerful gaze upon him and his staff synced deeper with his powers than he had ever imagined. The jewel at its top burned an autumn color before returning to its cool state. Elven ears followed his eyes as his head immediately turned to his daemon. *Glacier Waters ... a tornado ... and a storm bear.* Much weaker than last night, his insight was growing. They must have been separated from each other. Still, the stars were given their gratitude as he stood. The cycle was still unbroken but not from lack of trying.

Something has changed within the cycle, the deep voice of his daemon confirmed as he stood. A furry, medium-sized monkey jumped down from the bed behind him. The size of a husky, he walked on two legs, slightly wobbling as he kept his balance. His golden-tipped tail danced as he sat down in front of him.

It must be them. We must tell her.

Hearing the deep voice of his daemon was enough for him to act. He grabbed his staff, and the golden-tailed monkey said nothing more as he followed his mage into the largest room in the straw home. In the center of the room, a stern woman sat. Her hair was just as blond as his, but her skin was much milkier. She was an Elf, like him, living among non-Elves in less grand conditions. Brown linen and a jeweled necklace hung from her neck. She looked at him with kindness in her eyes.

"I keep getting the same feeling, Mother. Three visions. Water, wind, and earth. They must be the magi who have returned from the Terran system, yet the strength of the cycle is fading. I think they may have been separated," Kalaerede said.

"Which ones?"

"The water image has been the same, but wind and earth are stronger."

"I was hoping you wouldn't say that. An insatiable terror has been returned to us. Kalaerede, have the Gemini Sisters returned? Are they here?"

He shook his head. His mother was more disappointed than he was.

"Do you know where they are? Do you have any idea?" she asked, very quickly. Again, he shook his head. "What is your first thought, Kalaerede?" she asked very calmly.

"I've had these feelings for a couple days now, but they are getting strong. I feel as if something has changed."

As Kalaerede looked up to his mother, he could not explain his feelings. From the moment they arrived, everything had been so clear. He felt their pain of crossing worlds, their confusion and even a little anger. Yet today, there was distance between them. Water was slipping from them down a foreign path while wind and earth were putting more effort into the cycle. The water mage was the first. Without him, the rest were subject to fail.

"Kalaerede, we have waited long enough. You must seek out another mage. I have sent a scout to Farmer's Hill to find the fire mage. She returned this morning," Shi'larra said.

As his mother summoned the scout, Kalaerede looked to his daemon. He had long sensed another mage was not far from him. Yet the suddenness of leaving his mother and her people was too great. This was not what he had expected. The magi were to unite in the order in which they were born. Nolan would come to him. The wind would lead to the heart, fire to light, earth to hope. The cycle would once again be whole. It seemed this was not meant to be. By seeking out the fire mage in Farmer's Hill, Kalaerede would be disrupting the cycle. Moments later, a woman who was much tanner than either of the Elves stood with him. Blood-red hair ran down to her shoulders. She bowed in front of his mother.

"What have you learned from Farmer's Hill, Tara?" Shi'larra asked.

"My Lady," Tara said. "The fire mage is no longer among the Kanes."

"Then where, Tara?" she demanded.

"I heard news of blue fire among the Farmer's Hills," Tara said quietly.

"Blue fire," Shi'larra said in the same quiet tone. "Are you sure?"

"The Kanes assured me an Ankkn with blue fire offered to be the child's archmage. They are in a cottage not far from Mare Lake," Tara said.

Kalaerede had never seen his mother look so shaken. Every muscle in her face was weighed down with grief. She stood up, as he knew she would. Pacing helped her clear her mind. Her grief began to morph in front of him as a beacon of anger rose from her chin.

"Annu, I need you to take him to Mare Lake. If you find the cottage, ask for blue fire. Please, hurry, if you run as fast you can, you should be make it by sundown!" she shouted.

"But, Mother—" Kalaerede began.

"Kalaerede, *please*. There is a plan set in case Nolan breaks from the others. Just do as I say," she said.

"Yes, Mother. Annu, are you ready?"

His daemon led him outside where they would have enough room. Kalaerede didn't know what to say to his mother, but he could see the urgency in her face. In a large area behind the beautifully crafted straw house, Kalaerede placed his staff on his daemon's head as he said the ascending spell: "Daemon of the mind, mage of the kind, powers in sync and powers in twine, raise a daemon of expected fame, show yourself as I proclaim!" A brown circle seemed to swallow Annu, and when he left that circle, a bright new daemon appeared. It still had a tail and fur that was the color of burned coffee. Nearly three times his normal size, he grunted as he looked at his mage.

"Kalaerede, we must leave now," the deep-voiced monkey said.

Kalaerede didn't say anything to his mother or anyone as he got on his daemon's back. Annu jumped out from the back of the hut and over the wall and ran north. He was running faster than his thoughts, passing through trees like the wind. All the while, he wondered if the legends of the Ankkn firebirds were true. It was said that the stars had blessed one family with the firebird seal centuries ago for their undying respect for daemons. The last known blue fire was believed to have died alongside the Southern Magi in the Civil War. Perhaps they had survived.

Was this what death felt like? No matter how many times Nolan tried to move or open his eyes, nothing but darkness surrounded him. With no one to hear him, Nolan was alone with his impending death. He should have been used to this by now. Nolan was only a child, forced to listen as so many children asked him where his parents were. *I have my grampa*, he would say. *Well, everyone has that, but you only get one mom and dad.* He hated that number; it really was as lonely as that depressing song suggested. They reminded him of the one pair of words he had never cried out in the middle of the night. Nolan was all by himself now. That was what he was forced to repeat in the shadow-less cloud of thought.

One day, it all changed though. Miss Dereks was a first-year kindergarten teacher with a hunger to fill young minds with hope and purpose. Day one she was smiling and eager. By day five, she had mastered the mom-eye. They worked wonders on Emmett. Henri laughed. Those two were terrible together. Back then, Nolan was the vigilant onlooker of their tricks and cruel pranks, like shouting Miss Dereks's name whenever she turned her back or clapping excessively when they laughed. During the second week, she told him it wasn't nice to shoot spitballs. Nolan remembered crying. At recess, Emmett was the one who apologized. Henri said he was aiming for the kid behind him. They exchanged names, and there were jokes about the girl with buckteeth or the boy who picked his nose and even the kid who rode the short bus. That was when the parents and grandfather were called. Henri's mother was the one who demanded a stern hand and an educative play date about children with special needs. If all mothers were that terrifying, Nolan wasn't sure if he wanted one. From there, a full-fledged friendship was formed.

Now all that was in danger because of yet one more day. Maybe this was Nolan's fate, and it had finally caught up with him. Henri and Emmett should have left when they could before whatever forced this loneliness destroyed their bodies in a way he couldn't even imagine. Maybe his parents should have done the same to that sweet child kicking his mother's stomach as his father smiled. Then he wouldn't be lying dormant as his body moved of its own will, terrorizing a world he didn't know existed. Nolan's parents tried to keep him away from it, but they weren't there to help him. *No one was.*

8

A Sudden Change

JAAHN HAD SPENT the better part of the morning forcing smiles. The tales of their origin, especially of the now tearless mage, had bored him to pieces. This was beginning to cost him more than time. The daemons had found them a small breakfast of fruits and berries. It seemed Nolan's stomach had already grown accustomed to the natural sweeteners of his own world. After breakfast, Jaahn convinced them, which took little effort, that it was time for them to find his friends in Farmer's Hill. He hated walking through the Green Valley when he could have been teleporting, but the risk was too great. Jaahn had become the leader of their adventure, despite their ignorance of his true intention. The silver seal he was growing to detest even more was no longer the only being constantly at his side. Raymond, Amelia, and her daemon, Bast, were a few feet behind him, talking among themselves.

Probably more of her constant apologizing. Why she was ever given my sister's blessing, I will never know.

You know what that curse is, Pani said.

Jaahn couldn't help but smile.

So the connection has been made, has it? I'm sure the Dea would be proud. No matter. Your thoughts will no longer be welcome in my mind, daemon!

Pani strained for a second, but no one else noticed because he kept walking. Jaahn smiled. A few hours passed. They felt like moments for Jaahn, but his companions were not as strong as he was. Their legs had gotten slower, making the distance between them even greater. This was an advantage to him. He no longer had to hear the distant whispers of the two of them. Their ignorance, at first welcome, was now becoming more and more tiresome. However, the mage and her daemon made their way alongside him.

"Are you sure he said Farmer's Hill? That's such a long way. You should go to the Meians first to find the mind mage, then Blackheart, then Farmer's Hill, where the Kanes live. How did your friends and you get separated like this?" Amelia said.

"A potion, I believe," Jaahn said convincingly. "Deconstruction? He said it may not work that well our first time."

"Wow," Amelia said. "Zachariah wanted fosters to use deconstruction? That's really dangerous."

"What did you call them?" Raymond asked, making his way near them as well.

Jaahn sighed as his quiet time was interrupted yet again.

"Fosters," Amelia said. "Because they've adopted the ways of the Terrans. It's a good thing though, their being in Farmer's Hill. If something went wrong with the potion, I'm sure Farmer's Hill has herbalists, maybe even a transferor. And, Raymond, your family would be there just like mine."

Jaahn continued to walk on, ignoring the mage's comments. She insisted on taking the lead, as if her shortcuts would get them there any faster. Jaahn grunted to himself. Only the silver seal stayed behind with him. After another hour, the mage's conversation with him restarted. The annoying girl asked him if he knew how to teleport. Admitting to control of his powers could ignite something he wasn't ready to face. Jaahn's face was stern for a second time as he caught up to her. But it would all be worth it once she gave him her curse. So in his most innocent replication of Nolan's whiny little voice, he spoke to her, although it was not as convincing this time.

"I'm not from this realm. I don't know anything about magic. My friends and I only arrived a couple of days ago," he said.

"I forgot. I'm sorry. I mean you don't even have your staff yet. I didn't mean to—"

"It's fine," he said, slightly aggressive. "But you're right. If we're going to walk there, we'll need some food for the journey. Why don't you and Raymond go gather some and I'll stay behind? I wouldn't want to get lost."

Amelia agreed. Raymond nodded, looking at Jaahn. The two of them walked carefully to the edge of the forest lying south of them while Pani and Jaahn waited. Pani waited a few inches away from Jaahn. He looked deeply into Nolan's eyes before he opened them suddenly. A screeching pain struck Jaahn like a bullet to the head. Pani did nothing but watch. Nolan's body fell to its knees, not uttering a word.

What are you doing to me! Give me back my body! Nolan thought.

Or what? What are you going to do to stop me? Jaahn thought.

What are you? Where am I?

Is it beginning to settle in, Nolan? Feeling cut off from the world, restricted, lonely, *doesn't fit so kindly when it's happening to you, now does it? Forty years, you kept me locked away in that insufferable cage, cutting me off from all that is natural to me.*

What are you talking about?

Once I find a way to consume the girl's soul, I will tell you.

You're gonna eat her soul?

We've been searching for her power for centuries, and now your grandfather has sent me straight here. He is insufferable, but it is the one thing I need more than keeping you alive. Soon no one shall have the power to stop me ever again.

Again?

"Enough," Jaahn said. "I grow tired of sharing."

Jaahn's attention was shifted to the daemon to his left. The daemon couldn't hear his thoughts with Nolan, but somehow he was able to sense Nolan's sudden awareness. As much as he wanted to retaliate, Jaahn was more curious about Nolan. Something else had happened—something he feared more than anything. Suddenly, Jaahn saw a smoky mist appear in front of him, which stopped him cold in his tracks. A heavenly white light appeared as it took the form of a young Dea. The girl had wavy brown hair. Her clothes were plain, less than a peasant's, but her youthful beauty was unmatched. Her body appeared to be thinner than normal, and light bounced off her every movement. She wasn't there. Not really. He stood there a moment longer, seeing her for what she truly was.

"Jaahn," the girl said sternly, "let him go."

"You!" he shouted. "How did you find me!"

"Don't do this, Jaahn. Just give him back! He's more important than your little temper tantrum," the girl continued.

"Are you calling me a child, *child*! I will not be forced to lie in wait again!" Jaahn shouted. Jaahn stretched his hand out. Grabbing at nothing in the center of her chest, he gripped what Pani assumed was her heart and pulled it from her chest. Screaming, the astral projection vanished before his eyes.

"Damn it! They must be close. I need a soul quick before they awaken."

Focusing all his energy, Jaahn breathed slowly, summoning the proper spell nonverbally. Another was moving at an incredible speed. It was a mage, Nolan's soul mate. *Perfect*, Jaahn thought. When he consumed it, the cycle would be broken and the awakening would be no threat against him. He figured this mage may be easier to acquire than the girl. It was like she said; he was supposed to find the mind mage first anyway.

"Come. We must go. I don't *need* you, but I can't very well leave you here to speak hope with the whiny one and Raymond."

"Won't they be even more suspicious when you're not here when they return, *Mage?*" Pani asked.

"The one I seek is much weaker than they are. This will not take long." Jaahn placed his hand on Pani. His body became a golden orb before absorbing the silver seal into it.

Nolan opened his eyes, with the same sheering pain from the last time. Everything was misty just as before. There was nothing around him—no light or people, just an empty vastness spreading on for more than he could see. Even his hands were hidden. Whatever this thing was, he knew what it was after: a soul. *Eating a soul?* He knew it was crazy, but so was everything else in this place. How much had his grampa hidden from him? Alone in the darkness, there was little he could do. If he tried hard enough, he could almost look out his own eyes again but never for more than a second or two— hardly enough time to get help. And besides, whom would he call? His grampa? Zachariah? Lucian? There was nothing he could do but think—one continual thought. His parents. As angry as he wanted to be for being raised an orphan, he couldn't help but be excited. If his parents were alive, they would have so much to catch up on. Where would he start?

The fire. Yeah, that was a good place.

He had so many questions. His grampa had obviously told him that so he wouldn't have to tell him the truth. But the fire. Why such an awful memory? There had to be tons of other things his grandfather could have made up for him but the fire. Why was that so important to maintain? If he would have just told him they'd died in a fire that might have been enough. However, Nolan couldn't answer his own hypothetical question. He had never thought about how much the fire had affected his life. At some point, it was just easier not to talk about it, not to think about his parents. His grampa had been a great parent, but then again, he'd had decades of practice. Figures. The one time he wanted to talk to his grampa about the fire, he couldn't.

Every time he closed his eyes, Nolan thought about that painting of them. *Theodore and Illariel Wylie.* They looked so real. He wanted to know what had happened to them. Why had his grampa told him they were dead? There had to be some explanation, some reason for why they'd been separated. Maybe they didn't want him, like that blond-haired man had told him, but that painting in the summer palace. They didn't look like parents who weren't happy to welcome their son into the world. And then almost as quickly as the thought formed in his head, he thought of its counter. *What if they are dead and someone's just playing with me?* Zachariah didn't say no, and he wanted to believe him, but after everything that had happened to him, he wouldn't know the truth if it looked him in the eye. Nolan desperately wanted to talk to Pani. Pani had protected him from Daedalus. He saw into his eyes, crystal blue. Nolan tried as hard as he could to summon whatever connection Zachariah was talking about or even just speak with him. No matter what he did, however, Pani didn't respond.

9

Listen to the Monkeys

HENRI AND EMMETT were still following Zachariah as he led them through the forest, but his attitude had changed completely. What before could have been said to be a pleasant worry was now frantic. His walk was more spacious than ever. Henri and Emmett were beginning to wonder if he even knew they were behind him. Every few seconds or so, he would pause and look around the endless trees, but then after another second, he would keep speed walking forward. They wondered if the blue sun had anything to do with it. Midday was approaching, and they still hadn't found any of the other magi. The Alphas were still inches away from their respective magi. Their protectiveness was new despite whatever Nolan did to them.

"What do you think he's looking for?" Henri asked.

"I don't know," Emmett said, barely above a whisper. "He didn't mention looking for anything before."

"Why are you whispering? It doesn't really matter; he's probably already reading your mind," Henri said.

Emmett grunted and continued to whisper, "You think the animals know what he's looking for?"

"I think they would have told us. Out of everything that's happened, they're more honest than anyone. Besides, we are *their* magi. I think their loyalty is more to us than him."

"That must be why your animal wouldn't find a way out of the maze when I asked it to," Emmett said.

"*It* is an owl, a daemon. And his name is Oris. All day you've been calling them 'animals' and 'those things.' Don't you see by now they're more than that?" Henri said.

"Yeah, they're ticking time bombs," Emmett said. "Nolan put some kind of spell over them—remember?"

"Of course I do, but there's nothing we can do about that. You heard what Zachariah said. We'll cross that bridge when we get to it."

They felt like they were being watched from every direction in the forest. Their daemons were only inches in front of them but a good foot behind Zachariah. Strange sounds burst into their ears, but it was nothing like a trip to the zoo. There, the sounds were the occasional grunt or maybe even a moan, but here, it was as if the daemons were talking to each other. Daemonic tongues ran back from one side to the other, following them at every tree branch. Zachariah was the only one who looked terrified, despite his new sense of urgency. The daemons walked and flew with their heads held high. Another hour passed before mortal words were welcome.

"Do you know what they're saying? The daemons?" Henri asked Oris.

The honey-back owl turned his head as he flew next to him. "No, I do not know the tongue of the primates."

"Language?" Emmett said. "You have your own languages?"

Oris grunted at Emmett.

"Yes, Emmett. Each species of daemon has their specific tongue, or language, as you call them. Only an Alpha is able to speak all the tongues of his family."

"His family?" Henri asked.

"All those who reside in his element," Oris continued. "As the wind Alpha, all tongues belonging to wind daemons are one with me."

"So you're like a translator?" Henri asked.

"When I speak, it will always be in owl tongue, but if I am talking to a non-owl, they will hear it in their own tongue, and vice versa. To a Dea, it would sound like two different tongues, but we would hear it as one."

"But neither of you speak primate?" Emmett asked.

"Neither of us *are* primates," Oris said. "Primates belong to the element of the mind. Only its Alpha will be able to understand what they are saying. But do not worry, young Emmett. No wild daemon would dare cause harm to the cycle. It is sacred to all daemons."

"These primates were probably sent to watch over us by Emperor Amos," Gebb said. "He knows how important the cycle is. Even a Dea respects the power of Mother Maia."

"Who's that?" Henri asked.

"Maia, the patron goddess of all daemons. She is to daemons as the sun and moon gods are to skinned magic," Oris said.

Henri laughed when he heard "skinned magic."

Henri and Emmett were curious to ask how Mr. Wylie could have sent primates to them, but it was easier to just go with it at the moment; he was obviously a bigger planner than they had thought. Before long, their attention was drawn back to the Dea leading them. Zachariah turned to them, his neat red hair shining under the sunlight. Whatever he was looking for, he must have found it. Zachariah came back holding a thick scroll in his hand. There was a jewel in the center. It was blinking white. Holding it in front of them, Zachariah continued to smile. He wasn't saying anything to them. When he looked closely at the color of the blinking jewel, however, his smile shrank. Henri and Emmett walked closer to him, and their daemons did as well.

"This is a telling scroll, left by Emperor Amos, with two different messages left inside. You see this jewel here? It tells us which message the scroll is going to tell us."

"It chooses its own message?" Emmett asked.

"Based on the situation, yes," Zachariah said.

Zachariah then pressed the white jewel and threw the scroll high into the sky. They watched for a second before the sun blinded them. As the scroll fell in front of them, it opened, dropping like a curtain. The telling scroll stopped in front of Zachariah's face. It was just as tall and wide as the portraits back in the summer palace. An image began to appear on the scroll, an image they had all seen before. It was Amos Bartholomew Wylie dressed as the high emperor. The vivid picture looked blank as he stared off into nothing. Then he spoke.

"Magi," he said, "my worst fear has come to pass. The alter ego of my grandson has risen. While it is unfortunate Jaahn has regained control, do not place your blame with him. He knows not what he does. If you are hearing this, the cycle is being threatened. I have asked the primates to watch over the magi who walk this forest. Their magic combined with my own should be more than sufficient protection. As I speak, I am gathering the Gemini Sisters. Only through their awakening can Jaahn be forced back to his resting place before he consumes our last chance against the Makaians. The five of you must unite as the Gemini Sisters prepare for their return. As you know, four of the magi have been sent to the Terran system and four remain in our world. This is also true of the sisters. They should arrive before the next rise of your sun. Stay in the shadows, young magi, until the light shines again."

The telling scroll quickly closed itself and fell to the ground. The white jewel turned black as Zachariah picked it up. He put it in the pocket of his robe.

"Jaahn?" Emmett whispered. "Who is—

"Who's the other mage!" Henri shouted.

"I believe you are already know, Henri, don't you?" Zachariah said.

Emmett looked at Henri's burning black hair. Gebb looked up at him. The storm bear's eyes matched his deep voice. Oris flew closer to Henri.

"Lilith," Emmett whispered.

"What was he talking about?" Henri said. "What did he mean by only the sisters can bring Nolan back before Jaahn consumes them?"

"Lilith and her Gemini Sister are the only ones who can help Nolan. They alone can protect him from causing any permanent damage."

"What do you expect Lilith to do? She's just a kid! My sister is just as lost to this place as we are. We're the ones hiding in the forest. I won't let you do this to her!"

"Let me?" Zachariah said, walking closer to Henri. "Do not be confused, young Henri; you may be the wind mage, but you do not understand the danger Jaahn possesses. The Gemini Sisters are our last chance. Otherwise we all are in danger."

"All?" Emmett said.

"Yes, Emmett. All Deas fear the great soul eater, even the Northern Magi. They will do whatever they can to restrain him," Zachariah said.

"Soul eater? Is that what he is? Nolan is a *soul eater*!" Henri shouted. "That's what he does! That's the big threat! And you want my sister to go against that?"

"She must! It is the only way. The Gemini Sisters' awakening will restore Nolan to his natural balance when they complete the cycle," Zachariah said.

"Bullshit!" Henri shouted. "There has to be another way."

"There is none, Henri. It must be Lilith and her Gemini Sister!"

"To go up against, Nolan! We should be the one fighting him, not her, not camping out in some fucking forest with a bunch of fucking monkeys!"

"So hope and light affect the moon?" Emmett asked.

"The mage in him, not the Moon Dea," Zachariah said. "The cycle indicates that only the elements of the most internal duel can reverse the effects of such a powerful force, but only when they first unite. Hope and light are split: male and female, brother and sister. The Gemini Brothers have already awakened, years ago. The only chance we have left are the Gemini Sisters. This was why Emperor Amos insisted on a separation of the two. In case the worst were to occur, he could unite them and restore Nolan before anything ill occurs. The prophecy does not mention a fight. There should be no harm to any young Dea! They will be safe."

"Like we were back in the palace?" Henri said. "How do you know they'll be safe? How do you know Nolan isn't looking for them right now? He's the only one who can go home."

"Emperor Amos would have taken steps to prevent that, I'm sure," he said.

"So you don't *know*!" Henri shouted. "And what about the mob, huh? Maybe they'll let Jaahn eat our souls."

"Then they would be next! The Makaians want him to return as much as we do. They will help the Sisters unite if they must!" Zachariah said.

"What! Now you're saying the mob is going to help us! You have no idea what you're talking about, do you? Putting your faith in the enemy! Or Mr. Wylie halfway across the world! All while putting my sister's life on the line while we stay behind and *hope* she's okay! You don't know what's going to happen to her!"

"The cycle …"

"Fuck the cycle!" Henri shouted. "It hasn't done us any good, has it? We're just as powerless without it."

"Henri," Zachariah whimpered.

"Fuck … your … cycle! I won't risk my sister to save *your* world!"

"Me either," Emmett said softly. "Whatever magic any of us have, it's weak. You rely so much on your precious cycle, you don't even look around. You're talking about people's lives, Zachariah. We won't sacrifice anyone. Not for this!"

Zachariah placed a quick hand on his chest. Oris and Gebb were staring at the sun as if they were in a trance. Without saying a word, they ran in separate directions. Henri and Emmett tried to follow them, but Zachariah wouldn't let them. They tried to push past him, but he shouted at them to stop.

"No! We must what until after the transformation. Listen!" Zachariah said.

Henri and Emmett did exactly that. There was nothing—no daemonic communication, no strange monkey talk, not even the wind was making a sound. They were alone in the forest for what felt like the first time. The silence was unnatural, terrifying to say the least. Everything had just stopped. Henri and Emmett looked around frantically, wondering the same thing: Jaahn?

"What's going on?" Henri asked.

"What you said! What both of you said. It's clear that you meant every word of it, so much so it brought out an unnatural reaction in your daemons. They are linked to you. I've told you time and time again to respect the relationship and bond between you and your daemon, but now—now it is too late. I can only pray your short time with them will be enough."

"Enough for what?" Henri said, his attitude still as strong as ever.

"Enough to change them back, Henri. Whatever spell Jaahn cast on them, it made them more sensitive to your spirits, your energy, and your *feelings*. That must be why they were so close to you after it happened."

"What good will that do?" Emmett asked.

"To convey the soul of a living being, you must remain close to them physically. This will establish a kind of reading of the interior of the soul. Once this is done, the connection is created. A person of great power can abuse this relationship. It is one very similar to love. Jaahn hoped there would be some strife between one of you so that he could bring something into the world that has not been seen since the Civil War."

"What?" Emmett asked.

"A temperamental daemon also known as an unstable daemon. This was how the relationship between mage and daemon was fully realized. Emperor Magnus waited too long to bond daemon and mage, causing a kind of chemical reaction. A temperamental daemon will assume all of the emotions of its mage without any concern of its own. This can be disastrous. Daemons and their magi require more than a physical bond; they *need* a spiritual one as well. Body and spirit are one with us all; when one is weak, the other will fall. Oris and Gebb have lost control of their bodies to *your* angry spirits. Until *you* are stabilized, they will be as vicious as a horned daemon."

"So we just have to be calm?" Henri said. "I can do that."

"It is not a simple task, Henri! You cannot fool your own spirit. Come! We must find Oris first. As the only daemon that can fly, we need to get to him before he decides to leave the Outlands in a desperate attempt to return to Earth. If he does, I'm sure Jaahn will be watching."

10

Beasts of Mare Lake

VICTORY TASTED SO sweet as he opened his eyes. Had he finally done it? Pani was next to him, looking grimly at a cottage about a hundred feet away. Nolan had tried for so long to get control of his body again, to speak to his daemon, the only living thing from this world he could trust. For a few seconds, he just enjoyed moving his head when he wanted to, wiggling his fingers, looking out into the world that he had nearly consumed. In the distance, a small cottage with a large chimney was blowing light-blue puffs of smoke into the air. There was someone walking up to the cottage very timidly. There was a daemon beside him, a monkey. It reminded Nolan of the white-palmed gibbons back at the summer palace.

"Nolan?" Pani said.

"Yeah, I'm back, but I don't know how long. He just … let go."

"It seems your grandfather was right," Pani said. "Before we left your Terran home, he told me the Gemini Sisters would find you.

And all I had to do was be patient. They could use me as a way to find you."

"Grampa knew?" Nolan said.

Nolan tried to hide his anger. It was a part of his plan. Despite not knowing what a Gemini Sister was, he knew one thing: he was back. One image kept popping back into his head, something Jaahn had tried to grab—that girl's heart. He wished he could have thanked her or at least given her a face. The only thing he could vaguely remember was how young she looked. She couldn't have been much younger than Lilith. Then again, how old was *he*? Jaahn said something about being trapped for forty years. What did that mean? As he tried to summon Lucian as he did in the oasis, he wasn't too shocked that he wasn't responding. Nolan wasn't even sure that he was doing it right. There had to be some way. Jaahn had always made using magic seem so easy. He didn't understand what or where Jaahn came from, but he knew he was connected to him somehow. The next thing he did was look down to his medallion. Taking it off was out of the question. He remembered that much. A white tiger with black stripes had never looked so frightening. Every piece of him wanted to blame that tiger for everything—the palace, the fire, his friends, his parents ...

"Did my grampa mention my parents? Did he say anything about them?" Nolan shouted.

Pani was obviously expecting this question as he shook his head. Emperor Amos, he had said, had only told him of the Gemini Sisters.

"I do not know much, but their tale is one of legend, Nolan. Theodore was the first Wylie prince to marry an Elf. Every other male in the Wylie family has married an Ankkn. Their life spans are the closest. According to legend, Theodore and Illariel were to be married in the Elven tradition, but on the eve of their wedding night, there was a terrible storm. The Elves foresaw this as a sign of impending danger for the couple. They had to postpone one year. Soon after their marriage, Illariel became with child. The Makaians sent every known assassin they could find to kill your mother before she gave birth. Theodore teleported his young family around the world throughout the entirety of her pregnancy. It was only when teleporting proved too great for her that they stopped in the Outlands. Within weeks, you were born in Aurean Clouds. But not soon after, the three of you were captured. It was then that the prophecy of the next generation of magi was revealed. As the others took their first breaths, it was confirmed that you still lived. Shortly after, Emperor Amos privately entrusted the power of the empire to the High Council. It was assumed that he had set you and your parents free, but over forty years have passed since—"

"Forty years! What are you talking about? That would make me … I don't even know."

"The year of your birth was the year 148, the beginning of the southern cycle. The year now is 191, which would make you the tender age of …"

"Forty-three!" He had never gotten this angry this fast. It was one thing for his grampa to keep Deva Prime from him, another thing to tell him that his parents were dead, but his own *birthday*! He was eighteen, an alumnus of Middlecreek High School, a member of the fucking Honor Society. There were twenty-five years of birthdays he had missed. For forty years, Nolan had been kept in the dark!

"Nolan?" Pani asked.

He instantly knew why his daemon had spoken so softly to him. His medallion was glowing again. Wanting to fall down to his knees, Nolan felt his body being pushed back into itself. Attempting to open his eyes was useless. He knew this feeling all too well. *You are beginning to understand, aren't you, Nolan?* Jaahn said calmly. The dark voice spoke to him without moving his mouth. There was a sense of compassion in his tone.

Imagine being imprisoned here for forty years. It makes one rather unhappy.

Look at what you're doing! Why would anyone allow you to leave? I wish you'd never gotten out!

I was just thinking the same thing about you.

"So that is how they were able to find me," Jaahn said to a saddened Pani. "I underestimated you daemons. Tell me, the mage moving in front of us, which one is it?"

Pani's calm tone had suddenly shifted to an obedient response. He explained that the daemon in front of them belonged to the primate family, which represented the element of the mind. Thus, the mage in front of them was the southern mind mage. Looking between the daemon to his left and the still walking mage, a plan quickly formed in Jaahn's head. Nolan tried to peek out his own eyes again. He could hear his own voice saying words he didn't recognize. Then he saw two more pale-blue lights before everything went dark again.

The bright light of the world was quickly leaving them. With his hands still holding on to his staff, Kalaerede looked up to see the sun was setting, which meant that he was getting closer to blue fire. He insisted they walk the last few miles on account of the great journey Annu had made from their home. Traveling across the East Thunder Mountains was no simple stroll, but thankfully, in his ascending, his speed increased along with his size. Kalaerede carried nothing as he walked alongside Annu back in his natural form. The two of them were speaking telepathically from the moment he descended. Kalaerede asked Annu how much he knew about the firebird seal and by extension the four Maian seals. He was not surprised by Annu's knowledge of daemonic lore.

The goddess Maia created four daemons before any others: the blue firebird, the green hippopotamus, the white-tailed king primate, and the yellow starred lions. The first four daemons were known as the Founders. Maia created the Founders with a mixture of the two elements: fire and wind, water and earth, light and mind, hope and heart. However, this power was too great for one daemonic family. The four kingdoms then became eight. As the Founders grew older, their excess power was placed into four seals, a collective extension of their powers. Once Maia created the seals, she hid them from the world. *Only those who are righteous and true shall find the power of the daemons two.* Two seals had been discovered: the firebird and the hippo. The rest, as they say, were a mystery. This legend intrigued Kalaerede. This blue fire archmage was blessed. For this, he had earned the respect of the Elf mage.

They came at last to the cottage spewing blue smoke into the heavens. Kalaerede looked to his daemon. The cottage couldn't have looked any plainer. The area behind them was full of grass, not a single flower in sight. While they were only a few hundred miles away from the village of Blackheart. Kalaerede thought it comforting to know that the fire mage was training in an area away from danger. From what he knew of the elements, fire was the most difficult to control but the easiest to react, just as it was in nature. He wondered what his training would have become if he had had an archmage. Still, he could no longer hold his excitement at meeting with another mage. Even though this was not the way, it was supposed to happen, he was ready. They had been separated for too long.

What are you waiting for? Kalaerede's daemon spoke to him.

Kalaerede walked up to a wooden door on a small cottage in the middle of nowhere, but the engraftment on the door amazed him most. There was a symbol of what he assumed was the firebird seal. An angry blue firebird with wings spread wide stared down at him. Kalaerede couldn't take his eyes off the door. It continued to amaze him until remotely he put his fist up, leaving his staff to stand on its own. He knocked. It was not a man who answered it but a tall girl who looked about his age with a blue firebird at her side. Gaping slightly, Kalaerede stared at the daemon.

"Blue firebirds are extinct?" he said.

"Nearly," the girl said. "Are you an Elven mage? I thought the light mage was coming to *collect* me? Something must be wrong. Come on in," the young girl said. Her long brown hair swayed as she ushered him in.

"I am here in search of blue fire," Kalaerede said.

"Archmage *Medhas* of Blue Fire, he's the only blue fire I know." The young girl laughed.

As he walked inside, his staff attached itself to his right hand. Without another word, Kalaerede stared at the man behind the counter. His hands were behind his back. The red skin tone told him the archmage was Ankkn. He had never seen one, but the legends were true. They were very tall men. Long black hair was tied in a scarf behind his head as he stood in the kitchen.

"Archmage Medhas, do you know a woman by the name of Shi'larra?" he asked, his staff still tight in his grip.

Kalaerede knew at that moment that this man must have at least heard of his mother's name because he dropped whatever it was he was cooking. The iron skillet fell to the floor and the sound alone could have awakened the dead. As it rang on, Kalaerede waited.

"What do you what to know about Shi'larra and why?" Archmage Medhas asked in a stern voice.

Kalaerede had not wanted to, but he had to know. He concentrated on this Archmage Medhas, reading his mind quickly. He saw visions of him and his mother together, kissing and smiling. His mother had never mentioned a man in her life other than his late father.

"How dare you read my mind, mage?" the archmage said. The fire in the chimney began to grow as he walked closer. "How do you know, Shi'larra?"

"She is my mother; my name is Kalaerede, the Southern Mind Mage," he said.

Archmage Medhas stared at the boy in front of him. "Shi'larra has a son?"

"Yes," he responded. "How do you know my mother?"

"That does not concern you. If you are a southern mage, where is your daemon?" Medhas asked.

"He's probably outside," Kandace said, interrupting. "He's got the staff. We only get those after we bond with our daemons."

Kalaerede heard her, but he shared a look with Archmage Medhas. He looked down to his left, hoping for an answer. *What had happened to Annu?* He was just there a second ago, but when he heard the door close, he knew that he wasn't beside him. Something took over him. Remembering the beautiful engraving on the door, he thought perhaps *someone* had—but that was impossible. Only another mind mage could cast a mesmerizing spell. He turned around to the mage behind him.

"I have to find my daemon, Annu. Can you please help me?" He knew what her question would be before she could speak.

Annu, where are you? What happened? There was a few seconds of pause before Annu responded. Annu must have been farther away.

I was taken to a lake somehow, and there's something coming out of the water.

"He says something is coming out of a lake? Is that near here?" Kalaerede requested.

Kandace and Archmage Medhas shared a look of fear.

"The sleepless beasts of Mare Lake," he said. "How in the world did your daemon get all the way out there? Are you that careless, mage?"

"Yeah, everyone knows to avoid that lake," Kandace added.

Kalaerede couldn't give them an answer, but he knew they weren't really looking for one. Before he knew it, her daemon and she were leading them out of the cottage.

"Your name is Caw-la-red? I'm Kandace, and this is Raia, but you probably already knew mine being the mind mage and all," Kandace said. There was no time to correct the pronunciation of his name so he followed her silently.

"Wait! Wait!" Kandace yelled. "We're not walking there? There's no need to run."

"Yes," Archmage Medhas said from behind them. He was quick for his age. "There are much faster ways to travel. Kandace. Raia, can you accommodate the young mage?"

She nodded.

"Quickly," Kalaerede said. "We don't have much time, Mage Kandace!"

"Are you ready, Raia? Just like we practiced," she whispered.

"I'm ready when you are," Raia said.

Kalaerede just stood there watching; Kandace touched Raia with her staff, closing her eyes, focusing her energy. She said the ascending spell.

"Daemon of fire, mage of the kind, powers in sync and powers in twine, raise a daemon of expected fame, show yourself as I proclaim!" Kandace shouted.

Holding his staff, thinking only of Annu, Kalaerede wished he could have said the ascending spell over his own daemon. A bright red light consumed her as Raia had become a new daemon. The only thing on her body that had not become inflamed was her claws, which had a golden cover on each. She appeared to have bright blue and white feathers. Kandace jumped on her back with her staff at her side. Kalaerede was behind her. Within seconds, they were soaring through the skies of this attractive land.

Kalaerede was about to ask about the archmage but before he knew it, Archmage Medhas was propelling himself through the air. Blue fire pushed beneath his feet as he followed a few feet ahead of them. Kalaerede had never seen the land from this height before. He wasn't afraid, even with blue fire so close to him. *Magic of the blue firebirds*, he thought. Medhas may not have explained his relationship with his mother, but he was very helpful in this search.

"How does your mother know Archmage Medhas?" Kandace asked.

The question caught him off guard. "She couldn't tell me," he replied.

"I'm sorry. When did she die?" Kandace asked.

"She's not dead; she is the Lady Lioness of the Meians," Kalaerede said.

"Isn't your mother an Elf? The Meians are Kingskin, well, women that is, my kind of warrior. I didn't think Elves, let alone a guy, could live there."

"Is that the lake there?" he asked, not feeling comfortable explaining how his mother became the Lady Lioness while simultaneously putting missing pieces together. She asked the wrong questions. Annu was in danger!

"Not much for small talk, are ya? Okay, I guess I'm without words with a mage who reads minds. Yeah, that's fair," Kandace said.

Before sundown, they were near the lake, the last source of fresh water before the Reaping Desert. Raia didn't go too high but from Kalaerede's view, the land was simply magnificent. Mare Lake was not the largest lake, but it was the deepest. It was ideally placed between the East Thunder Mountains and the Dry Lands. The smell of the freshwater lake steamed up into the air. Kalaerede saw Annu.

"Mage Kandace, what are those things around Annu?" Kalaerede asked.

"They are the sleepless beasts. They're mystical creatures who only protect the lake. They must think that Annu is a threat," Kandace replied.

The sleepless beasts were large, tar-skinned beasts with two large yellow eyes and patches of gray along their slippery backs. It was impossible to tell the difference between males and females. Kandace warned him of their silver tongues. The quickest touch could poison them. Their tails were black like their bodies with a triangular spike at the tip. While the beasts lived within the lake, like some daemons, they could leave the water and still breathe normally. Twenty of the stronger ones were surrounding Annu in a large circle. He stood there growling at them but not attacking. Since Annu didn't know what they were, he wasn't taking any chances. They would have to attack first.

"I thought this land belonged to the archmage," Kalaerede said.

"He doesn't *own* it. High Emperor Amos secured this section of the land using protective spells. Besides, Ankkns don't believe in owning land—houses *definitely*, but not land. Come on, Raia. We have to get closer to him," Kandace explained.

They landed inside the circle of beasts, about twenty feet wide, with more still emerging from the sea. There had to be at least thirty of them now. Kandace and Raia were preparing for a battle. Kalaerede ran to Annu with his staff in hand. He didn't want to fight against a mystical creature, but if he didn't have a choice, he would. Archmage Medhas landed next to them, immediately walking toward the beasts. Kalaerede watched as Kandace tried to calm the sleepless beasts. They snarled as they looked at Medhas, not convinced. He still walked forward, insisting the magi stay behind him. The beasts were now staring at the large blue firebird behind him. Kandace told them she was friendly, but they were not convinced. The beasts made their way to the archmage, growling. He positioned himself firmly, defending the magi and their daemons. Blue fire rose from his hands.

"Stand back!" The fire expanded, becoming a wall between them. He turned to Kalaerede, telling him to quickly recite the ascending spell over Annu. There was a battle brewing. As Kalaerede touched his daemon with his staff, he still wondered how the two of them had been separated in the first place.

Nolan was only able to open his eyes for a few moments, but he could tell his feet were moving. Jaahn was laughing, but there was more to it, a quick, splashy, repetitive sound. Looking down for another few seconds, he figured out what it was. He was walking on water! Pani was beside him doing the same. Now this was the magic he wanted to learn how to do! Like the stuff they saw on TV. But at what cost? Jaahn was so much stronger than he was and a master of all things magic—though he didn't seem to care too much for mages and daemons. His knowledge of magic felt older than that, as if he really was a god. It made his little telepathy look like child's play. What was he and how could he do things Nolan couldn't? Maybe he only claimed power by taking it from others, like soul eating. The idea alone filled him with grief. Nolan had brought this into the world because he was too childish to accept the truth. His parents were *legendary. And I'm a soul-hungry monster waking up from over forty years of isolation?* How long had Nolan been in this land—a few hours, a few days maybe? And he was losing his mind. Jaahn's constant pain was all too familiar to Nolan.

He couldn't remember a time when he didn't have nightmares about the fire. The worst lesson was explaining it when Henri and Emmett slept over at his house for the first time. They must have been in second grade when his screams woke them. Nolan was expecting his grampa to run into the living room, but he didn't. Henri and Emmett listened, and then it got very quiet. Emmett said they had to bury it. His father told him when something hurt too much, you buried and forgot about it. Henri reminded them dreams weren't real, so they decided to bury the blanket instead. The ceremony led them outside with Nolan's blanket in hand and his Gameboy Advance to light the way. Henri tried to find a good place to dig, but eventually they settled for the red mulch in the back garden. He didn't have the fire nightmare for a while after that. Emmett and Henri helped him forget the constant terror that plagued his dreams. Jaahn had no one for years. As much as he wanted to sympathize with a soul-eating monster, he couldn't forget why he was alone. He wanted to eat people. Jaahn had to be stopped by whatever means necessary. If it couldn't be Nolan, maybe the mountain of blue fire rising in front of them could. Jaahn must have felt him peeking, as Nolan's eyes were forced close again.

11

Find What Is Lost

HENRI, EMMETT, AND Zachariah were running through the now-silent forest. The cries of the shifting daemons were the only thing they could hear. Zachariah was running much faster than either of them, making it difficult for them to catch up. Using his telepathy, he was able to help them find each other if they were ever momentarily separated. The sun had already begun to set. Neither of them felt any closer to finding Oris. Zachariah told them the transition must have been complete. He ran faster. Over the next few minutes, all they could do was run. The forest was becoming an empty shadow, with no sound other than their feet smashing into the ground. Zachariah placed his arm out in front of him, forcing the magi to be quiet. *He's here.* Zachariah told Henri to go deeper, where they would communicate via telepathy. Henri questioned him. Zachariah said Oris would not harm him. However, Emmett and he were fair game. He implored Henri to listen to Zachariah's voice.

Henri reluctantly walked deeper into the forest. Fear rained down his face like a monsoon. He turned his head to see Emmett looking sternly ahead. Oris was in front of him. The honey-back owl was slightly larger than when he ascended back at the summer palace. Gray shadows fell from his eyes as he stared into Henri's eyes, towering over him.

"You—you can't hurt me," Henri said. "I—I'm your mage."

"True," Oris said, but the voice wasn't the same.

"You—you have my voice? That's me?" Henri took a moment to process this before he returned his attention to the large owl staring him down. This was talking to yourself on a different level of crazy.

"Oris, we need you to come back, okay? Whatever this is …" Henri started.

The owl walked closer to him. "How are you going to protect Lilith if I do?"

"Lilith is in the Terran system; we're here. She's fine," Henri said.

"She's in danger, and you know it," Oris-Henri said. "Don't worry; I'll take care of it. I'm going to kill Nolan," Oris said.

"What! That's not what I said," he said, defending himself.

He is a part of you, Henri. Do not feed wood to the fire. Stay calm.

"You—I—we would never hurt Nolan. He's been my best friend since kindergarten."

"Who is going to eat my sister's soul! Without him, there's no need for her to come here. She can stay normal," Oris said.

Henri couldn't deny it. The thought had crossed his mind, but he would never actually do it. Kill his best friend? Nolan didn't even know what was going on. Neither of them did. He couldn't live with killing an innocent.

Tell it to him, Henri. You need to hear it out loud.

"But … this isn't Nolan. He's … something else." Henri walked closer to the owl. "This thing, whatever it is, I know it's not him. He needs my help."

"Lilith needs my help! I won't let Zachariah sacrifice her," Oris said.

"But we can't help her like this," Henri said. "All of the magi need to unite, and if Lilith is a mage, like us, she'll have to get here eventually."

"I will not lose someone else to this world! This is not my home!" Oris shouted.

Henri looked up at the blue sun as it made its final resting place in the western skies. The stars were beginning to come out. Emmett and Zachariah were still waiting a few feet behind him, hiding in the trees. Facing his daemon again, he knew he, Oris, was right. That was what hurt the most.

"But what if Nolan goes there first?" Henri asked.

"What?" Oris-Henri said. "Zachariah said Amos would prevent that."

"Zachariah was wrong before. Nolan is the only person who can travel between the realms. He's the one who brought us here. If he knows where Lilith is, she won't be safe anywhere. She has to come here, with her Gemini Sister or whatever. Here we can really protect them," Henri said.

"Protect her?" Oris-Henri said.

Henri nodded.

"She needs to come here with us. Nolan can't find us here. That's why he sent those spirit attacks. The only thing I can do for Lilith is bring her here. She needs to be here *with me*. It's the only way. She'd have to be here eventually," Henri said.

"And what about Nolan? Do we just offer her up on a dinner plate, huh?" Oris-Henri said, less aggressive.

"No one said they had to meet. Maybe there's something else. Maybe Mr. Wylie is already telling her what she needs to do. He said in that message that he would be sending them. She has to know something. And when she gets here, we can ask her," Henri said.

"Where is she going to be?" Oris-Henri asked.

"Probably in the forest. Mr. Wylie already knows we're here because of the scroll. Where else would he send her? She could already be here! We're wasting time!"

"She—" Oris said.

A white light surrounded the gray-eyed owl. The transition back was very fast, leaving a weak honey-back owl, lying on the ground. Henri smiled for a second before he walked up to him. He placed his hand on the owl's back. It was like a swift wind pushed down on him. *Smack!* Henri looked to his left. A long dark-brown staff was planted in the ground as if a meteor had crashed a few feet away from him. On its crown was a gray jewel, glowing in the night. Zachariah and Emmett walked out of the forest. Zachariah was glowing with wonder as his eyes doubled before them.

"The stars have seen your plight," he said. "And they have blessed you. It is said the staff of legend will only be given when the magi have accepted their responsibility to the cycle. Take it; it is yours."

Henri grabbed the staff tightly. He didn't feel much different. But then again, he wasn't sure what to expect. Oris was still lying on the ground. Henri picked him up, leaving the staff. He tried to lay it down, but it refused.

"That which is a weapon and a teacher shall never lie on its back like a creature," Zachariah said confidently.

"So my new wood is always pointing up?" Henri said and laughed.

Emmett rolled his eyes.

"Yes, to put it simply?" Zachariah said, slightly confused. "I can carry Oris if you like?"

"No," Henri said, releasing the staff to its own. "I can do it." He picked up Oris, and then he grabbed his new staff.

Zachariah smiled again.

Zachariah's face was warmed by the moments he had just witnessed. Helping Henri up, he told them they had to press forward. Gebb the storm bear was their next target. He said Gebb wouldn't be able to leave the Outlands, but if he left the safety of the Meditation Trees, he was outside the protection of the emperor's magic. They had to move quickly before he too was lost.

"I am sure Gebb will be much less ..." Zachariah turned to Emmett. "Convincible."

Finally some good news! For so long, Nolan had watched as Jaahn roamed freely, using Nolan whenever he needed information or wanted someone to torture. He didn't know how or who was summoning the blue fire, but something was stopping him like no one else had done. If Nolan could see a mirror, he knew he would be smiling; it almost made him laugh. Jaahn had been enjoying the luxury of his body without a cage. He must have forgotten he wasn't the only magical threat on Deva Prime. Nolan was ready to accept whatever consequence was coming his way. It was worth it to put that soul-eating monster back in its cage. He had taken Nolan's body! Met people! And pretended to be him! The world he never knew he belonged to was meeting a lie, but not for long. The blue fire would stop him or at least make it difficult for him. Payback was a bitch.

Junior year at Middlecreek High, Henri started to consider himself as the unofficial class stud. He treated the girls like a vending machine. Spent a few coins, savored the taste, and then threw them away. Emmett and Nolan were different. They liked to keep their fucks steady, like a good drummer. No matter how many times they warned him, he wouldn't give in. *Newer is always better*, Henri had said. Until one day, the new clashed with the old. Her name was Bridgette. The other girl's name was Liz. They both had the same last name. And why wouldn't they? For nine months, Liz was living off Bridgette like a hungry parasite. His uncle, Principal Drake, wanted to penalize him, but the age of consent in Texas was seventeen. Legally, there was nothing he could do. That wasn't good enough for Liz, so she found another way to torture him. Thus, the motherfucker was born. At first, it was funny. All the guys' high fived, but as Henri's efforts got harder and harder, reality was setting in. Nolan and Emmett could only laugh.

What would they call Nolan when this was all over? A murderer? A soul eater? *One person could change the world, Nolan.* Those were Zachariah's words when he described the influence the last southern water mage had on the cycle. Only because of him did the other magi born after him stay true. The cycle protected the others from Makaian influence somehow. Zachariah spoke about it as if it was repellant for dark forces. It wasn't working. Jaahn didn't care about the cycle or the magi or especially the daemons. As much as Nolan wanted to believe the blue fire would stop him, it was becoming less likely by the second. Blue fire was great and all, but Jaahn had the body of the water mage and knowledge of magic Nolan didn't. Jaahn could win. Either way, when it was all over, Nolan would have to live with the aftermath of what one person had done to this world. Would Henri and Emmett one day laugh about all this, or would they would never get the chance? Eventually Jaahn would find them just as he found the others. Where could they possibly hide from a god?

"We have to find him," Raymond whispered as he wondered why Nolan had left. Had he found someone else to threaten?

"Maybe he got restless? He's probably just looking for food. Don't worry; his daemon is with him. I'm sure he'll be back any minute," Amelia said.

Raymond was with the heart mage, Amelia Channing, and her rose tiger cub, Bast, waiting in the place where they were supposed to meet. Amelia had managed to find a lot more berries and fruit than Raymond had. She was sitting in the center waiting, as her daemon patrolled around them. She didn't seem worried, but the blue sun was nearly setting. The soft rises of the red moon were already beginning to show in the western sky. Whatever fear she was denying doubled within him at every passing moment. She obviously didn't know how dangerous Nolan really was. Was this a test to see if Raymond would betray him? He would never. Nolan would kill his parents without an ounce of concern. This wasn't the divine prince everyone said would protect the world. Raymond was quick to make his way next to her, as if Nolan was watching. Adding his small stack of berries and what looked like nuts to her rather large collection, he took a seat. After an hour of uncomfortable silence and Amelia explaining to Raymond that some of the berries he picked were poisonous, Raymond looked for a way to pass the time. Bast lay down beside her mage. Amelia's staff was standing on its own next to her.

"How is that possible?" Raymond asked, pointing to her staff.

Amelia turned her head, looking at her staff. "Oh, that. Our staffs will not lie on the ground. They always point up. That which is a weapon and a teacher shall never lie on its back like a creature. It's from the magi spell book. It's on the inside cover. I can show you."

Raymond didn't understand, but Amelia stood up and gripped her staff tightly. He watched her eyes close and her focus magnify. Bast sat up and watched her. Pulling her hand back slowly, Amelia extracted magenta-colored energy from it. The energy rested in her hand for a moment until it became a spell book. It was a large book, thick with pages. On its cover was the divine symbol of the heart. Raymond's eyes were as wide as the ocean as the magic unfolded before him. Amelia made it look so easy as she smiled in front of him. She handed him the book. Raymond took the book, which had considerable weight. Opening it, he read the inside cover aloud.

"Protectors of the elements the chosen vessels of the gods, will need to unite as the world comes at odds. With every birth of the truest eight, the falsest ones shall follow in wait. They will be seen as true for the world to view, with lessons of the wise, given by heaven's eyes, contained in that which is a weapon and a teacher, one that shall never lie on its back like a creature. Similar they may be, enemies are they too. One day the time will come when the truest eight shall wake, and we the world must accept our fate."

The magi prophecy, he thought. He had heard it before, but holding it in his hands was an unparalleled comparison. Books were written testimonies of a world he wished he knew. The knowledge within those pages made Amelia a legend in the making. One day, people would want to know her words, her testimony of the world before. What glorious words would she share with them? Beneath the prophecy, there was a small symbol, which looked like three jagged mountains. Raymond pointed to it, showing it to Amelia.

"That's the symbol of the mountain choir, the seers of its temple. They gave the prophecy of the two magi before their temple was destroyed," Amelia said.

Raymond read the prophecy several times, holding history in his hands. After his third read, he gave the book back to Amelia. How could one with so much power be so easily deceived? Did she not use her magic against Nolan, or did she know of his darker motivations? Raymond had heard the path of the water mage influenced the others, but it couldn't have been that quick. No one had seen Nolan since he was a child unless he spent all this time slowly bending the other magi to his will. Amelia didn't seem as willing to kill him as Nolan was, but the uncertainty of which side she was on was more nerve racking than before. At least with Nolan, Raymond knew he was in danger. Vigilance would keep him alive.

"Where do you think Nolan is? Shouldn't we look for him?" he asked.

"It is getting kinda late," she said.

Raymond watched her grab her staff as her daemon followed her into the setting colors of the blue sun. Green Valley was very different as night approached. Its welcoming appearance turned lonely. The blue sun was not yet setting, but the differences were becoming clearer. On eastern part of the valley near the city of Blackheart, there were shadows growing larger by the second. The western valley leading to King's Forest and Thunder Mountains was still welcomed by the sunlight. The three of them were walking to the west.

Long moments of silence passed as Raymond started to keep his distance from Amelia. She kept looking down to her daemon. They must have been communicating through telepathy. What were they deciding? How to use that book against him? He looked around, trying to find a possible escape route. If only he knew where he was. Blackheart was in the Southlands, but that was all he knew. While his head studied the environment, he tried to change her focus, hopeful that his loud words would silence her dangerous thoughts.

"S-so do you have any other way to find him? Can't you use magic?"

"I would need something of his to track him. He didn't leave anything behind."

"He's smart like that, isn't he?" he asked quickly.

"He's much more than that. With Nolan here, every mage will follow behind him. The world will finally see the cycle as it always was," she said.

Why did her words sound strangely ominous? Was Nolan's dark influence spreading still? He sighed as they walked throughout the Green Valley. The rose tiger kept her eyes open, trying to pick up on Nolan's scent, or was she just keeping an eye on Raymond? He wondered how long they had been looking; his legs were getting weak. Even with an escape plan, he couldn't outrun a tiger. He heard the magi could make their daemons stronger and faster with a few words. He would be dead before he knew where he was.

"So were you born in one of the neighboring villages?" Amelia asked.

"I'm actually from the Outlands. I was born there," Raymond said. He had said too much the moment he opened his eyes. How much did Nolan tell Amelia? Soon, she would open that spell book and know the truths of his heart. Would Nolan say he betrayed him and rip out his parents' throats as he said he would? Raymond couldn't take that chance.

"Really?" Bast asked, speaking for the first time toward Raymond. Her powerful, maternal voice didn't fit her small frame. "You've traveled a great way to get to the Blackheart from the Outlands."

"It was very sudden. Where do you think *Nolan* is?" Raymond asked quickly.

Raymond kept trying to figure out what was going on here. He wanted to tell Amelia everything, but he didn't know if he could trust her. Nolan was more powerful than she was, but he didn't tell her much. Raymond was already on thin ice. He blurred the lines between truth and lies, hoping they would find Nolan soon so he could return to being their silent shadow. He told her his parents lived in the Stormy Forest, which was true. He said they didn't travel much, which was also true. He said that his father wanted to leave the Outlands one day, which was true and false, and that they used passes to cross the barrier, which was false. He said that Nolan had found them wandering around Blackheart, which was true and false.

Her questions stopped for a while. Raymond was relieved. She kept saying she was sorry they had to meet like this. When she asked what he saw in Blackheart, he was speechless. He looked up as the sun was still moving slowly across the early evening sky. Yet every time it descended, he started to sweat a little more. He knew she was testing him. He didn't see anything, he said. Thankfully, he thought the truth had kept her from digging, but he knew she was hiding something. The shadows from the east were getting stronger. They had made it out of the forest, exchanging the unfamiliar forest for more familiar space. Raymond was beginning to get worried. How much longer would he be stuck between legends and horror? They had to find him.

Raymond looked up as Bast led them closer to their original campsite. Amelia kept talking and *talking*, trying to pull information from him. Nolan would be proud he kept his mouth shut. He didn't mention Daedalus or the kidnapping or Nolan's hand around his father's throat. Amelia could be dangerous, but even a lonely boy from the Outlands knew she couldn't defeat the divine prince. What if Daedalus and Nolan weren't enemies? They were both Wylies. Daedalus killed his brother. He hunted Nolan's parents. Obviously he found them and trained Nolan to follow in his footsteps. Raymond wouldn't break. Whatever Amelia didn't know about Nolan and Daedalus's plan, she wouldn't learn from him. The cycle wasn't worth his life.

"Isn't this where we started?" he asked.

"I've been tracking his location, but I've haven't found him," the rose tiger said. "This is the last place he was. One second he was here; then he was gone. If I didn't know any better, I would say he teleported."

"But he said he didn't know how to do that," Amelia said.

"Then where did he go?" Raymond asked.

12

Leaving Middlecreek, Again

HOW DID I get here? she wondered. The yellow sun was falling over the horizon as a young girl was standing behind the abandoned playground around the corner from her home just as she had been asked. Henri, Emmett, and Nolan used to come out here at night when they slept over at her house. A small forest opened up beside a creek in the back. They walked for a few minutes until her father said it was a good place to stop. Lilith's black hair touched the bottom of her shoulder blades. Short like her father, Lilith had her mother's face. She was told her parents wouldn't be able to go with her. Nevertheless, they were standing a few feet away from her on patrol. Her mother, Iris, was a tall, skinny blonde with blue eyes. She was staring at her with worry and excitement. Her father was a little shorter than her mother was. His eyes were green, and his hair black, like both of his children's. It was nowhere near as long as Henri's but just as graceful. How could one person change so many lives?

"We don't have any syrup," Iris said as she checked the kitchen cabinets the previous day. "How can we have pancakes with no syrup?"

Samuel got up from his chair to help his wife. Lilith, however, stayed in her seat and chuckled to herself as her parents looked for some.

"And what's so funny, Lilith?" Iris asked, still searching the family kitchen. "Do you know where the syrup is?"

"No," she said, "but I had a dream you would forget the syrup."

"Tell me about it, Lilith," Iris said.

"Okay?" Lilith said. "I was sleeping then I saw you looking for some syrup. We didn't have any, so Dad said we should just eat it with fruit like his mom used to do. Then I woke up with a huge headache, so I took some aspirin. Then I put on my clothes and came downstairs. And that's my morning? We all caught up?"

"You had a headache *immediately* when you woke?" Iris asked. "Are you sure?"

"Yeah, it was a pretty big one, so I took like four. What's the big deal?" Lilith asked.

Iris immediately turned around and said a few words to Samuel. Lilith couldn't hear them until her father said, "We should tell her."

"Tell me what?" Lilith asked.

Her parents then walked over to the table and stood across from her. The look on their faces told her they were hiding something. They looked at each other, and then her mother spoke.

"Lilith, Henri isn't staying with the Wylies like we told you. He's gone home," Iris said.

"Okay? So he's sleeping in *again*," she said.

"No, not here. To our real home," Samuel said.

"We are home?"

Iris and Samuel took a seat at the table on opposite sides of their daughter. She looked at each of them, confused.

"We all come from the same place, but it's not Greece like we told you. It's a different system we call Deva Loka. It's where we're all from—a planet known as Deva Prime," Samuel said very intensely.

"Your father, your uncle, Nolan, Amos, and even Markus all come from this place. We moved here when you were an infant because of a prophecy," Iris continued.

Lilith sat back in her chair and laughed, but when she saw her parents not returning the chuckle, she said, "Okay, real funny. I'm gonna go back to sleep. My headache's coming back."

Iris looked at Samuel, and he nodded. He stood up and put his hand on her shoulder. He told Lilith he could prove it. Her father positioned his hands inches from each other as if he were holding a box of cereal with his palm on each. Lilith could see a gray stream appear from his hands. Within seconds, it turned into a tornado. Lilith backed away from her parents, hitting the wall and then laughing.

"Wow! That's a neat trick, Dad. How do you do that?" she said.

"It's not a trick, Lilith. It's my gift," Samuel said. "I, along with your brother, are descendants of the true magi. Our powers derive from the element of wind. On our home world, we are known as the raven-haired Rolands."

"What? They're at Nolan's. I just talked to him the other day," Lilith said.

"That was a spell, Lilith," Iris said. "A spell written by Amos to conceal his voice."

"So now Mr. Wylie is a witch and Dad shoots the breeze?" she said. "You can stop."

"An emperor," Samuel corrected, urging Lilith to take her seat.

Iris then walked over and opened one of the drawers. She pulled out a black journal and walked back to the table. She then pushed it toward Lilith and told her to open it. Lilith did. She looked through the pages, and it appeared that someone had written through it with a gel pen except it was very precise and easy to read. From what she could read, there were four colors: black, green, rose pink, and blue. She skimmed a few of the entries, but she was confused.

"What is this supposed to mean?" Lilith asked.

"They're visions, Lilith, visions written down by your ancestors and mine. What you're holding is called a rose record. Lilith, you are the youngest in the line of rose seers. We can see into the future," Iris said.

"Like a cheap fortune-teller? They had one of those at the carnival. A carnival where Henri ditched me." Lilith then put the pieces together. "So you're saying that dream I had today was really a vision *of the future*, of today?"

"Yes."

"So I'm a seer and you're a seer. Is Uncle Joshua a seer too? Are we all just a bunch of *seers* and *windy people*?" she asked.

"It's only females that carry the gene. Your grandmother, myself, and you are the only ones in our family," she said.

"We are all considered Deas," Samuel said. "Your mother is a seer, and I am an elemental. Some of us have a different power, a different gift. You, Lilith, have been blessed with two."

"Two? What do you mean?" she said quickly.

"I'll explain that later," Iris said, still looking at her daughter. "Are you okay?"

"Am I okay?" Lilith asked, placing her hand on her forehead. "You just told me I'm from a different realm and I'm not normal. How am I supposed to feel?"

"You're completely normal to us."

"Then why wait? Why am I here and not there with them!" she shouted.

Iris and Samuel looked to each other again. This time, Samuel spoke. He said the high prophetess had had a vision of a mage born outside their realm in the Terran system. His birth would become the bridge between the two worlds. He would provide a safe haven against the forces that threatened their world. Joined by three other magi, he would return to a home foreign to him and save that which he did not know he was born to protect.

"They were talking about Emmett," Iris said. "He will be the bridge between our worlds."

"That doesn't answer my question!" Lilith shouted.

"Lilith," her mother interjected. "Your father and I came here because the prophecy willed us here. Your destiny, along with theirs, was to be raised outside of our realm. We do not question why. Since

Nolan has returned, along with Henri and Emmett, now we wait until you are sent for as well."

"Sent for? I don't wanna leave my home!"

"Something has gone wrong in Nolan's arrival. He needs you. Emperor Amos has told us this," Samuel said.

"That's why Henri didn't ride the Ferris wheel with me? He was in another realm!"

"Yes," Iris said. "We must return to our world."

"You mean *your world*! This is my home. I have friends here. I go to school here! I have a life here! Obviously, there was something wrong with that other place. Let's just stay here. Why do we need to move! That will *never* be my world!"

Lilith couldn't believe this! The Ferris wheel was tradition. They were covering for Henri. He probably wanted to meet up with that girl from the smoothie place. But what about her dad? That was the weirdest magic trick she had ever seen. Lilith backed away from the table and ran up to her room to cry. Iris soon followed after.

Lilith's room was the smallest in the house, but it was impossible to tell. Her bed took up most of the space with small stuffed animals and plenty of awards on her dresser. Her walls were painted baby blue. In front of her large bed was a dresser of equal width with a wide mirror attached. Lilith sat on top of her white-and-red comforter with her pillows behind her against the headboard. She had tried to close her door, but she didn't do it strongly enough. She even wanted to cry, but no tears were coming out, so instead Lilith sat up on the side of her bed, holding her face, trying to make sense of this. Within seconds, her mother walked inside, holding her rose record. In the comfort of her room, Lilith and her mother had a long talk. Iris tried to make her understand, but Lilith kept shaking her head. Lilith looked as her mother turned to a blank page and pointed her index finger. She started to write her name, and as she did, the same blue color appeared. Then Lilith started to listen.

"The headaches will fade. I had the same problem when I first came here. Because we're so disconnected from our world, our visions here are weaker. They have to go through more channels, I assume. Sometimes they can even seem insignificant. Look at this one here."

"Don't buy syrup," Lilith read. She chuckled a little.

"I had that vision two months ago, and I haven't bought syrup since. Eventually, I forgot completely until today," Iris said. "Now I know why."

"You were supposed to not buy syrup so I could have a vision that we didn't have any syrup."

Iris nodded.

"So your job? Dad's?"

"All thanks to Emperor Amos. When Henri and you were children, he helped us blend in to this world and got us jobs. The Terrans have great potential, but they are still so young and divided in many other ways."

"You said Terrans? Are there not humans in the other realm?"

"Kingskin look most similar to Terrans. I think that is why Emmett was born here, so that we may understand the link between our two realms."

"But we look like Terrans too?"

"Because your father and I have ancestry in both Kingskin and Deas, as most Deas do. That is why we blend so well here. We look just like them," she said. "Which makes me wonder why?"

Lilith was heartbroken but still unsure of what her life would be like now. Her mother said they were waiting for their chance to go home, but this was home to her. She didn't want to leave. As she looked around her room, she thought of all the things she would miss—her bed, her friends. Hell, she would even miss school. They said freshman year was the hardest, but after that, it was a cakewalk.

"I know you're having doubts, Lilith," Iris said. "But we must trust in ourselves and trust in our powers. They will never deceive you."

Iris then took her rose record and placed it on Lilith's lap. She told Lilith to touch the other side. She said strange words, but the last was her name. Instantly, a soft bounce landed on the bed. It was another book. Iris smiled as she handed it to her daughter. Lilith opened it. Iris then led her to flip through the pages to see that their journals were identical. Then she turned to the inside cover and told her to write her full name. Rather than question her, Lilith looked at her left finger. Hesitantly, she moved her finger down gracefully. As she did, she saw a bright purple light appear as if it were ink. *Lilith Miriam Roland.* Iris smiled.

"When will I see Henri again?" she asked.

"Very soon, I hope," Iris said as she walked toward the door. "We wait for the sign."

Lilith spent the remainder of the day in her room. She had heard the door open and close, and she assumed her parents had left her. A few hours later, she heard someone shouting her name. When she woke up, she hoped this had all been a bad dream. Instead, Lilith saw a girl she had never seen before. In front of her bed was a young girl who was a little taller than she was. She had a soft light-brown skin tone with long beautiful wavy brown hair. She was dressed in horrible ripped black cotton pants with a shirt that was too big. Her eyes were blue whirlpools, and she was staring at Lilith, who noticed this mysterious girl wasn't wearing any shoes.

"Are you Lilith, daughter of Samuel and Iris Roland?" the girl asked. Her voice was soft and every syllable could be heard perfectly as if she was singing slowly.

"How did you get into my room?" Lilith asked.

"You don't know?" she asked.

"What now?"

"My name is Cassandra. Together, you and I form the Gemini Sisters. I'm going to take you to Deva Prime to save Nolan," Cassandra said.

"This is too much. Too soon," Lilith said against her bed. "No, I'm not your sister."

"Lilith, we don't have much time. Your brother's life is in danger. We need to see each other in order to help him, to help everyone," Cassandra said.

Hearing word of her brother, Lilith nearly dropped all of her worries. If he was on that planet her parents had talked about, he was the only person who could understand what she was going through. Their parents had lied to both of them.

"What do you mean he's in danger?" Lilith asked.

"You have to come back to our world. If you do, you can save his life. Otherwise," Cassandra said, softly, "we can lose all of them. I can get us there, but we have to leave quickly."

"What about my parents? I can't just leave them."

"This isn't about them," Cassandra said softly as she lowered her head. "We have to do this alone."

"I won't just leave my parents!"

Cassandra paused for three seconds. "You're not the only one who has to."

Something changed in that girl, as if she knew exactly how Lilith was feeling. A guilty stone broke her glass house. Her mother had just told her a few hours ago that they were waiting for a sign. Was this what she meant? Damn that was quick.

"I'm not ready to deal with this. How do I even know I can trust you?" Lilith asked.

"Because someone I love too is in danger if we don't act," Cassandra said.

Lilith waited for a second, balancing out the options. Hearing Cassandra's plan, Lilith had many questions, some of which Cassandra answered. Apparently, their magic would bring them together and take them to a safe place in Deva Prime. The way Cassandra said it, it was some kind of portal. Cassandra knew the spell to open it, and once she did, they would have only seconds to touch each other's hand before it disappeared. She told her to meet her in a safe place in one hour of their time. Cassandra recommended it be outside, away from people.

Lilith didn't understand. Then Cassandra was gone. She ran to tell her parents. They were not surprised at the quickness. Time was different in Deva Prime. They took her to the abandoned playground she knew about. Her parents were holding each other now after they stopped in the trees behind the swing set. They had already hugged and shed their share of tears. Lilith was holding nothing but her new rose record. Exactly one hour from the time Cassandra arrived in her room, they saw the change. A cloud began to form around the trees, and then as if nothing were happening, a portal began to form. It was sucking in everything around it; the trees were being pulled as if their roots would soon follow. The portal was a swirl of purple, yellow, brown, and green. Lilith began shaking as her heart trembled with fear. The portal opening only lasted a few seconds before a young girl appeared in it. The girl seemed vaguely familiar, but she was dressed in a brown cloak and her head was covered. Her hand opened, and her arm was stretched out. She called out Lilith's name. After one last look at her parents, Lilith stepped inside.

What was happening out there! The anticipation was making Nolan's mind race longer than a million-mile marathon. Jaahn shut him out just when things were about to change for everyone. Nolan didn't care what that blue fire did to him or his body as long as it meant that soul-sucking sinister creature went away for good. The hope of someone coming through made him try to take control again even if just for a moment. If he could feel his feet, he knew they would be shaking. No longer would be shackled to this beast who pulled him everywhere he went like a great Dane on a small leash. Nolan hadn't felt this chained since Lindsay. For the first time, he was relieved he didn't go to that carnival. Lindsay was a grade younger than he was, a fucking gorgeous girl. Her chest sat up just like it was supposed to; she kept her hair smelling good, hmm. It almost made her bat-shit, crazy-ass attitude worth it. For over a year, they stayed together for all the wrong reasons. *A year*, Nolan thought. Jaahn said he had been *here*, wherever that was, for forty years.

Time must have been much longer on Deva Prime than it was back in Middlecreek. He wondered if his grampa was still there, pining away at the lies he had told him over the years, well, decades in Deva Prime time. He had to have known about Jaahn and what he could do. That fucking apple juice. Couldn't he have given him some lighter version that didn't suppress everything? Magic could have made things easier. He could make Lindsay forget him. Nolan's thoughts about playing with magic made him remember how all this started. Here he was feeling impatient and ready for someone to put Jaahn away as if he weren't the one who opened the door. The moment he played with magic, Lucian had to take him to the oasis to save him, making him vulnerable. Nolan was just as guilty of burning down the summer palace as Daedalus was. In such a short time, Nolan had threatened an entire world. One person changed everything. What would have happened if Jaahn got loose on Earth? Temper tantrums would turn into thunderstorms and typhoons. Who would help him then? Lucian hadn't been much help since Jaahn took over, and his grampa was who knew how many miles away? Nolan was single-handedly tracking down magic. Now he *hoped* someone else could undo his mistake before Jaahn consumed blue fire quicker than drinking a flaming Russian.

Principal Joshua Drake was enjoying the childless summer vacation every principal deserved. Each muscle in his body blended into his couch like the perfect Long Island iced tea. His days were limited before summer school began and a stressful job became slightly less stressful. He wondered how the children were doing back on their home world. They would have had so many questions, especially Nolan. His grandfather had dropped by nearly every day, authoritative with decisions he didn't need to worry about. It would all be clear very soon. Questions would flow from the divine prince like water from a hydrant, but it was for the best. For a long time, each of them knew this day would come. Preparation and acceptance weren't often rivals. As the shaggy-haired principal watched the golden orb move into his living room, he kept his eyes opened, muted the television, and sat up straight. The golden orb before him transformed into the high emperor. Joshua's two dogs, Rocky and Bailey, barked with excitement as they ran up to him. They looked like golden retrievers, but their coats were a little brighter. Joshua rose from his seat half-smiling, but when he saw the look on Amos's face, he knew that he was still worried about micromanaging all the issues they had prepared for since they arrived.

"I just got off the phone with my sister, Your Highness," Joshua said. "Lilith has met with her Gemini Sister. They should be arriving in Deva Prime any moment."

"Good. Then we can finally put Jaahn behind us. But I'm afraid our troubles don't end there, however." Amos sighed.

"You mean Veronica?" Joshua said.

"I don't know what more I can do outside the truth. What do you suggest? Your modern Terran knowledge is much greater than my own."

"My sister shared a vision of her going to Deva Prime so perhaps we should use this time to our advantage, Your Highness," Joshua said.

"Your sister had a vision?" Amos said. "Why was I not informed?"

"It was some time ago, only fragments at a time. She was finally able to piece it together when Lilith left," he said.

"It is for the best then," Amos said. "But I'm still not sure what to say to Veronica. I'm sure she will be asking questions come nightfall. And with Lilith gone …"

"Do you think you can use the spell again, Your Highness?" Joshua asked.

"I can but …"

"I know you don't like to use magic on Terrans, Your Highness, but sometimes you don't have a choice. We've gone all this time without being discovered. Let's leave here as quietly we came. I don't want to keep her in the dark, but I don't know what else to do. I only hope that my sister's vision will occur sooner rather than later," Joshua said.

"We must do something to keep her from worrying. A voice on the phone may not be enough," Amos said.

"I've been around these Terrans for years now, Your Highness; a phone call should give us, at minimum, a few more days. If nothing changes by the end of an Earth week or two, then we have to weigh other options."

As Amos nodded, he teleported back to the home that was once full of children. Joshua sat back down on his couch with his dogs at his feet. He unmuted the TV and got comfortable again. Joshua loved watching the shows where Terrans were talking about the different kinds of animals that lived among them. He took issue with how blandly they described nature, as if they were half-asleep. Nature was a beautiful wonder that pushed the world through so many changes. It always was and always would be. Joshua could watch them for hours, from insect to lion to whale; all these animals reminded him of his home and the life he exchanged. Now he had to watch them through very large televisions, as if it replaced living. Nothing would ever compare to walking among the leaves and the trees, hearing the beasts around cry into the days and nights, declaring their admiration for all the Mother had provided them. Terrans would never understand how enchanting their world could be. Instead, they locked nature in cages for amusement and shows. What Joshua wouldn't give to be one of those voices in the jungle, but they all must make sacrifices, no matter how much they hurt.

13

Mage against Mage

THE THREE OF them were so deep in the forest, they could barely see if the sun or the moon was out. Oris was beginning to regain consciousness, but he was still very weak. Zachariah said that it was normal for this to happen. Regaining your own spirit took some time. Emmett wondered if the same would happen to Nolan when they fixed him. Finding a storm bear in the forest was proving to be more difficult than they would have thought. Zachariah tried asking Emmett to see if he could feel his daemon's presence, but, of course, that was out of the question. For what felt like an hour, Emmett was right beside Zachariah as he walked and ran through the Meditation Trees, searching for the only temperamental daemon in the world. Every time he turned around, he saw that old piece of wood Henri was holding in his hand. Had he not been through the same thing? At the same time? Henri was given his staff, and he was still waiting. The only reason Henri got his staff was because of Nolan's spell. Were the almighty stars rewarding the actions of a soul-sucking beast? They should have given him one too. Maybe it could help him find Gebb. Or were they making the half-Terran earn his visa with a little more conflict?

The primates in the forest were still very yielding toward the magi. They were also afraid of the temperamental daemon let loose in their home. Emmett wished they were still talking in the distance. It was better than the frightful silence. Maybe they could tell him where Gebb was. Damn, he missed those monkeys. Zachariah told them they were getting closer to Titan Lake, the largest lake in their world. The lake was in between the two main forests of the Outlands: Meditation Trees and the Stormy Forest. They had to get there as fast as they could.

"Gebb, the *storm* bear is from the Stormy Forest, isn't he?"

Zachariah nodded.

"I'm guessing we're trying to beat him there."

"There is nothing more dangerous than a natural playing field," Zachariah said.

The three of them continued to walk until they made their way to Titan Lake. By this time, Oris was completely awake, with little memory of what had occurred. Emmett kept his thoughts to himself as he listened to Henri retell his tale of self-discovery. He already knew his own future discussion with himself wouldn't be easy. His mother said he was stubborn like his father. Stubbornness was misunderstood, his father would say; he said how he used it made all the difference in the world. Emmett's mother, Veronica, said she had hated his father when they first met. He was cold and old-fashioned, but Markus Bradley was smitten with the highbrow daughter of the Van Dammes. Her parents didn't like him, and her friends thought it wouldn't last, but he didn't care. *Because I'm stubborn like that.* Stubborn people were unbreakable; they weren't distracted or easily tricked. Emmett was proud to be stubborn; no one could tell him his father was wrong. Because he wasn't.

Emmett nearly bumped into Zachariah as they approached Titan Lake. The lake was wide enough to be an ocean. They couldn't see anything but tiny blue waves bouncing off in the sunset as the winds pushed them away. Zachariah told them Titan Lake was known not only for its size but for its delicious badger-fish. Zachariah said he hoped Gebb would be there feasting on his species' natural delicacy. On the edge of the lake, staring into the water, Emmett was looking for any sign of the storm bear. Zachariah asked Oris to join him as they searched. Emmett stayed behind with Henri and his new staff. Emmett kept his attention narrowed in on the lake for as long as he could until he heard Henri grunting behind him. He kept trying to lay that staff down, but it wouldn't lie down. Now it was official, Henri really was magic.

"Do you feel any different?" Emmett asked.

"Seriously? Not really. I'm not sure what all of this means. I'm guessing it'll be helpful but why the wait? Why did everything have to go wrong before it was given to me?"

"Must be like a test or something," Emmett said.

"Yeah, maybe, but why do we need to be tested? We're the magi, whether we like it or not. If we die, then their precious cycle is thrown off balance. They should have given this to us from the start."

"You mean the stars?" Emmett looked up. "What do you think they are?"

Henri shrugged.

"They've got to be some kind of magic. I bet they have my staff up there too."

"Probably and Nolan's too. Do you think they want us to use them to fight Jaahn?"

"That's what they called Nolan, right? Maybe it's like the Phoenix to his Jean Grey," Emmett said.

"The what?"

"X-Men. Alien force that took over Jean Grey. It was some powerful shit, man," Emmett said quickly.

"Oh, yeah, *The Last Stand*," Henri said. "Real fucked-up movie. Worst one yet."

"Not that horrible movie," Emmett said. "The comic book, man."

"Never read it. I must have been too busy getting laid," Henri said laughing. "Anyway, I'm pretty sure the Phoenix didn't eat people's souls. I wonder what he does with them."

"I hope we don't find out."

Zachariah and the honey-back owl came running up to the two of them. Only a few minutes had passed, but Emmett could tell they had found something. With slight hesitation, he followed them. Emmett was going to talk to a *bear* with *his* voice. No matter how many times he thought about it, it was still unimaginable. Zachariah reminded him that Gebb wouldn't hurt him. He tried not to get pissed that Zachariah was reading his mind again. How many ways could Emmett tell him he didn't like that before he *actually* stopped doing it? This world made him rethink everything in his life, but he wouldn't let the world take his mind. Never.

Despite how Kalaerede had already recited the ascending spell over Annu, he had yet been given little chance to use his skills. Archmage Medhas was extremely protective of the two magi under him; he was single-handedly fighting against the sleepless beasts of Mare Lake. The most interesting feature of the battle was the way in which Medhas attacked them. It was never to kill them or even burn them; he was scaring them with his blue fire, pushing them back to their sacred waters. Kalaerede had heard that Ankkns respected mystical creatures more than daemons, but he never would have expected this to be associated with battle. The fire mage beside him had been starving for a battle. Kandace did not respect her archmage's wishes as she flew up with her daemon, Raia, leaving Kalaerede to wait patiently as the blue fire bolted through the air.

"Kandace! Get behind me! This is no time for theatrics! Stay with Kalaerede!" Medhas shouted.

"I won't let you do this alone!" she shouted.

The sleepless beasts continued to launch themselves against the outsiders, scratching and biting anything they could. They were coming from everywhere. Kalaerede felt defenseless as one of them made its way past Medhas's firewall, but he remained obedient to the archmage's command. One of the leathery beasts slipped through the wall of blue fire. As it did, his ascended golden-tailed monkey punched it back into the water. Annu stared at the lake before turning back to Kalaerede.

There's a daemon in the lake, an Alpha.

Another mage? Perhaps it's Nolan or one of the others. We have to get to them.

If one of the foster magi had heard the commotion, he or she would probably be confused and frightened. Kalaerede tried to read whichever mind was out there, but he sensed a thick wall rather than an open door. The mind mage wouldn't allow that to stop him. The cycle was in danger. Kalaerede made his way onto his daemon's back as they ran toward the lake. Medhas tried to stop him when he said there was another mage on the lake. One of the leathery creatures distracted him as Kalaerede and Annu moved closer to the water. They were stopped on the edge of the lake. Withdrawn of his free will, Kalaerede's body appeared to be bound tightly by rope just as Annu's had been. In an instant, Annu was tossed aside by an invisible force. Flying away from him, Kalaerede's body continued to lift itself gently into the air. At last, he saw the daemon. It was a silver seal, walking with despair in his eyes. To his left, there was a young Dea with wavy brown hair and a silver chain. Kalaerede's eyes widened. The moon medallion hung around his neck. It couldn't be. Nolan was the only word he could say.

"Water and mind will be joined again as they were always meant to be," he said.

Kalaerede watched as Nolan opened his mouth to an unnatural size, drawing him more and more to him. Kalaerede tried to fight, but he foresaw nothing that could undo this fate. Then blue fire hit Nolan square in his chest, knocking him onto the ground. Kalaerede's body fell instantly. Archmage Medhas shot with fury, running past Kalaerede as he pushed the Wylie back further and further. A large wave of water rose from the edge of the lake, quickly pushing them back onto the ground. Kalaerede watched the sorrowful eyes of the silver seal as it lowered its hands. Medhas quickly rose, looking everywhere for the Wylie after he helped Kalaerede up. Medhas reached in his pocket and pulled out two vials with blue liquid inside.

"You know what this is?"

Kalaerede shook his head.

"It's a refined potion known as deconstruction. Take your daemon and use it to take you to Meditation Trees."

"But …"

"There is no time! Jaahn will be back soon and with his daemon. We have to get you to safety!" Medhas shouted.

"The great soul eater!" he said.

"The very same! Kandace!" Medhas shouted.

Grabbing Kalaerede, Medhas rocketed into the air. He gave the second vial to his pupil. Kalaerede heard the same fear in his voice boom a second time. A jet of water hit Medhas, pulling him down onto the ground. Kalaerede saw the angry creatures growling as he fell to them. Raia barely caught him, but she was unable to do the same for Archmage Medhas. Kalaerede looked for Archmage Medhas as held on to the blue phoenix. Medhas rocketed himself toward Kandace and Kalaerede, launching more blue fire toward the wall of water. He secured a place for them to land.

"Go now!" he shouted.

"Not without your daemon," Jaahn said.

Kalaerede looked down to see Annu held up in the same invisible rope constraint he had been trapped in only moments ago. To Kalaerede's surprise, the sleepless beasts were at the Wylie's side.

"Why aren't they attacking him?" Kalaerede asked.

"We're not the only ones who respect the patron gods," Kandace said.

Jaahn then began to speak to the sleepless beasts in a language Kalaerede had never heard before. A great number of sleepless beasts started to gather around him, listening to his every word. Medhas turned to the two magi, whispering.

"When I give the signal, you two take your daemons and go to Meditation Trees."

"But Annu …" Kalaerede began.

Medhas pointed to his head sternly.

Kalaerede, he is speaking in Divine, the language of the gods; this is not the divine prince you think you know. When I return your daemon to you, drop your deconstruction potion and think only of Meditation Trees. Do you understand?

Kalaerede nodded. Medhas turned in front of them. As he looked down to his hands, blue fire streamed down through him until they became whips. He swung them down to the ground, digging into it. Raia descended back into her normal form. Kalaerede and Kandace were stricken with wonder. Kalaerede heard more of the Divine whistling through the air, but it wasn't from Jaahn. Medhas was speaking. Jaahn turned to him, just as shocked, then he started to laugh. Lines of blue fire ripped through the air as the beasts started to make their way. Slowly each of them ran toward the archmage, but none of them was able to make it through his fire whips.

Jaahn let go of his hold on Annu. The sleepless beasts launched themselves against the magi, but Medhas cut them off. Annu ran as fast as he could to his mage after Kalaerede told him what their steps were. Jaahn turned to grip him again, but Medhas's fire whips distracted him. The beasts tried to capture him too, but they failed as well. Archmage Medhas continued to impress and surprise the mind mage as his daemon descended into his natural form beside him. Kandace was the first to drop her deconstruction. The blue smoke covered her body and engulfed her daemon's before it went sailing through the sky. Kalaerede thought of only Meditation Trees, which wasn't difficult since it was Annu's home. He smashed the vial on the ground, watching as it spread to the golden-tailed monkey. The last thing the Elven mage heard was Jaahn screaming.

Emmett was following Henri, Zachariah, and Oris as closely as he could. The smell of dead badger-fish was nauseating, overpowering every sense in his body. The dead fish were leading them around the lake to the barrier between Stormy Forest and Meditation Trees. Zachariah told them to be careful. Mr. Wylie's protection spell was limited to the Meditation Trees. At the corner of the two large forests, Zachariah stopped them. Emmett knew what this meant. A part of him was both excited and nervous. He didn't want to be the only one without a staff. Keeping his head up, Emmett walked slightly into the Stormy Forest, following the foul stench of badger-fish. Gebb, who he had assumed had ascended on his own, was now the size of bears Emmett had seen in the zoo. Only his eyes were different.

They were shadows of gray beneath them. Sighing, Emmett took a step further. As he did, he stepped on a branch. The sound made Gebb's eyes pop open. Emmett was careful not to turn to his friends, hiding on the opposite side of the lake, bordering Meditation Trees.

"Gebb?" Emmett asked.

The storm bear continued to eat the fish raw, very noisily as Emmett stepped forward.

"Yes," Gebb said in Emmett's voice.

Emmett was prepared for this. He had heard Oris speak with Henri's voice just hours ago.

"I don't know what to say," Emmett said.

"That makes two of us," Gebb-Emmett said.

"I ... sorry. I didn't mean for this to happen ..." he began.

"I'm only human," Gebb finished. "You're right. I *am* human. I don't belong here. I've always known that. I should have left when he gave me the chance. This is not my war. It's theirs. They're the freaks, the aliens," Gebb-Emmett said.

"I ... I didn't say ..." Emmett wanted desperately to turn around and explain himself. "We-we're in this together."

"Together? I wish I had never met either one of them! They're fucking freaks! All of 'em! They took everything from me!" Gebb then pointed to the same location where Zachariah, Henri, and Oris were standing. The storm bear rose, and Emmett backed up.

"They have to pay for what they took from me!" Gebb-Emmett said.

"Stop!" Emmett shouted, standing between them. Gebb looked down to him. "They didn't hurt you! They've been trying to help you—me, I mean. They're not the ones who brought me here."

"Nolan is," Gebb said. He stared down at Emmett. "He's the one who brought me here. He's the prince of freaks!"

"Yeah ... but he didn't ..." Emmett stuttered.

"He didn't mean to? Don't be stupid! He and Mr. Wylie have probably been planning this for months! They're the ones ..."

"That's not true—it can't be. Then that would mean he knew about his parents, that he knew about all of this," Emmett said.

Emmett, be careful not to ... Zachariah said telepathically.

"You know I hate when you read my mind," Emmett said.

"How many times do I have to tell you?" Gebb said.

"No," Zachariah said in a whisper. "Their bond is strengthening but not in a good way."

"It's time we took the fight to Nolan," Gebb said. "If it wasn't for him, none of this would happen. I would be back at home, with my mom, not here with these fucking freaks."

"We … we can't. Nolan is our …" Emmett said.

"Enemy. That's why we need to stop him before he gets to us. Do you really want to keep hiding, like cowards? What would Dad think? That's probably the only thing this world got right about him. He was no coward."

"Henri, don't!" Zachariah shouted.

"We're not cowards!" Henri shouted. "Don't believe him, Emmett. He's just baiting you!"

Emmett turned around as Gebb walked closer to him. The storm bear growled softly as Henri walked into Stormy Forest. Oris quickly flew alongside him. Zachariah told him to return.

"No! I won't sit back here and watch while another one of my friends is tricked into self-pity. Emmett, don't let him use your dad against you. That's how they got to Nolan! Your parents are not your weakness."

"And what do you know!" Gebb shouted, still in Emmett's voice.

Emmett stood behind him, watching. "You haven't lost a parent like we have. How could you possibly understand?"

"You're not the only one whose parents kept secrets! They lied to all of us!"

"It's so much more than that, Henri! You'll never understand how we feel!" Gebb said.

"This isn't the way, Emmett! You're not you! You're Jaahn, or whatever he is! Emmett, listen to me, we're not hiding; we're preparing. We can't run in on him half-cocked. Lilith and her Gemini Sister … that's our plan. We have to find them before we save Nolan, and we can't do that without you."

"Save him?" Gebb said.

"Emmett, listen to me!" Henri shouted. "We know what we're doing. Don't pussy out!"

"I'm not a pussy!" Emmett shouted.

"Then get over yourself! Stop wallowing in your little pity party and get out here and help us!"

"I … I'm trying."

"Try harder!" Henri shouted as he pointed to Gebb. "Get some fucking enlightenment!"

The wind mage tripped backward. Emmett turned to see an angry bear. Oris flew in front of Henri just as the storm bear launched himself toward Henri. Zachariah was there to help Henri up. Emmett shouted as Gebb followed. Gebb stopped on the edge of Mr. Wylie's protection spell.

"I'm not a coward! I may be half-Terran, but I'm also half-Devanian. My dad was from here. I think he'd want me to be here."

"But Nolan, he is …" Gebb said.

"My friend," Emmett said. "And he needs my help, and I'm gonna help him!"

"The half-Terran wants to help *me*. How generous," a dark voice said from behind him.

Emmett backed up. The white light he once saw over Oris had now fallen over Gebb, reducing him to his normal form. His body lay on the ground as Jaahn stayed outside of Meditation Trees. Emmett watched as the silver seal slowly pulled Gebb's unconscious body outside Mr. Wylie's protection. Emmett raced over to him despite Zachariah's and Henri's timid nature. Jaahn quickly teleported into a golden orb, which then encircled Pani, Emmett, and Gebb as they were running into the Stormy Forest.

Did you enjoy the show, Nolan? Jaahn said to him.

Nolan could feel Jaahn pressing down on him as if he were kneading dough. The soul-sucking creature inside of him wouldn't shut up as he made Nolan watch his friends fail against him. *They think they're going to save you, but all they're doing is making my hunt that much easier. All the magi in one place! How delicious. And you will* watch *as I consume every one of them.* Nolan still had the haunting image of a gapped mouth trying to consume that mage from the lake. Nothing Nolan tried could stop him from witnessing it. Jaahn said he only needed one, and his insatiable hunger would silence Nolan the way he had silenced him for forty years. Jaahn promised to let Nolan watch. Was that how he did it, swallowing them whole like a two-legged anaconda—or would he spit out their bones like an owl? Nolan couldn't sit back and watch him eat Emmett, but he was running out time. Jaahn wouldn't play as much as he did back at that lake. His patience had gone, departed after the blue fire turned into blue smoke. Whatever Jaahn was planning, it would be quick and satisfying. Jaahn's confidence was growing as Nolan's last hopes were falling down in front of him.

For some reason, Jaahn couldn't eat the boy or the girl he had tricked into following him. Nolan was thinking about them more now. Were they Jaahn's weakness or his secret weapon? He didn't want to eat them, so they must have been special. Oh, shit, were they like him! Was there a set of soul-sucking siblings silently standing on the sidelines? The girl was special. Jaahn had let him peek into her story. Something about a curse. But the little guy? The first thing he remembered was how Jaahn had threatened his parents. Jaahn kept their names from him, but Nolan was more worried about the boy. From the beginning, he had submitted to Jaahn. If Jaahn could wreak all this havoc single-handedly, what would he do with some help?

The guilt pounded into Nolan once more like an angry baker. Calais was the one who had tempted him with the truth, but he wouldn't have found them if Nolan hadn't played with magic. What did they think would happen when they told the orphan his parents were alive? They tried to warn him. Lucian and Zachariah told him to be calm no matter what he heard. And with one slipup, they both ran away in fear of what lay inside of him. No one would be safe around him. The slightest flurry of feelings could turn this mild-mannered boy into a soul-sucking beast, and like the Hulk, he was unstoppable. For the rest of his life, Nolan would be a visitor in his own mind. Occasionally, Nolan might see the outside world or hear himself laugh when he swallowed another soul until eventually he became the old man sitting quietly in a nursing home with nothing but memories of the one mistake that plunged his world into a bottomless stomach, hungry to consume a world he never should have returned to.

174

14

Five More to the Forest

AS THE WORLD plummeted into the third passing, Kandace and Kalaerede entered Meditation Trees. Each of them had heard the terrible rumor about using deconstruction. They were both grateful neither of their bodies had been either left behind or combined with those of their daemons. Staying close was the only thing that made sense. Annu, the golden-tailed monkey, quickly climbed on the trees in front of them, tossing several delicious red papayas down for Kalaerede and Kandace to eat. As he did this, the chatter of the primates returned. He listened and responded. Kandace asked Kalaerede if he knew what they were saying. Kalaerede shook his head and ate. The two of them ate in silence, listening to the strange monkey chatter among the trees. More primates eventually came to listen as well. They were soon surrounded. After eating a few more pieces of fruit, Annu came back to the ground.

"They were here not too long ago," Annu said. "The other two magi with another Dea. Emperor Amos asked the primates of this forest to watch over them. They did this until two temperamental daemons were summoned."

"Good," Kalaerede said. "We all must face ourselves at some point. I am glad they did so under the safety of the high emperor's protection."

"Yeah, it can get pretty bad," Kandace said. "Where are they now?"

"I have asked them to locate the other magi. I only hope they remained in the forest. Emperor Amos has restricted the magic to these borders," Annu the golden-tailed monkey said. "If they leave Meditation Trees, the emperor's magic can't protect them."

"Well, that was smart," Kandace said. "It'll be easier for us to find each other now."

A large amount of blue smoke appeared feet away from the two magi. They backed away slowly until the smoke settled, revealing Archmage Medhas unscathed. He walked out with his hands behind his back. He walked over to them. Kandace was quick to tell him what they had just learned. As she was talking, he picked up one of the stray red papayas, wiped it on his shirt, and took a big bite.

"No fruit can ever compare to a ripe red papaya," he said. "Temperamental daemons, you say; tell me, which elements do they belong to?"

"Earth and wind," Kalaerede said.

"And how do you know this, Call-law-reed? Am I saying that correctly?" Medhas said.

"Yes, yes you are," Kalaerede said. "And it is obvious, Archmage Medhas. The Dea who attacked us at Mare Lake was the Divine Prince Nolan Wylie, first of the magi. He arrived here with the foster magi two days ago. They were separated and placed here."

"Do you see the benefits of your spiritual training, Kandace? It is not enough to be physically strong; you must be spiritually strong as well. Thank you, young mage. Raia, Annu, will you assist the primates in locating in the other magi while we make camp here?"

"Camp?" Kandace shouted. "We should be out looking for them!"

"In order to be found, one must stay still. Daemons, find all the magi in the forest. Return as quick as you can," he said.

The blue firebird and the golden-tailed monkey quickly disappeared through the forest.

Medhas continued, "Call-law-reed, tell me, where is your archmage?"

"I have no archmage. The mage before me died before his bloodline could be continued," Kalaerede said. "Like the foster magi, I am to begin a new bloodline."

"Then it was your mother, Shi'larra, who taught you the art of spiritual understanding," he said. "She did a fine job."

"Thank you. My mother, along with my grandfather, taught me much, but they are not archmages. I still have much to learn," Kalaerede said.

"Lord Beluar, if my memory is correct," Medhas said. "He is originally from Aryvandaar. I'm sure he was able to teach you more than an archmage could."

"Yes … but how did you—"

"Call-law-reed, will you join Kandace and find some mammoth leaves," he said quickly. "It will be dark soon."

Kandace and Kalaerede nodded. Mammoth leaves were easy to find. They hung from the trees neighboring the red papaya. Kandace used her staff to shoot controlled fireballs at the stems of several leaves. As they fell, Kandace and Kalaerede grabbed them by the stems, and then they pulled them back to camp. Medhas explained that mammoth leaves were large enough to hold them, but they were also very soft. After making a small blue fire, he showed them how to make them into beds. Before long, they had lain down in a circle around the blue fire, waiting to be found.

Is that a blue sun? Everything her parents told her was right. Another world really existed beyond the stars. The forest around them had plenty of thick trees, barely covering the sun. It was blue! For every moment she thought she was dreaming, that blue sun hovering above her reminded Lilith that all of this was real. Aliens were crazy rumors back home. They filled the movies and shows with imagination and the possibility of a limitless world. Lilith never imagined she would be the proof extraterrestrial life existed outside of Earth. This world looked very similar to where she grew up. This forest looked like the rainforest she talked about with her Uncle Joshua. He said he used to live in a rainforest. Did he mean this place? They even had monkeys here. Lilith only saw them through shadows as they bounced through branches, but they were real too. They grunted and yelled as if they were speaking to each other. Were they following them? Lilith followed close behind Cassandra, the girl she had only met hours ago in an attempt to save her brother. Cassandra was taller than Lilith but not by much. Her hair was smooth with natural bounce at its ends. Wind could surf from it. Dressed in the same rags Lilith had seen only yesterday, Cassandra continued to look up at the blue sun as if mesmerized. She asked her if she knew where they were going.

"I think so."

"You think? How did we even get here?" Lilith asked.

"The portal was supposed to take us somewhere safe," Cassandra said, "but I don't know. I've never made a portal before. The magic was really tricky," she said still looking up.

"This is your first time!" Lilith shouted.

"Yes, but the portal only works for us. I would have had no other reason to create it. We have to keep moving."

"Are you sure we're even in the other realm? What if we're on the wrong planet or something?" Lilith asked.

"We're in the right place. See those fruit? They're called red papayas. That tells me that we're somewhere in Meditation Trees."

Lilith was comforted by Cassandra's limited knowledge of the land. She said they had to keep an eye out for the others. Lilith didn't know how many other people they needed to be looking for, but her thoughts were only on one person: Henri. Somehow, he had gotten to the same place she was in. Something must have happened. Lilith should have known when he wasn't on the Ferris wheel. Henri was a lot of things, but he was a stickler for traditions. Every Sunday, he made sure he was home for dinner whether he wanted to be there or not. Sometimes, he reminded her of their mother. If believing all this stuff helped him, how could she say no?

"Do you mind telling me *again* how all of this happened? I'm still a little confused. How does this help Henri?" Lilith asked.

"Sure. We are the Gemini Sisters, the magi of light and hope," Cassandra said. "You and I represent the last elements to leave this world in the trust of mortal flesh. Henri, Emmett, and Nolan are magi as well. When they returned here, they woke a vengeful soul that is determined to consume magic. He'll start with the foster magi, like you and Henri, because you're the weakest. But you and I can stop him. When we unite, there is something of mystical awakening that every soul of magic is said to feel. It is the completion of our cycle."

"So what do we have to do?" Lilith asked.

"According to legend, we find that which is protected and claim it as our own. Then we will have truly accepted our place and the world will know it," Cassandra said.

"What is it we're looking for?" she asked.

"I think it's our staffs, but we would need our daemons as well," Cassandra said.

"Daemons?"

"Like Terran animals. They're our daemonic equivalent, our protectors. If we find them, we should find the others," Cassandra said.

"And what do these day-mons look like?" Lilith asked.

"Don't worry; they'll find us."

Over the next hour, or what Lilith assumed was an hour, they walked the forest steadily. They could still hear the sounds of what she thought were monkeys echoing throughout the forest. Lilith wasn't prepared to do this much walking. Her feet were starting to hurt. When they got to a river, she asked if they could stop and rest for a minute. Cassandra told her the river was known as Whitetail. It was the only river in the forest, and it led to the Maian Gulf, leading to the Latean Ocean. When Lilith asked if there was any edible food nearby, Cassandra told her there were dragon-berry bushes behind them. They were slightly sweet, like peaches. Lilith took a handful more and ate them before sitting down. She offered some to Cassandra, but she refused.

"Do your parents know you're here with me?" she asked.

"Yes, they saw me off just like yours did," Cassandra responded.

"I bet yours gave you a better send-off than mine. They just told me about the place yesterday," she said. "I already miss home."

"In the Terran system? You were born just as I was. I'm sorry things happened this way. I've known this day might come for decades, but it doesn't make it any easier."

"Decades? How old are you?" she asked.

"Forty, which makes you forty, too," Cassandra said.

"What!"

"Your parents didn't tell you? The Gemini Twins are born in the same year. We're Deas; we age slowly," Cassandra said.

"You're telling me I'm forty years old here! That's impossible! I don't look forty!" Lilith shouted, nearly spitting out her food.

"It's just a number," Cassandra said. "But it is also a fact. I was born in the year 151, to Illariel, my mother, and my father is High Prince Theodore Petruos."

"Are you saying that your ancestors are rulers of this whole realm?" Lilith asked. Why did those names sound familiar to her?

"Half of it. There's also a royal family of the Northlands," Cassandra began.

"Well, doesn't that make you like some kind of princess or something?" she said.

"Technically, I'm the High Princess of the Southlands. Do not think of me as a princess, Lilith. As the light mage, my responsibilities are to the cycle before my own family," Cassandra said.

"Then shouldn't we be in a castle, not some forest?" Lilith said. "And no offense, why are you dressed like that?"

"I've never lived in the palace," Cassandra said with her head down. "After my mother and her family requested to be sent to their sister city of Telardon, my father met her during his studies with the Kintiar Elves. They fell in love and became one. Once my mother gave birth to Nolan, everything went wrong after that."

"Nolan is your brother?" she said. "That's where I've heard those names before. Those are his parents?"

"He's the brother *I'm* trying to save. I tried to talk him earlier, but something was wrong. That's when I knew I had to find you."

"Nolan is your brother? But his parents are dead. How is that possible?"

"They're not dead. They're lost," Cassandra said.

Before Cassandra could continue, Lilith saw two daemons fly toward them. Cassandra smiled. She said they were spectrum butterflies. They were the biggest butterflies Lilith had ever seen. Each of them were the size of small child, flapping in front of them with shades of purple, yellow, red, blue, and green. All the colors wrapped around each other like a ball of rubber bands. Black beady eyes concentrated on the two of them as they stood frozen in their path. Heavy winds pushed from their fluttering wings calmed the two lost sisters, as they were captivated by the daemons' style and grace. Lilith had never felt less threatened and safer on an alien planet.

"My name is Urra. You must be Cassandra, the elder of the Gemini Sisters," the butterfly in front of Cassandra said. Her voice was strong yet gentle; it did not fit her small body.

"They can talk?" Lilith asked.

"And you must be the foster mage, Lilith. I am Mahl, your daemon and protector," Mahl said.

"I was hoping you'd find us," Cassandra said. "Have you been looking long?"

"We arrived at the same time as you," Urra said. "The portal you summoned brought us here as well, just a little ways off."

"How?" Lilith asked.

"We are connected to you. We will always be," Mahl said.

"Are you what we're supposed to be looking for?" Lilith asked.

"In a normal situation, no. We would be given to you by your fifth birthday, when your soul is settled in its new host. What we are looking for is your staff, young mage. Granting the stars are as all-knowing as they seem, we are hoping they will give them to you soon, given the urgency," Mahl said.

Lilith didn't know what Mahl meant by "the stars," but nonetheless, she followed, keeping her thoughts on Henri. Cassandra led the four of them along the bank of the river. She asked Urra if she had seen any other magi since she arrived. She said no. Cassandra told Lilith there had to be a reason why the portal took them to Meditation Trees. Lilith wondered if her brother was close by when they stopped.

"Why are we stopping? Is Henri here?" Lilith asked.

"Don't you hear that?" Cassandra asked.

"The monkeys? That's weird, right? I mean animals grunt and stuff on Earth too. But I think they're following us."

"They're not grunting," Mahl said. "They're talking."

"We must be getting close," Cassandra said.

Lilith continued to follow Cassandra and the two butterflies, hoping they were getting closer to Henri or Emmett or Nolan. She secretly hoped it was Henri. They walked on, with the blue sun burning down on them. With the trees as high as they were, Lilith was expecting some kind of shade; however, nothing could block the size of that blue sun, reminding her of everything her parents had told her yesterday. Even with the occasional flutter of butterfly wings, the heat was pouring down on the improperly dressed foster mage. They had walked deeper into the forest until the river was nowhere to be seen. Cassandra continued to look up at the sun with an impatient frown developing on her innocent face. When Lilith looked up too, she saw a light shining down on them.

"What's that light?" Lilith asked, pointing up.

"It's about time," Cassandra said.

From the light came two loud *smacks* as something landed directly in front of them. They landed hard on the ground, leaving deep impressions like a crater fallen from the sky. Each staff was made from black wood with distinguishing features. They were reflections of each other in all ways but one. The first staff had a yellow jewel, and the second staff had a purple jewel. Vines twisted around the jewels, protecting them as the thick wood stood at their height.

"How do we know which one is—?

"Yellow is the color of light, my element, and purple is the color of hope, yours. Are you ready?" Cassandra asked.

"If it helps my brother," she said.

They grabbed the staffs at the same time. A beam of purple and yellow light shot into the air like a laser, almost hitting the same place where it came from. Cassandra and Lilith felt an enormous sweep of power as a giant wind burst from beneath them, lasting only a second or two. They fell onto the ground, but they quickly got up. Lilith didn't have to ask what they were looking for anymore. This was it.

15

Dragons and Dungeons

JAAHN GASPED AS he looked up at the sky. They were too late. He had already safely procured his meal in Daedalus's house where it all began. Soon, he would consume Emmett and end their beloved cycle before it ever began. But first, he had to prepare the two treasures he had left outside of Blackheart. He no longer needed to play along with Daedalus and Amos. Once Emmett was consumed, he could take from the girl what he truly hungered for and Raymond could finally know why he was so valuable to him. With a sullen daemon beside him, the ravenous Jaahn teleported back to Blackheart. Jaahn and Pani walked toward Bast, Amelia, and Raymond, furious. The sun was making its way across the skies. The three of them were sleeping before he teleported in. Bast was the first to wake with Amelia and Raymond last. Jaahn's eyes flashed black as he looked at them.

"What's wrong with your eyes, Nolan?" Amelia shouted.

Jaahn shouted one word and Amelia's body quickly fell to the ground, as if her legs had just stopped working. Bast tried to do the same, but when the word was repeated, she too fell. Pani was speechless.

"You—you can't use Divine offensively like that! It's against the law!" Pani shouted.

"Mortal laws mean nothing to a god!" Jaahn shouted.

"What did you do to them?" Raymond shouted.

"They're just sleeping," Jaahn said calmly. "I still need the girl anyway."

Jaahn walked a little closer to Raymond. He looked up and around; the Green Valley had been much prettier the last time he was there. He didn't have much time left. The Sisters had already awakened. That much he had seen from the sky, but there was still time; he knew it.

"You really have no idea who you really are, do you?"

Raymond was still confused.

"I'll explain it to you after. For now, you just need to stay close to me. Maybe later we'll go hunting for old time's sake."

Before Raymond could run, Jaahn teleported into a golden orb. The orb then turned around Amelia, Bast, Raymond, and Pani. Within moments, Jaahn stood proudly in the center of Daedalus's house. He saw Raymond vomit violently on the ground, but he ignored it. Jaahn wiped his hands over Amelia and Bast, and they disappeared in a green smoke. He turned to Raymond and pulled him up to his feet. He put his hands in the center of Raymond's chest. His eyes pulsed black as he ignored Raymond's fear. Once it was done, he told Raymond to stand up.

"Protection plant!" Jaahn shouted.

Quickly, a large root broke through the floor, six feet long. It stood with green spikes on its sides as Jaahn walked over to it. When Raymond tried to run away, Jaahn tightened his fist. Raymond was immediately bound by invisible ropes and floating behind him as he struggled violently.

"What are you doing to me?" Raymond said.

"I'm here to rescue you, you idiot," Jaahn said as he turned to the plant again. "No one enters this house! You hear me!"

The plants nodded before descending back into the ground. He heard the earth move as large vines surrounded the house with a god's magic pulsing through every one. That would give him some delay before the Gemini Sisters' magic reached him—but not much.

"Pani, go keep an eye on our guest," Jaahn continued. "I'll be down shortly."

"Which one?" Pani said sternly.

"The girl. Wouldn't want you spilling any information to the half-Terran, now would I?"

Pani obliged as Raymond's floating body hovered behind him. It was time Raymond learned how similar Daedalus and Amos really were. Again, Nolan's former body was transformed into a golden orb, taking Raymond and him to another section of the house. Jaahn could recognize what was in Raymond from the second he saw him, even in his foreign form. He was curious how Daedalus knew it, but there was no time to question it. Amos and Daedalus both tried to tempt him, and both of them would fail because of it. There would be zero chance of disturbance. As long as Raymond was confined within the White Room, Jaahn would have time to consume the one soul he needed before the Sisters tried to force him to sleep again. He released Raymond when they were in the hall. His sorrowful cries made him weak and pathetic. But all of that was about to change.

"It's time," he responded quickly.

"What are you going to do to me?" Raymond asked.

"You'll find out soon enough," Jaahn replied. "Keep walking down this hall until you see a white door. I can't walk inside myself, but I was able to summon it for you." Jaahn said. "Don't even think about running. Daedalus has given me everything I needed! Now go!" he said, teleporting.

I gotta get out of here, Emmett thought. He opened his eyes to see nothing but complete darkness. He tried to stand only to find that he was chained at the ankles. The window above him was barely out of his reach. A door stood out in front of him; it had three slots through the single window so it was easy for someone to spy on him from afar, but to his right, he saw that he was not alone. A shadow was chained as he was, and Emmett knew who it was by the bushy tail that lay on the floor like a furry rabbit. It had to be Gebb, and from the looks of it, he was still asleep. Emmett sat down and tried to get Gebb's attention. He kept calling out his name, hoping he would wake up.

"Emmett?" Gebb asked. "What happened?"

"I don't know, but it can't be good. Nolan or Jaahn or whatever captured us just after we broke the temperamental spell. I'm sorry about that," Emmett replied.

"Believe it or not, temperamental daemons are expected for young magi. Every mage will go through it," Gebb said.

"Good. You boys are finally awake." A dark figure smiled from inside the cell.

"*You*! Where's Nolan?" said Emmett, startled.

"Yo think you know who I am, do you," Jaahn said sarcastically. "How little too late."

Emmett watched as Jaahn's mouth opened larger than normal, but he couldn't keep it open. Emmett could see him struggling to control himself. He started grunting and talking to himself. Then Emmett heard his name, but it wasn't Jaahn's voice.

"Nolan?" Emmett said.

Emmett and Gebb looked at each other with shock; they knew that something was wrong, but they didn't know what had just happened. Jaahn teleported away, quickly, grabbing his head. Emmett and Gebb sat in their dungeon, trying to think of a way to escape. What the hell was going on out there?

Seconds after Nolan teleported, his legs started to move against his will. Raymond marched down the lonely hallway, clawing at anything he could get his hands on to stop himself. The hallway Raymond was forced to march down was brown with many other doors leading to endless possibilities. Raymond got an eerie feeling about the house. There were pictures in this hallway; they were believable at first—pictures of an ocean, or a group of children—but then this. The picture hung from the wall, ceiling to floor. An image was laid out in front of him. Three horns of a trident were staring at him. The middle horn was a little longer than the other two. Raymond had never seen that before, but it felt familiar. What did it all mean? Nolan had said he was going to save him, but Raymond didn't need to be saved! He needed to return to his parents, to the Outlands where he was safe. What kind of game were these Wylies playing? Daedalus and Nolan must have teamed up from the start. He said Daedalus gave him what he needed. This must have been his house. The Wylies were terrible people, just like his mother had said. They used their magic to strike fear in everyone who didn't submit to them. Raymond thought by being respectful and fearful, he would be spared of any malevolence, but obviously he was wrong. Nolan was never after his parents. He was after him, but why?

At last, Raymond made it to the white door Nolan had talked about. It was large and out of place. On the front of the door, there was a strange black dragon with its body spread out. The mystical creature took up the entire door, looking ferocious and massive. The dragon's frozen eyes looked at him as he stood in front of it. Instantly, the dragon's eyes flashed white for a second before opening. Nolan's magic continued to make him march. This was where it would happen! Raymond cried out, but no one could hear him as he was pulled inside. When the door closed, Raymond regained control of his legs, but the door had disappeared. He was trapped!

The room was the size of his room back at the cottage but painted white, with symbols on the wall he couldn't read. Raymond could also see more of the dragons from the door on the wall, but they were much smaller. Running his hands on the walls, Raymond wished that he could tell what they said, feeling the letters was nothing more than teasing him. He had no idea what the symbols meant. Raymond stood in the center, shouting for someone to open the door. The room started to spin around his frozen form like he was the sun above Deva Prime. Each of the tiny dragons began to peel itself off the wall and fly around him like a mad tornado contained in a box. He screamed, but they continued to encircle him. As the tiny black dragons continued to move, Raymond lifted his head. He screamed as the dragons started to claw at his chest in the same place Nolan's hand had once been. He didn't feel any pain, but his head froze. His head snapped back like a twig as the magic overpowered him, changing his bright-blue eyes to black as coal.

The blue fire had been snuffed out as the morning cracked above them. The magi of fire and mind had grown restless waiting for their daemons to return. Somehow they had fallen asleep on mammoth leaves before they knew if their daemons had joined them. With a dangerous Dea on the loose, neither wanted to lose those who were most precious to them. Archmage Medhas tried to keep them calm, but neither Kandace nor Kalaerede were responding to benign words. Kandace, the fiery mage, demanded they be allowed to go out and search for them. Kalaerede agreed with her, but her aggression was much louder than his was.

"What do you mean *no?*" Kandace said.

"Kandace, now is not the time for aggressive attitudes. Raia and Annu are perfectly capable of taking care of themselves! They are not your pets. They are Alphas, kings and queens of the Outlands," Medhas said.

"I hate when you ask her to do stuff without asking me. She's my daemon, Archmage! You had no right!" Kandace shouted.

Archmage Medhas walked up to Kandace; his eyes burning into her. His hands moved from behind his back and swung in front of him, covering each other as they rested on his belly button. Kandace and Kalaerede stood back, but he pressed forward, turning his face before them, making sure both of them were witness to his words.

"Have I forgotten my place, Kandace Kane?" he said mildly. "Tell me who I am."

"My archmage?" she said slowly.

"Yes," he said as his voice boomed with every word that followed. "An archmage is an elemental Dea responsible for the guidance and care of young ones within the sacred cycle. A title, which was given to me by the grand archmage himself. As an archmage, my pupils are not limited to Deas. For Deas are not the only examples of magic within the cycle. This extends to Deas *and* daemons. If both of you feel as if I have wronged you or stepped outside my authority, *please*, challenge me. You will both learn *very soon* that your daemons have more purpose than you know. So am I being challenged?" Medhas said.

"No," Kandace whispered.

"I did not hear *you*, Mage Kalaerede," he said.

"No, I understand, Archmage Medhas," he said.

"Then there will be no more reason for either of you to question me again," he said.

They waited in silence after Medhas handed each of them more fruit to eat. Kandace and Kalaerede kept to themselves, wondering when their daemons would return. Hours passed by as the blue sun was reaching midday. Medhas stood up as a pounding breached their camp. Before Kandace and Kalaerede could open their mouths, there was a steady rhythm hitting the ground. Annu broke through the forest trees. Kalaerede jumped up when he saw his daemon. Yet the sound grew louder, but neither of the magi was moving. Suddenly, two colossal red spotted apes walked up behind the Alphas. A large red spot fell from the top of their chests to the bottom of their stomachs. Each of them walked with their hands pounding on the ground in front of them. Annu quickly walked over to them and spoke. They responded and continued to speak for a moment longer. From behind them, Zachariah, Henri, and Oris walked into the forest.

"Archmage Medhas," Zachariah said. "It's been too long."

"Zachariah Kingsley," Medhas said. "It's good to see you again. But where is the earth mage, Zachariah? He should be with you," Medhas said.

"Jaahn took him," Henri said at last. "He came in last night, and he took him! And we couldn't do anything to stop him."

"You are the wind mage, correct? A raven-haired Roland. It seems tradition has reigned as strong as history tells," Medhas said.

"Yes, Medhas, this is Henri James Roland, the southern wind mage. He arrived here with Emmett Bradley and Nolan Wylie a few days ago. Emmett has gone missing. I trust you know why," Zachariah said.

Medhas nodded. "We ran into him at my cottage. This is my pupil Kandace Kane and Kalaerede, the mind mage. He came to me from the village of the Meians. His mother is Shi'larra."

"Shi'larra of the Kintiar Elves? Medhas, it has been—"

"Mage Henri?" Medhas said quickly as he walked past his old friend. "Do you know where Jaahn may have taken him?"

"No, we just got here. We never left the island until *that thing* took over Nolan. What is that thing in Nolan?" Henri said. "Why is he doing this to us? He's our friend."

"You haven't told him," Medhas said, turning to Zachariah.

"Emperor Amos told me—"

"He is not here, is he, Zachariah? As much as I greatly admire the high emperor, he cannot expect us to wait until his return to teach them the ways of this world," Medhas said.

"Henri," Medhas continued, "you know what your friend is, do you not? He is the Moon Dea, the reincarnation of the moon god, and with that comes certain conditions. One of which is the soul of a god. This much you may know as well. What you may not know is that certain souls contain so much of a presence they can create a personality all their own. Reincarnations of the patron gods have souls such as these. Originally, these personalities were used as a kind of self-defensive mechanism. However, it was discovered that once they were released, they developed their own ambitious goals. It was then that they were imprisoned, forced to serve their reincarnated masters. Now they are a tool for certain afflicted Deas to achieve the highest degree of power imaginable. As with any power, they must be trained and understood. Your friend, the young Wylie, has yet to be trained, and now you see why he must be."

"So … Nolan isn't under a spell?" Henri said.

"Not anymore," Cassandra said.

Raia was flying ahead of them, followed by Urra and Mahl. Kandace raced over to her daemon as Cassandra and Lilith made their way into the small gathering of magi. Each mage was holding a staff when Zachariah and Medhas walked over to them.

"Who are you?" Henri asked.

"Henri?"

"Lilith?" Henri looked past the wavy-haired girl to his own sister's long black hair. He ran over to her, picked her up, and swung her. Mahl and Oris flew close by.

"When did you get here?" he asked.

"Just this morning. You'll never guess who brought me here," Lilith said.

"That hair?" Zachariah said. "It looks just like … I … I am Zachariah Kingsley, senior librarian, and you are …"

"High Princess Cassandra Alèynor Wylie and the mage of light," she said.

Zachariah, Medhas, Kalaerede, and Kandace dropped to one knee. The daemons each bowed their heads. The only ones not bowing were the Rolands.

"Wait a second, High Princess," Henri said. "We saw your picture frame hanging in the summer palace, but your portrait wasn't there."

"It's not supposed to be," Cassandra said. "Those frames become engraved every time a Wylie is named. A portrait doesn't hang in them until we come of age. I'm not the only Wylie hanging there, am I?"

Henri shook his head. "So you're Nolan's cousin? I didn't know Mr. Wylie had any siblings?"

"He doesn't. I'm Nolan's sister," Cassandra said.

"But his parents are, oh yeah, but that doesn't make any sense. How is that possible? How do we know you're not lying?" Henri said.

"Anyone ever tell you about the one thing all Wylies can do? Our inheritance from Magnus? You've seen Nolan teleport?"

Henri nodded. Cassandra quickly turned into a golden orb and swung herself around in three circles before taking shape again in the same place she was before.

"You can teleport?" Henri said.

"Because I'm a Wylie," Cassandra said.

"How is that—" Henri began.

"I'd love to explain it, but now really isn't the time, Henri. Which of the magi are here?" Cassandra said.

"Great, someone who can bring us back to the reason why we're here. I like her," Kandace shouted. "Now, Cassandra, before we do anything, I just want you to know I'm not gonna be calling you Your Highness or anything. As far as I'm concerned, you're a mage first, princess second, got it?"

"Kandace!" Medhas said. "Have I taught you nothing?"

"No, it's fine, Archmage Medhas. I prefer it this way. Informalities often have deeper impressions than formalities," Cassandra said. "Besides, I've never felt like a princess."

"Okay, now, since the two of you have awakened, I guess it's safe to assume Jaahn was put back in Nolan's subconscious, right?" Kandace asked.

"Right, he should be back to normal very soon, but I'm sure Jaahn will put up some fight," Cassandra said.

"What about Emmett? What if he's ..." Henri said.

"Oh, come on, Henri, don't be crazy; we're connected. If any of us are killed, don't you think we would know it? We need to get to the others. We're still missing the heart mage. Last I heard, she was in Blackheart. I think we should go there."

"Hold up there, firefly," Archmage Medhas said. "Just because we have five out of eight does not mean *any of you* make the decisions here. Zachariah and I have our instructions. We are to take all of the magi to the grand archmage. There you will begin to finalize your training."

"The grand archmage!" Kalaerede said and gasped. "He's the oldest and most powerful Dea in the world. It's rumored that he's immortal."

"He is the Dea who taught Magnus Wylie and Sophia Conrad," Kandace said.

"Who?" Lilith asked.

"Sophia Conrad," Zachariah said. "She was the Sun Dea, the empress of the Northlands. She was the equal of Magnus Wylie until—"

"Until he killed her," Kandace said. "For bringing us into a Civil War."

"Kandace!" Medhas the archmage shouted. "Do not interrupt. Terran magi, we haven't time to give you a history lesson. If I'm not mistaken, we have a spell casting Dea among us, do we not? Then may I suggest we spend this time finding the necessary ingredients for deconstruction."

"Cassandra can teleport us like Jaahn teleported Emmett?" Henri asked.

"I can't teleport all of us there. Besides, we would still need passes for everyone here. I don't have one, and I don't think Lilith has one either. But, archmage, deconstruction is a grade-six refined potion," Cassandra said. "Are you sure we will find all the necessary ingredients? I don't know them by heart."

"I do," Zachariah said. "And I have faith in your grandfather. We will find everything that we need. This is a wonderful beginning."

"I'll end it all, Nolan. Let me do, this!" Jaahn said as he began to form the energy ball outside Emmett's cell door. Grunting, he closed his hand again. Jaahn had made it down the hallway when the unspeakable happened; Nolan had somehow managed enough strength to teleport himself to the floor above him, away from Emmett. Nolan was getting stronger. Jaahn's defenses would eventually be broken. Teleporting had required much of Nolan's energy, leaving him weak while Jaahn took control again. Jaahn had managed to teleport himself back to Emmett's dungeon cell. Nolan summoned every ounce of energy he could to stop him. The awakening had made him stronger now but also more foolish. The cycle had to be destroyed; it was the only way! For centuries, the small-minded Deas did not see the risk their beloved cycle could unleash upon the world. Jaahn had to destroy it all before it began. *Fine*, he thought. If he couldn't consume Emmett, he would kill him and every reincarnation born after him! As Jaahn was raising his hand to blow down the door and everyone inside, he saw a strange shadowy figure in front of him. With a colorless glow, the figure placed its hand on Jaahn's chest.

You'll regret this, Nolan!

16

The Last Magi

SATISFACTION AND A side of smiles ordered Nolan to touch his face again, not because he had to but because he wanted to! He could move his hands and his fingers, blink, shout, whisper; the simple choices of life were returned to him in the blink of his own eye. Nolan didn't know how, but he was back, and that was all that mattered. He didn't feel angry anymore; he was the definition of calm. Before Nolan had a chance to speak, his powers teleported him one floor up. When he finally could clearly see again, Pani stood in front of him outside a room. He heard his name. Nolan could barely keep himself up. He leaned against the wall, repressing the vomit building in his throat. The young Wylie opened his eyes. He blinked several times to make sure he wouldn't be forced back into the blackness of his own mind. As much as he didn't know about Jaahn, Nolan knew enough. The one time he had control over his body, he lost it. Whenever he got pissed off, Jaahn took over. What kind of fucked-up life was that? Was he supposed to just be calm his whole life?

Calm down.

Lucian! Lucian!

Calling out to his ancestor had scared him. Maybe Jaahn did something to Lucian so that he couldn't speak with him anymore. Maybe he would snap back. Nolan looked at his daemon, hoping he would be able to explain everything that had happened to him.

Nolan?

Lucian?

No, it's me.

Nolan looked up to see the silver seal smiling at him. He was looking for Lucian to be the voice in his head, but he wasn't unhappy that his silver seal had responded instead. A vague memory of Jaahn telling Pani to stay out of his head popped in.

You can read my mind now?

After everything we've been through, the ability to understand each other is a gift.

Nolan listened as Pani filled in the gaps of their time together. He couldn't believe all of the things Jaahn had made his body do, what he made Pani do. Some things he knew because he could see them, but other things were completely new to him. The boy's name was Raymond, and Jaahn locked him in a room; the girl was Amelia, and Jaahn put her to sleep. Kandace and Kalaerede were the ones he saw at the lake, and the Gemini Sisters saved him. He wanted to thank these Gemini Sisters most of all. It seemed that he had met most of the Southern Magi except for the Gemini Sisters. Who they were was probably the biggest question of all, even bigger than his missing dead ancestor.

"I have to find my friends," Nolan said at last.

We will.

"And I have to figure out how to wake up … Amelia? And what about Emmett? He's going to kill me! Does he even know what's going on? Oh shit, what about Raymond or Henri and Zachariah? They could be anywhere. How am I gonna—"

Pani placed his hand on Nolan's shoulder as he bounced back and forth from one side of the hallway to the other side. The two looked at each other.

We are going to figure this out, Nolan. Don't worry.

Nolan's face lit up like New Year's Eve in New York. The silver seal had been with him from the moment he arrived in Deva Prime. Pani never left his side, not when he heard the truth about his parents, not when he almost ate two of the magi's souls, not when he kidnapped his best friend and locked him up in a dungeon, not when he confined a boy to a room, and not when he put a girl to sleep and not in the fun way. And most important, Pani never lied to him.

"First things first," Pani said. "We need to get Emmett out of that dungeon. Do you remember the way back?"

Nolan was immediately calm as he followed the silver seal. Then there was a bright distant light coming down toward him. His first thought was Jaahn, but then the light got stronger. There was a loud *smack* a foot in front of him. A long piece of wood with a blue stone wrapped in brown vines stood in front of him, glimmering in the night. He asked Pani if that was what he thought it was. Pani told him it was. Nolan walked over to it. Firmly grasping it, he looked up, wondering where it came from. Who had sent it to him? He unlocked it from the prison and ran behind his daemon.

Emmett remained locked in a cell, jangling his chains back and forth, trying to figure out what the hell had just happened. He knew it was Nolan somehow trying to stop that thing from eating him, but that hadn't worked for anyone yet. Emmett had to get out. The cell was small but with enough room for him to see his storm bear on the other side. Besides the door with its three slots, there was no other way for him to get out. He longed for the open forest of Meditation Trees, even if it was with a temperamental daemon. *That which is a weapon and a teacher.* Zachariah had told Henri that when he got his staff. A part of him wanted to know what it could teach, but to be honest, he was more concerned with the whole weapon aspect right now. Nolan was fighting back—that much was certain—but how much longer would he be able to stop him. Emmett couldn't put all his faith in Nolan, not after everything they had gone through. His best option was to break out of there and fight off Jaahn. And then as soon as he got to land, he would just make a run for it. The rest would have to come to him later. *But how do I get those damn stars to give my staff? I really need it*, he thought. Whatever those things were, they sure weren't very helpful. Emmett needed an answer. He needed something, someone to help him.

They don't call me a guardian for nothing.

Emmett's eyes popped. He knew that voice; it was the storm bear. He heard his voice in his head! Even in the dark corners of the cell, the bear's brown eyes looked up at him.

"Is this normal?" Emmett asked.

"Daemonic telepathy? No, it is not a skill we naturally possess. Only Alphas and their individual mages can share minds such as this," Gebb said.

"So eventually, it would have happened?"

"Eventually, yes."

Emmett wasn't a fan of mind reading; that much he knew was clear, but one person, especially someone who was supposed to protect him, eh, why not? They spoke back and forth for a few minutes, trying to figure out the best way for them to burst out of those chains. It probably would have been much easier if Emmett knew even the slightest bit about his own magic, but Zachariah had told him basically nothing. His focus had always been on bonding with Gebb, and now that he finally felt that he was, nothing good could come of it.

Emmett heard footsteps coming down the hall. He knew it had to be Jaahn. Conversation turned to desperation as Gebb and he tried to figure out a way out. The more they tried, however, the more those shackles just rattled in the darkness. Suddenly, there was a light above, one they couldn't escape. It broke through the ceiling. *Smack!* In between Gebb and Emmett, there stood a wooden staff with a green jewel wrapped in branches. The jewel lit up the room. The chains around Emmett's and Gebb's wrists rose into the air. They broke instantly. Emmett made a run for his staff, as did Gebb.

Now what? Emmett thought.

Use it.

Emmett grabbed the staff and pointed it at the door. He kept telling himself it was a weapon, a way to focus the power he never knew he had. Remembering what he did at the summer palace, Emmett tried his best to concentrate on that power he felt that day—not that it was too different from what he was feeling now, except now he needed it. Closing his eyes helped him more than he wanted to admit. Another loud smashing sound forced him to open his eyes. The wall was blown to pieces, nothing but rubble and dust rising in the air. He ran.

His name was called out from behind him, but he didn't waste any time. With Gebb at his side, Emmett ran faster and faster, pretending he was back on the football field. Having no idea where he was going, he asked Gebb, telepathically, if he had any idea where they were. No.

They turned around to see that the dungeon door had put itself back together. *Living relic spell with auto repair*, Gebb told him. They at least knew they were in the home of a spell-casting Dea, but that didn't give them too much information. As far as they knew, the summer palace wasn't the only spell-casting home in this world. Again, Emmett heard his name called out, but he kept running. Jaahn was *not* going to eat his soul. Running up and down hallways had proved to be his only option. His legs were hurting, but he kept going.

"What the—" Emmett shouted.

Before he knew it, Emmett was slipping, as if he had run onto ice. He couldn't stop himself. So the wall did it for him. Gebb and he opened their eyes at about the same time. Pani and Nolan were standing above them. Nolan kept saying he was sorry as Emmett held his head.

"What did you do to me?" Emmett said.

"Well, I'm the water mage. I guess that means ice too," Nolan said.

Emmett opened his eyes. That voice, he knew that voice. He had heard it every day since kindergarten, but he still had to be sure.

"How do I know you're you?" Emmett said, holding his staff toward Nolan.

"The Sisters. They must have done something. It's me, Emmett," Nolan said.

"Not good enough! Tell me something only you would know!" He backed up as Gebb followed, defending him.

Nolan stuttered for a second, looking to Pani. "Oh, oh, I got it! At Maci Ramirez's party last year, you got really drunk and pulled out your—"

"Okay! Okay! It's you!"

"… dick and ran around chasing every girl you saw!"

"Yeah, yeah, I remember! Okay, you're Nolan!"

"Damn, that shit was funny!" Nolan said. "I think I still have that video on my phone."

"You-you shouldn't keep videos on your phone; it-it drains the memory," Emmett said, stuttering.

Nolan laughed. Relieved, Emmett stared at his confused daemon. That was not a story he enjoyed reliving, but he knew who the person was in front of him now. Standing, he looked at Nolan and smiled. It had been too long.

"So you're back," Emmett said.

"Yup."

"And you're not gonna eat my soul?"

"Nope."

"Good." Sighing, Emmett and Nolan smiled. "You did some fucked-up shit, man. What the fuck was wrong with you?" Emmett said.

Emmett then explained and listened as all the pieces came together. Nolan was especially curious when he said they talked to his grandfather, but Emmett couldn't remember how Zachariah had explained that.

"Did anyone say anything about my parents?" Nolan asked.

"Zachariah did. They're not dead, not as far as he knows. What Daedalus and the blond-haired guy said was true. They're alive, but they're imprisoned."

"Like in a jail?" Nolan asked.

"I don't know."

Emmett knew his words had given Nolan slight comfort, but he couldn't help but be a little selfish. They had never found his father's body. Could he be alive too somewhere back home or here? Magic was suddenly opening up new possibilities for the half-Terran mage.

17

A Deconstructive Discovery

URROUNDED BY A sea of strangers, a familiar face opened new doors to a world undiscovered. With his sister by his side, this world became more truth than lies. Zachariah had divided them up with a mission to find one of the eight ingredients Mr. Wylie had left for them. The eight ingredients for the refined potion deconstruction made it the first and most complicated potion Henri had ever heard of. It required a half a cup of water from Glacier Waters, eight black clovers, one cup of water from Latean Ocean, six spoons of timber sap, one cup of water from the Eoltic Ocean, one cup of water from the Thrzian Ocean, and two large spoonfuls of reaping sand. All to be mixed in the proper cauldron, as Zachariah said. Lilith and he were asked to collect the black clovers as if they had any idea what they looked like or where they were. Mr. Wylie was becoming more impressive by the second. For another world, he had planned every possible scenario to a T. He expected Nolan to freak out as he did because apparently it was the only way to free the Gemini Sisters. That was a *huge* risk, and everyone knew it, but for some reason, everyone trusted him and followed his instructions obediently. And here they were. All the magi were staffed, equipped with daemons, and most important, alive. Nolan almost destroyed the cycle, and Mr. Wylie was there to stop him without showing his face.

"Can you believe this?" Lilith said. "This place is real. They were right about *everything*. Where do you think we're really from?"

"Some place with raven-haired Rolands. What did Mom and Dad tell you before you left?" Henri asked.

"They told me that I had two powers: one was a seer and the other I'm guessing was this. Then Mom handed me this," Lilith said.

Henri opened the rose record and flipped through the pages, but there was nothing. Lilith took it back and opened it.

"You really can't see them?" she asked. "They're right here!"

For the next few moments, Henri tried to see what Lilith saw, but he couldn't. "Must have been magic," he said.

The trees were nearly touching the sun, and the smell of the red papaya was sugary sweet. Primates of different shapes and sizes were constantly around them, following them, talking. They moved a little more slowly now so Henri could see them. Each one he saw had a dancing tail. Oris explained that the dancing tails were well known among primate daemons. There was a saying among the Ankkns: "Monkey dance. Monkey live." There had to be at least four or five different kinds of monkeys around them. Some were large, like the ones Henri and Zachariah had met, but others were smaller like chimps. He watched a couple of them playing as they continued to search for black clovers. Uncle Joshua always talked about how beautiful nature really was. Mr. Bradley and he used to take them all on nature hikes and camping trips when they were kids. If Emmett's father and his uncle *were* really from this world, he was starting to understand they loved being outside. Zachariah said they traveled the world looking for artifacts. What more did this world have to offer?

"So you're the wind mage and I'm the hope mage," Lilith said. "I knew I got the crappier element. Who would have thought there would be four parts to a person's spirit?"

"Well, you and Cassandra are about the only ones who've done any real good. I mean, seriously, without the two of you, it was only a matter of time before Jaahn ate our souls," Henri said calmly.

"Nolan would never let that happen. He's our friend."

"Yeah, *our* friend, but he doesn't even know the other magi. Shit! He doesn't even know he has a sister, does he? How is that possible? Did she tell you anything?"

"Cassandra says she grew up in the place where their parents were held prisoner. It was really dark too. She said she's been there forty years! Can you believe that?"

"What I can't believe is that she's the younger sister? How can she be forty and Nolan just turned eighteen?"

Henri looked up at his daemon. His voice was in his head. Oris explained neither of their Terran ages were accurate here. In Deva Prime, time moved much slower. The first of the magi was born forty-three years ago. Over the next three years, seven magi followed him.

"*Seriously!*" he shouted.

"What!"

"According to Oris, Cassandra's one of the *youngest* of the magi. He says Nolan was born in the year 148. The last two magi born were you and Emmett. That's why we couldn't come here until after your birthdays!"

"But my birthday isn't for another two months!" Lilith shouted.

"Yeah, on Terran standards. It must have just happened here!"

In all his time with Zachariah, Henri was beginning to realize how much information he kept from him. He wished he had had an archmage like that loud girl Kandace had. Archmage Medhas wasn't waiting around for permission to share things with them. It was starting to make sense though. With Emmett's and Lilith's birthdays passed, their powers had reached their maturity, which meant they were ready to be explored. The cycle was now complete. It started with Nolan and ended with Lilith.

"Did he tell you that without talking? My daemon can talk. Can't yours?" Lilith said.

"Mine can too," Henri said. "The more you're around them, the closer you get. Telepathy is a way for them to speak to *just* us. It's kinda cool, but don't tell Emmett I said that."

Walking through Meditation Trees was strangely calming for the dark-haired Rolands. With the monkey chatter, the sugary smell of red papayas, and a gentle breeze on a late morning, not even the nightfall would make them nervous like walking through an under crowded park on a Sunday morning. Henri didn't know how much time had passed, but he was enjoying being back with his sister. Somehow, this made up for the Ferris wheel ride he missed. The silence was inevitable but calming as Henri wasn't surprised. His sister and he were still accepting this new part of their lives. And right now, he wanted to enjoy every second of it.

"So who do you think he is? This grand archmage?" Lilith asked. "Is he some kind of teacher? Like Professor Xavier?"

"Like in X-Men?" Henri said, shaking his head. "You and Emmett need to get out more. Anyway, I don't know, but I'm wondering why we didn't go there from the start. He probably would have known what to do with Nolan. He could have prevented all of this."

"What if he couldn't?" Lilith said. "What if Cassandra and I really were the only option?"

"What did you guys do anyway?" Henri asked.

"Our staffs fell from the sky, we grabbed them, and then boom, she tells me Nolan is back to normal," Lilith said.

"There has to be more than that?" Henri asked.

"Your guess is as good as mine," she said.

"I found it, Lilith!" Mahl said. The spectrum butterfly flew high in the trees until the two Deas saw a small black bag hanging from one of the branches. She picked it up and handed it back to Lilith. The bag read "*Eight black clovers*." On the bag, there was a symbol of a white tiger behind the red moon. There was a large "W" in the center of the red moon, with three stars in the background. Henri had seen that before. It was all over the summer palace.

"Wylies?" Lilith asked.

"Must be a family crest," Henri said. "Maybe it's got something to do with Nolan's medallion."

"Oh, yeah, that is a tiger, isn't it?" she asked.

"Mr. Wylie thought of everything," Henri said.

Oris turned them around as Henri followed them back to camp. He couldn't believe that a few days ago, he was walking through the same forest, scared shitless that some soul-sucking version of his best friend was tracking him down. He walked comfortably now, listening to the primates playing.

Nolan was still a little cautious of walking through Daedalus's house, especially since he knew he had something to do with his parents' disappearance, which started every lie he had ever heard. Emmett said he didn't have to worry about Jaahn coming back, but Nolan still tried to keep his cool. Yet with everything he saw, he wanted to burn it, hoping Daedalus might feel something if a portrait was ripped down or a vase was broken. The temptation of letting out the crazy alter ego was too fresh to let him show it. Luckily, Pani had told him about the protective houseplants. Nolan wondered if they would be able to help him if Daedalus returned or came looking for them. He hoped they wouldn't let him down. It was easier to be calm with Emmett and Gebb on his side too. Seeing their nervous, smiling faces made him almost forget he was the reason they were locked in a dungeon. Emmett and he tried to make their walk as normal as they possibly could, but they couldn't stop staring at their staffs. Nolan was expecting something a bit cooler.

"I mean I get that it's a weapon, but how are we supposed to learn how to use it? Is there like a manual or a spell book or something? Zachariah didn't tell us what to do once we have them," Emmett said.

"Yeah, I'm starting to realize he only tells us what he is supposed to tell us," Nolan said.

"I wonder who told him to do that," Emmett said.

"Exactly," Nolan responded.

"Zachariah Kingsley," Pani the silver seal said, "has always been a trusted friend of High Emperor Amos, even given his ancestry."

"His ancestry?" Nolan asked. "Is he in the mob?"

"No but his grandfather, Reginald Kingsley, was the northern mind mage who fought in the Civil War," Pani said.

"So he *is* in the Mob?" Emmett said.

"No," Gebb the deep-voiced storm bear said. "Reginald Kingsley is the only mage who was not welcomed back in the Mafia. He was a very powerful and crafty thief. After the war, he used his magic not only to steal from the Makaians but from others as well. Many often didn't even know they had been robbed until days after. It was then that Divine Emperor Magnus requested the assistance of the Mahellian Elves to help him discover how he did it."

"Why ask Elves?" Nolan asked.

"They were the ones who trained him," the silver seal said. "Before the war, the Elves cared not for squabbles between Deas."

Nolan was surprised and intrigued by Zachariah's ancestry. Despite it being his grandfather, he still had a bad rep. He smiled thinking of his grampa. If he was good enough to gain his trust, maybe Zachariah Kingsley wasn't all-bad.

"You know I've been hearing about this war for days now, but I don't remember what it was about?" Emmett said.

"We learned about it with SIMON, remember? The stone portal hidden in Snow Mountains," the storm bear said. "It is the door to a place of great imprisonment where the horned daemons were taken after the Second Daemon's War. Since they were not physically killed, their bodies and spirits remain intact, waiting to be released."

"So, the war," Emmett continued, "was fought to keep it closed? I'm assuming the Mob wanted to open it and everybody else didn't? They wanted to strengthen their magi to be like us with you guys, right?"

"Partially," Gebb said. "The Northland Empress Sophia wanted to open the portal but only to kill the horned daemons in a more permanent action. Emperor Magnus disagreed. The result of their duel was the beginning of the Civil War. Magnus defeated Sophia in what it is known as the first divine duel. After that, the Makaians gathered their magi and Magnus did as well to defend the portal. The war lasted fifteen years."

The memories of the summer palace were starting to come back. The last time magi fought magi, all but three of them ended up dead. Henri's family was one of the bloodlines that survived. A few of the bloodlines stopped during the Civil War, but he didn't know which ones. This wasn't over yet. The Northern Magi had an incomplete cycle since all their horned daemons were imprisoned in the Underworld. Suddenly, Nolan wasn't sure how he felt about entering a war that had so many magi fatalities. Those without a surviving bloodline ended the southern cycle. Pani told him this was why four of the Southern Magi were the first magi in their bloodline. The stars chose them to represent the elements. Emmett, Nolan, Lilith, and the last Gemini Sister. *And who would make a better water mage than the reincarnation of the moon god?* Nolan felt like he could hear Zachariah telling him that when he first got there.

At last, they made it to the room where Amelia was sleeping. Nolan gulped when Pani led them inside. The room was much bigger than it needed to be, but the view was amazing. They could faintly see the ocean surrounding the island he first landed on. Everything in the room was covered with a white sheet except for the bed. Nolan was tempted to pull them back to see why Daedalus had them covered, but he was too concerned with Amelia and her rose tiger lying on the bed. Whatever he did to them, whether it was a temporary or permanent sleep, it was his fault. And he had no idea how to reverse it. Emmett said she was cute. Nolan was nervous to get too close because of the tiger cub lying inches away from her. To the side of the bed, her staff stood on its own. Nolan wondered if it would react to him, as if it knew he had done it.

"What did you do to her again?" Emmett asked, having no idea his words cut like knives.

"A spell, I think, but it wasn't anything I've ever heard before," Nolan said.

"You mean you've never practiced spells before?" Emmett said. "Like it's all new to you?"

"No, smartass. I mean it wasn't English," Nolan said.

That's because it was Divine, Pani said. *The language of the gods. It is forbidden to use it offensively like this. I'm afraid I don't know how to reverse it. Have you tried contacting Lucian? All emperors speak Divine.*

Nolan had been trying from the moment he got back, but nothing came to him. The last few times he really talked with Lucian, Nolan had been asleep. Even without him, he had no idea how to drift to and from Suspension. Try and try he did, but Lucian never spoke. Pani told him to try summoning Lucian. He might as well have tried talking to Amelia. Emmett continued to comment on anything and everything in the room. Nolan knew he was just stalling, hoping Nolan would figure out what to do. Zachariah had told him his powers came from his emotions. Maybe that was the key to bringing Lucian back from where he was. He had to want it more than anything else. Focusing was a little easier. Jaahn had done so many things, but he knew magic, which meant *Nolan* knew magic. Having that much power had made him more confident in his own abilities, even if they were terrible and murderous. Jaahn never backed down; neither should he. *I need to talk with Lucian.* The phrase kept repeating slowly in his mind, wrapping itself over and over again. His eyes closed. Nolan focused on his breathing almost by instinct.

When Nolan opened his eyes, he saw the white outline of the room. And he wasn't alone. The outline of Pani was standing beside him, but he wasn't speaking or even acknowledging that he was there. There was just an outline of a silver seal standing next to him. After wasted effort trying to talk with his daemon, he kept thinking of Lucian. Another few precious moments passed before a spiral of golden energy appeared in front of him. Lucian looked calm. Nolan wished he could hug him.

"It's been a long time, Nolan," Lucian said.

"I thought you were gonna protect me? Where were you when Jaahn was here?"

"I could not reach you once Jaahn had arisen. He blocked me at every turn from the moment he woke up. He is *much* more powerful than I am. Only the Gemini Sisters could help you."

"And Grampa? Pani told me we went to my house."

"I can see this has been quite the bonding experience for the two of you. Only beings who share a connection can see each other in this realm and another," Lucian said.

Nolan didn't want to go too much into Pani being there. He wanted answers. Lucian must have known that because he didn't mention it again.

"Your grandfather," Lucian said. "Yes, I was able to speak with him partially before I returned to Suspension and inform him that Jaahn is resting once again. My body cannot travel the realms, Nolan, but my spirit can. The journey back, however, has left me very weak. I am sorry I was not able come to you sooner. However, it does my heart good though to know you learned how to summon me on your own. Your powers are growing."

Nolan was proud of himself. Who would have thought just a few days ago he wished he were back at home, drinking tainted apple juice. Since he knew his time was limited, he had to ask him if he knew anything about his parents. Lucian did not learn the truth until his grampa told him. He gave him a message.

"He said words could not express his sorrow, but it had to be this way," Lucian said.

"It had to be this way! That's not an apology! We mourned them! Both of us!" Nolan was getting angry again, but he calmed himself. He hadn't come this far just to let Jaahn out again. He had to change the subject and fast.

"What about Amelia? Can you help her?" he asked.

"Yes. Offensive Divine is a lesson every emperor must learn. If you wouldn't mind …"

"I don't even care anymore. At least this possession will do some good," Nolan said.

Nolan felt Lucian take over his body. It was strange to be back in his own mind, but watching from this view was much better. Lucian walked him over to Amelia and Bast. He placed one hand on each of their heads and said something else in Divine. Once this was over, Nolan heard Lucian speak to him again. *They will have no memory of Jaahn placing them under this spell. The rest is up to you.* Yeah, just leave it to him to explain how they got from one place to another.

He grabbed his staff and looked over at Emmett on the other side of them.

"Was that—" Emmett began.

"Yeah, it was Lucian. He fixed them, but he—"

"Where am I?" Amelia said, waking up alongside her daemon. "Nolan?"

"I teleported us here because we were in danger!" he shouted. "Are you okay?"

Teleporting was the only thing he knew his family could do. As long as she believed they got there by accident, he could make up the rest of it as it came up.

"I see you got your staff too. That's good," Amelia said, getting up. "That means your powers are growing. Who's this?"

"This is Emmett Bradley. He's a mage. He's one of my friends from home," Nolan said.

"Hey," Emmett said.

"Bradley," she said, turning to him. "Are you related to *Markus* Bradley?"

"That's my dad, yeah."

"Oh my stars. Everybody knows Markus Bradley. He's the most famous man in the world. Even the stars blessed him. They're the ones who made him a Dea! Your father is legendary around here. He must be really proud!"

Nolan's face turned as he looked at how Emmett looked at Amelia. Reliving memories about his father while translating Terran terms, Emmett was smiling heavily for a guy who was almost dinner less than an hour ago. Emmett was fitting in this world like a puzzle piece while Nolan was as welcome as a nuclear bomb. He looked down at his medallion. Nolan was supposed to be the prince here. However, the thought made Nolan relive the joys of being a prince on Deva Prime.

"And is it true that he sailed all the way from Oneiroi to the Secluded Isles on a boat leaf!" Amelia asked, getting up quickly. "No man has ever traveled to Oneiroi!"

"I'm sure it is. My dad was amazing," Emmett said.

"Was?" Amelia asked.

"He died a year ago back home," he said.

"Oh. I'm sorry. I ..."

"It's okay," he said.

Without even thinking, Amelia hugged Emmett. Tight. Emmett nodded to Nolan. Then he hugged her back, almost sniffing her hair. Nolan saw a crush developing.

"It's just, everyone has different stories about Markus Bradley. Some people in my village even say they met him. I can't wait to tell them I know his son. They'll never believe me," Amelia said.

"Where is your village?" he asked.

"Blackheart is in the Southlands between King's Forest and Green Valley," Amelia said.

"Maybe I'll come with you when you go back. They'll believe you then," Emmett said.

"Yeah," Amelia said, grabbing her staff. "That'd be nice."

Nolan knew talking about her village had changed her attitude. If only he could remember how a heart mage could scare away an entire village. It was a curse that Jaahn wanted, but Nolan couldn't remember the name. He didn't want to ask in front of Emmett.

"So where are we?" she asked. "And who died?"

"What?" Emmett and Nolan asked, looking at each other.

"Covering everything with a white cloth. It means someone died here."

"I think this is Daedalus's house," Emmett said.

"Daedalus!" Amelia shouted. "We have to get out of here! If he comes back—we just shouldn't be here!"

Nolan and Pani led the other magi and their daemons out of the room. Nolan told her some cock-and-bull story about him not knowing who died there so they should probably leave as fast as they could in case Daedalus came back. Emmett agreed with everything he said even if it wasn't very convincing to him. They walked the hallway for a few moments before Amelia broke the silence.

"So where's Raymond?" she asked.

"Who?" Emmett asked.

Nolan was glad he asked; he had forgotten about him.

"This kid who strayed into my village. Nolan, you found him. Do you know where he is?" she asked.

Nolan's mouth was open wide as he looked to Pani. Jaahn put him in a room somewhere in Daedalus's little castle. How would they know which room? And more important, why was he locked up in the first place.

Shit, Nolan thought. *What was Jaahn thinking?*

All thoughts were focused on the bubbling taking center stage in their magi camp. Zachariah stood over the pot, stirring with a thin, metallic rod. Everyone watched as Zachariah stirred the deconstruction in a small black cauldron. Watching him had been like watching a chemist creating a magical concoction. All the ingredients had been found, and all the magi had returned safely. Now they just had to wait until the deconstruction was ready so they could all leave safely. The blue sun had already begun its retreat for the night, giving everyone a chance to look at the red moon and reflect on its latest reincarnation. Not much was said among the magi, who were far from friends.

"Second time's a charm, right? That's what the Terrans say?" Zachariah said. "It's just about ready for the activation spell. It'll only be three or four more hours."

"Why can't we just make another portal?" Lilith asked.

"The barrier," Kalaerede said. "It prevents any kind of portal travel. We'd end up in the middle of the ocean. Deconstruction is our best bet. The potion breaks the body apart into pieces. The barrier cannot stop this type of travel, which is why—"

"Deconstruction is *kind of* illegal," Kandace said. "But since it's a refined potion, only spell casters can make it in the first place. They're a rare breed, spell casters. The only ones I know were the Conrads and the Wylies. That's the two ruling families for you fosters."

"What happened to the Conrads?" Lilith asked.

"Perhaps a history lesson is best reserved for your training, Lilith," Archmage Medhas said. "There will be much you do not understand."

"Well, then what are we supposed to do while the potion brews?" Kandace said. "Just sit here. We've been waiting all our lives to meet with the other magi and here they are."

"Maybe someone can explain this age thing to us," Henri said. "Oris says we're forty."

"Yeah, and?" Kandace added. "All the magi are about the same age, give or take a few years, even Caw-la-red, and he's an Elf."

"In the Terra System," Call-law-reed said, "you must have different years than we do. How old did you believe you were?"

"I just turned eighteen, and Lilith was about to turn fifteen in a few weeks."

"That's about right," Zachariah said. "Our year is two and a half years in the Terran system. Here, you and Lilith are three years apart. The same, I assume, as Cassandra and Nolan. Am I correct?"

Cassandra nodded. Zachariah continued to explain that while the Magi cycle was divided into certain months, it was normal for this cycle to be complete over a maximum of five years. Before the division of the magi, this allowed enough time for all sixteen to be born into the respective month. The months, he explained, were also not divided in the way Terran months were. They followed a pattern according to the season they were in. He used their current season as an example. The first fifty-four days of summer were known as the month of Pa. The next two sets of fifty-two days were known as Re and Lu, leaving the last forty-eight as the month of Mi. This cycle continued every season in the same order. Whereas in the Terran system they had three hundred and sixty-five days in a year, Deva Prime had eight hundred and twenty-four. Nolan was the first to be born of all the magi, so everyone followed his lead. Within the next year, Kalaerede was born, followed by Henri a few months later. This process continued in a three-year gap until the southern cycle ended with Lilith being born in the spring of Mi. Emmett was the only one who broke this cycle, being the only true Terran-born mage, but even with the math, he would have been born in the spring of Lu a few years before Lilith.

"What about you, Cassandra? Where did you live your whole life?" Lilith asked.

"As much as I would love to share my tale with my fellow magi, I would really rather wait until Nolan is with us as well," she said. "We have a lot to talk about."

"He *deserves* to be the first to hear who Cassandra is. We must not tell him. He should hear it from her," Medhas said. "But there is one question I have of you, Cassandra. Since your mother was an Elf, is it safe to assume she taught you the ways of light?"

"Yes, she was no archmage, but she taught me everything she knew," Cassandra said.

"I have long thought the Elves were a deeply spiritual race, like the stars themselves," Archmage Medhas said. "It seems the same has occurred with Mage Call-law-reed."

"The what?" Lilith asked.

"Cow piss," Kandace whispered.

"The stars, Mage Lilith," Medhas began. "They are the perfect, the immobile. Each star in our world is more than a nighttime light; they are celestial energy separating us from the gods. They are the watchers and the masters. Each star you see, night or day, has the ability to meet with us, showing us eternal wisdom, guiding us to the destiny we were meant to have. *Some* people don't believe the stars are beings. And had I not met them myself, I too would be a fool, but the stars, Mage Lilith, they give us the steps toward enlightenment."

Zachariah continued the explanation in a less philosophical manner. He explained the stars were viewed by many as less interactive gods. This, however, required some background that the foster magi lacked. There were three categories of deities in Deva Prime: supreme, patron, and symbolic. Supreme gods watched over the world. Patrons cared for the world, and symbolic gods pushed the world. The magi were the reincarnations of the symbolic gods. Divine Deas were the reincarnations of the patron gods. The stars are a blurry mix of patron and symbolic. They cared for the world in a purely objective manner to maintain peace. They were the ones who created the barrier between the continents. They made the prison portal for horned daemons. The stars reacted when the worst of the worst was beginning. They tried to prevent the world from killing itself.

18

The Three Ss

RAYMOND OPENED HIS eyes in the White Room. He had fallen onto the ground. Scratching his head as he stood up, he tried to remember what had happened: Nolan took him to the room, he closed his eyes, and then there were dragons picking away at his chest as if they were digging through his heart. He knew Nolan had done something to him, but he didn't know what or why. He still felt the same, confined in a room with no door, but unharmed. Standing up, Raymond felt a slight weight on his neck. Looking down, he gasped. Hanging from a silver chain was a talisman around his neck. He picked up the cookie-sized medallion, which was as wide as two thumbs meshed together. A dragon was stretched across the side. It was black with small white stripes on the cracks of its wings. On the back of it was markings, he was sure it was Divine, the language of the gods, but he didn't know how to read it. *No!* He tried to take it off, but it stopped itself just below his chin before it fell back to his chest. Nolan had one of these! Nolan did this to him! It made him one of the most hated people the world had ever seen.

There had to be a way out. *Where's the damn door?* Raymond turned again to face the opposite direction. Nothing. He turned again. There it was, appearing out of nowhere. It opened as he ran for it. Raymond had to find someplace to explain this to himself. Maybe it was a fake. Maybe Nolan was playing a trick on him. His mother said fake medallions were all the rage during the Civil War. Running through the house made him more confused than at ease. At the end of the hallway, he saw Nolan standing with Amelia and another mage. Whatever darkness Nolan had, it was spreading throughout the cycle like wildfire. He had to leave before Nolan saw him and finally make a run for it wherever he could. He never should have agreed to go with him. Then he thought about his parents. Nolan would have ripped out their throats and done this to him anyway. None of that mattered now as Raymond found the biggest door he could and ran outside, hoping no one saw him.

"Was that Raymond?" Nolan asked, after seeing the same blur. He must have been terrified. Jaahn took him from his parents and locked him in a room, no doubt to use him in some way. There was something on Raymond. Something Nolan had too, another medallion. Raymond was going to be just like him. Did Jaahn just switch bodies? Nolan tried to take his medallion off, but it was still magically linked to him. Was Raymond the one who would bring him back after everything they went through to lock him away? Nolan had to stay calm, and, most important, he had to make sure Raymond was calm too. Maybe Raymond would release a spark that forced Jaahn out of retirement. Emmett said there wasn't another way to put Jaahn back. If he got out again, Nolan was going to be put to sleep like a rabid dog. Amelia didn't know that about Jaahn, thanks to Lucian. Nolan tried to call out to him, but there wasn't enough time. Amelia said they couldn't leave Raymond there. They had to get him and leave before Daedalus returned.

"Then let's go find him," Emmett said. "That kid's got some legs."

Bast, the rose tiger, was the best at tracking, so Nolan and the others followed her with Raymond's scent. Amelia and Emmett continued to trade their stories of their drastically different versions of Markus Bradley, but it gave Nolan time to think, which was no longer alone time. Pani had seen the same thing he had: a medallion on a silver chain. The silver seal had had doubts about why Raymond had come to Blackheart on the *same day* as Nolan. Let alone when Jaahn was in control of his body. There had to be a connection between Raymond and Nolan. The only question was how did Daedalus know? Nolan was closer to Bast than her own mage, but he had to know. It made perfect sense. If he was the Moon Dea, there had to be a Sun Dea. Maybe it was Raymond. Had to be. Nolan's steady walk soon became a light jog and then a straight-up run. As the six of them made their way outside, they continued to follow Bast until she led them to the back of the house. There was a greenhouse a few feet away from them. Raymond was on the ground, knees down, yanking at the vines around his neck. They weren't letting him leave. Nolan slowly walked over to him.

"Just stay calm," Nolan said.

"What did you do to me?" Raymond shouted.

"I didn't do anything! It was ... well, it was ...

"You took me away from my family, threatened to kill them, and then you do this to me! Why are you doing this?" Raymond shouted.

Raymond held up his medallion for everyone to see. Nolan wasn't the only one who backed away. The vines around Raymond's neck loosened up, and he was able to stand. Nolan kept telling him to stay calm, but Raymond was walking over to him with fury in his eyes. Once they turned black, he knew it would be over. The first thing Nolan would do was run! He wouldn't go back to the corners of his own mind!

"Stay calm, Raymond!"

"Don't tell me to calm down after what you *did* to me!"

"You're ... the Sun Dea! Wow! That's really great!" Amelia said.

"What?" everyone said, staring at her.

"Don't you see," Amelia said, walking closer to Raymond. "You're the reincarnation of the sun god; he was the patron god of Kingskin! The stars must have given you the medallion! They must think you're worthy to replace Sophia Conrad. But, Raymond, you're not bad. I can tell. Everyone knows all the Conrads are dead. You get to replace them, just like the foster magi replaced the magi who died in the Civil War!"

Fosters? Is that what they call us? Nolan didn't like this new term, but at the moment, he didn't care. Raymond was calming down. He kept his attention only on Raymond. Guilt was setting in like seasoning. He felt responsible for this burden on Raymond. Jaahn was the one who had brought him along. It was the summer palace all over again. Nolan didn't want to be the Moon Dea, and now he had forced an innocent person to join him. Did Daedalus pick Raymond to torture him? To remind him that everyone he touched wished they had never met him?

"I don't *want* to replace Sophia," Raymond said, still trying to take the medallion off. "I don't *want* to become a Dea. Take it back, Nolan, *please*."

"I don't think I can," Nolan said. He tried to remove his medallion as well, but it still stopped above his chest before dropping back again. "I'm sorry."

"Just try, *please*," Raymond said.

Nolan didn't think it would work, but he moved closer to Raymond, looking at his medallion. There was a difference. Where Nolan had a tiger, Raymond had a dragon. Curiously, he reached down to touch it. As Nolan's hand felt the familiar two-thumbed-sized medallion, a force pulled the two of them apart. Streaks of blue and white light remained in the air while the two of them fell to the ground. Nolan stared up into it as it streaked through the skies before he was blinded. Only a few seconds passed before Nolan's eyes opened again. Emmett was above him.

"What the hell was that?" Nolan said. "It's like someone just junk-punched me!"

He watched as Amelia was helping Raymond up. Judging by the look on Raymond's face, he was just as confused as they were.

Nolan *really* doubted he could take it off now. Everyone's eyes shot to Amelia for an answer.

"Did you feel that?" she said. "It's like the legend of the Gemini bond. I remember feeling this a few years ago. It must have been when the Gemini Brothers met."

"You're saying that when two souls meet, there's some kind of force?" Emmett asked.

"Not just any souls. Sibling souls. That's what my mom told me. The most powerful magical souls in our world are related to each other. The three Ss: siblings seek siblings. Every magical soul in the world should feel what I just felt. You guys don't 'cause you're not in tune with magical energy. But it's incredible. Everything's gonna change now. We finally have another Sun Dea. You can undo everything Sophia did. You're gonna be legendary, Raymond."

Raymond and Nolan looked at each other from opposite sides of the greenhouse. Nolan wondered how long this sense of uncertain wonder would last. The two of them were connected now forever. He kept trying to think of warm breezes and soft sand, hoping Raymond was thinking the same. As long as both of them stayed calm, hopefully no one's eyes would turn black. They looked at each other with fear and hatred pouring out of their eyes. Between the two of them, a large root shot up from the ground. The root lowered itself like a hook until it was inches away from Nolan's face. He could see a mouth. It spoke to Nolan in Latin before it dropped into the ground as if it were never there. They all made their way around him. The daemons stood next to their staff-wielding magi. The soil resealed itself. Pani asked him what the root had told him as Nolan was processing what he had just heard. Nolan remembered Lucian telling him Latin was a language they shared with Terrans. He still didn't know why.

"Well, what did it say?" Emmett asked.

"Someone is coming," Nolan said, and as he did, they watched as a black light shined down from the sky.

19

A Starry Visit

EVERY PAIR OF eyes stationed in Meditation Trees was each frozen as they looked up to the sky with reverence and confusion. A sensation of misplaced joy washed over each of them as if they had just had their favorite meal prepared by their nemesis. This feeling emerged only seconds after the beam of light seen around the world. The magi born and raised in these lands were stricken with awe while those who lived with more experience were beside themselves as they wondered what the feeling meant. Only the foster magi who stood among them were unsure why everyone refused to share the reason for this stern silence.

"What happened?" Henri asked.

"The common bond," Zachariah said with his hand over his heart. "Siblings seek siblings. It's a kind of acknowledgment that two sibling souls have reunited. Most are moderately weak; others are as strong as the Gemini bond. But this one ... this was the strongest bond I have ever felt. Medhas, you don't think?"

"It must be," he responded. "But how? And who?"

"What's going on?" Kandace asked.

Medhas's eyes cut toward Kandace as she was stricken with silence.

"Bonds are not common, Kandace," Kalaerede said. "But those who are in balance between their body and spirit can often predetermine which type of bond they have experienced. If my knowledge is correct, Master Zachariah, this bond was between brothers. Then I believe it is true, Archmage Medhas. The bond we felt, with its power and magnitude, must have been the bond between two of the strongest brothers in our world: the Sun and the Moon Deas. We have witnessed one of the strongest bonds known to our world: the patron bond," Kalaerede said.

Everyone was going back and forth, trying to explain how the Sun Dea had returned to them. Kandace was sure it had to be a replacement for Sophia. Cassandra, Kalaerede, Medhas, and Zachariah, however, were unsure if the stars could grant someone the same powers of a patron god. There was something about the Alcove of Souls. Henri and Lilith were the only ones not questioning it.

"You don't think *he* had anything to do with it, do you?" Cassandra asked her group, bringing them all to silence.

"Who are you talking about?" Lilith asked.

"Lilith, do you remember when Zachariah was talking about how the gods were divided: supreme, patron, and symbolic? Every race calls them by different names, but there are three that are universal; they are the three separate faces of the supreme, the Triad—our Creator, our Sustainer, and our Transformer."

"The Triad?" Henri said after a few moments of silence. "You think one of them made someone the Sun Dea?"

"It is possible," Zachariah said. "As a supreme god, their powers are limitless, even beyond Nolan's power. It is possible they may have been able to steal the soul of the Sun. Legend says the Triad were one of the riffs that brought Sophia and Magnus to duel. If one of them is responsible for this, it is possible they mean to bring about another divine duel. We need to bring Nolan and his new 'brother' before the grand archmage immediately."

The daemons looked up at the sky nearly at the same time. The monkey chatter, which had provided excellent cover for their conversation, had stopped. A black light shined from the sky. It was getting closer and closer to them. Neither of them could move from the second they saw it. The small circle they had all been standing in was very soon overcome with black light. The black light stopped in the middle of them. They saw it morph into a figure. Its body was a swirling vortex of black and white energy contained within a silver enchanted cloth known as a celestial cloak. It ran like water off its body. The flowing gray cloak had a hood covering its head. When it lifted its head, they could do nothing but stare.

"It is a star," Medhas said quietly.

It looked to him.

"A star has blessed us!"

"Medhas, of the Ankkn firebirds. You have been well."

The star looked to him as if they had met before. Its voice sounded like a room full of people. Men and women, each of them blended into one, giving it a multitude of resonance. The way it spoke was very slow, as if every word had been practiced in deep thought. They were both terrified and nurtured. Medhas bowed his head, as did everyone else. When the star spoke again, heads rose.

"Magi Henri and Lilith Roland, welcome home," the star said, turning toward them. "The brothers have found each other on their natural course. The Alcove of Souls has not been penetrated. Such is the way it was meant to be, for no power in this world could separate three. So let it be as it always has, with a new brotherhood rising from the ash."

The star clapped its hands one time. As it pulled its hands back, a large golden sphere emerged in the center of the group. As the golden sphere appeared, the star's hands stretched farther than mortally possible. The forest around them shook as the star's hands clenched the sphere as if they were magnetically linked. It too began to move. They watched the sphere instead of the star. Within a few moments, the forest and the sphere stopped. The star's hands fell back to its sides. The sphere was still in front of them. In the multitude of sounds, the star said it was done. The celestial cloak was blown off, as if by the wind, revealing a large vortex of black and white in the shape of man. A burst of light was emitted into the air, blinding the Deas. The star was gone, leaving the golden sphere pulsing before them.

Zachariah spoke to all of the magi as one. *A star cannot survive the physical world. If they do so, they will die within the hour. We have witnessed the indescribable.*

The golden sphere fell into the ground and opened. In the center of the Deas stood two magi, three daemons, and the Divine Deas. No one said a word until—

"How?" Lilith asked.

"The stars are well known for their golden spheres and their ability to sense the energy of others," Kalaerede said, looking at Lilith. "And yes, Henri, there is a connection between them and the Divine Deas. With each reincarnation, they shared one gift, their blessings. I don't need to tell you which ones."

"About time. They were gonna leave without you," Henri said.

"They?"

Turning around, they saw all of the Deas around them. Introductions were quick and painless from their side until Nolan looked at Cassandra. No one said a word remembering Medhas's order. This was Cassandra's moment.

"I've seen her before," Nolan began.

Cassandra looked at Nolan, and tears began to roll down her face. Her hands began to tremble uncontrollably as she looked at him with joy. Despite his slight reluctance, she opened her hands to his. He placed his hands in hers timidly. As their hands touched, their bodies melted into two golden orbs of light. Instinctively, the orbs flew around their separate daemons, taking them in. The orbs flew into the sky as everyone watched. The red moon started to rise from the ashes of the blue sun as the magi all sat down, uncertain of the future, staring at another medallion standing before them.

20

One Magi

WALKING DOWN THE hallway, hearing the firm sound of the door closing, she made her way toward the staircase at the end of the hall. After opening the wooden door, the blond Dea walked up them slowly. The stone steps were wiry and long, but as she walked up these steps every night, it only felt like a couple of minutes. She came to an open door, which she walked through confidently as she saw him turn and smile. His face was a little less rugged than she liked. His shaggy red hair and hazel eyes, standing on a muscular six-foot frame, made her mouth water. He was dressed more appropriately for the cold night with blue pants and a thin white shirt. Her lover turned back around. One arm rested straight in front of him, and the other was dancing as if conducting an invisible orchestra. His body was standing on the top of the stone tower, but she knew he was bored. She shared his warm sense of accomplishment as it smoked through his mind. A god in training he was, and she would rule beside him until their end of days.

She walked up to him, smelling his flame-ridden hair. There was no other smell more seductive than smoke in the early parts of night. He could do whatever he wanted, especially to her. There was no one to stop him. She asked if the people were loud that night. The red-haired Dea said he heard the pitter-patter of feet running to their mothers and fathers. He said their clothes were covered in flames. She liked this village because they ran slowly. Gently, she moved his thick hair as he moved his right hand to guide his creation like a dangerous conductor. The sweet-faced lover made her way next to him. She placed her hand on his resting one. Her long blond hair was kissing the night's wind. Leaning against him, she could feel the fire within him. She hungered for it, for tonight was a night to celebrate. Her pouty lips kissed him on the cheek, a soft kiss; his playtime was over.

"That's the third dancing snake charm this month, Aiden," she said.

"I was celebrating, Celeste," he said. "We all felt the same bond, twice now. All the siblings have found each other under the moonlight."

"We don't need the attention, right?" Celeste said.

"Fine," he whispered.

Forming a fist in his still hand, he pulled it into his side. His fire magic disappeared yet again. They kissed more passionately, her pulling him in. She felt his fire breath as he was warmed by her cold embrace. They walked back into the castle and down the stairs, holding each other's hand, constantly close. They lay down on her bed, his arms around her.

"How was your training with the archmage today?" he asked.

The sweet blonde said, "Don't ask."

"You know he is your ancestor. If he wasn't strict, you wouldn't be you."

She ignored him, looking up at the ceiling. He was rubbing his stubble against her soft chin like a puppy hungry for attention.

"How do you think we managed to stay hidden from Jaahn?" Aiden asked.

"Daedalus was able to keep him off our trail by leaving a little surprise for him in that pathetic little village. He put a divine cloaking spell over the castle after that."

"He is crafty, isn't he?"

She sat up on the side of the bed.

"Come on. Don't be like that."

Her sweet face turned cold. She looked at the naked room in front of him. Her red-haired lover sat behind her. His arms were on her chest as he kissed her neck.

"I'm not saying I like the guy. I mean no one *likes* him, not even his kids. He's just … *crafty*," Aiden said.

"No," she said, standing now. "Obviously, you don't get it. I'm going to bed. Alone."

"Celeste."

Aiden scratched his head as his hands fell to his side. Moving his hair behind his ear, he looked at her. She didn't want to look at him, but she couldn't look away.

"Don't hate me too long. You knew what I meant."

"He—"

"Yes, I know, but that's how we do things here. He knew that long before Daedalus showed up. Everyone talks about how brave your father was. Let's put that anger to good use. We finally have someone to play with."

Celeste let him get closer to her. One arm wrapped around her. Her neck felt one kiss on each side. Aiden's face still near hers, he said they should go to bed and dream an honorable future. She smiled; then she kissed him as they made their way back to bed.

"I can't wait to meet the Southern Magi," she said.